BELONGING

The murders of Jane Sears Geehan and Garrett Sears on the Southside of Harbour Grace, 1871

PATRICK COLLINS

Dedicated to my sisters
Regina, Maureen, Madonna and Patricia,
to whom I owe a debt of inspiration

DRC PUBLISHING
3 Parliament Street
St. John's, NL
A1A 2Y6

Tel: 709-726-0960

E-mail: staceypj@nl.rogers.com
www.drcpublishingnl.com

Library and Archives Canada Cataloguing in Publication

Collins, Patrick (Patrick Joseph), author
Belonging : the Geehan murders / Patrick Collins.

Includes bibliographical references.
ISBN 978-1-926689-69-2 (bound)

I. Title.

PS8605.O4683B44 2014 C813'.6 C2014-900545-8

This book is a work of fiction which is based on real life facts. Some names, characters, places, events and incidents either are the product of the author's imagination or are used fictitiously.

Layout, design and front cover by Vince Marsh.
Back cover photo supplied by author.

Published 2014
Printed in Canada

We acknowlege the financial support of the Government of Canada through the Canada Book Fund (CBF) for our publishing activities.

PROLOGUE

"The Evening Post"

A Special Report from a St. John's Correspondent to the New Yorker

Her Majesty's Penitentiary, St. John's, Newfoundland, 1872
The Scene of the Execution
of Patrick Geehan and Johanna Hamilton

At five o'clock, Patrick Geehan was aroused from his fitful sleep, and recommended to prepare himself for the last offices of the church of which he declared himself to be a member. He then ate some muttonchops, toast, and coffee, with great relish, after which he said he felt, "plucky."

But the more worthy object of human sympathy in this case was the frail but lovely creature, Johanna Hamilton, who sat wearied yet sleepless upon the miserable pallet within her last abode on earth. Her tears had steadily fallen during the night; but when the priest announced himself to her, she cried aloud for many moments before speaking to him. At length he succeeded in calming down her grief, but only to hear from her the distracted and plaintiff appeal-"Oh Father! For the love of sweet Jesus, save me!" The priest then gradually led her thoughts away from the earth. She slowly grew resigned to her fate.

At six o'clock, a company of policemen marched into the yard, and upon hearing them the doomed woman shuddered involuntarily and had new recourse to tears. On leaving her cell at the request of the sheriff, she drew back and sobbed hysterically. Being quietly pressed to move on, she advanced a step, and again shrunk from the terrible journey. At length it was found necessary to employ violence in removing her from her cell; but at the request of the clergyman he was allowed to re-persuade her to obey the sentence of the law. The priest finally succeeded in taking her into the passage, where her dress was looped, her arms pinioned, and the fatal noose adjusted. In the meantime, Geehan, dressed in a suit of black, had been fitted out for his leap into death, and he stood before his beautiful accomplice.

"Poor Johanna," said Geehan aloud; but the condemned woman did not even raise her eyes towards him. She held down her head meekly, and seemed fully to realize her shame. But her tears had all dried up, and her sobs were hushed; nothing save an occasional sigh was left of the grief and distraction of her last night on earth.

"Are you ready?" asked the sheriff, and Geehan answered promptly. "Yes, sir."

Geehan then received the white cap, as did also the unfortunate Johanna. Geehan, accompanied by a clergyman and two deputy sheriffs, led the way to the cortile of the penitentiary. Approaching the platform upon which the fatal trap-bars were, the doomed woman again shrunk back and cried bitterly. But again encouraged by the counsel of her spiritual advisor, she went courageously up to the platform. There she knelt and prayed ardently. Geehan also prayed. Their prayers being finished, they arose and the white caps were drawn over their eyes by the deputy sheriffs, and the noose of each was adjusted to ropes, which dangled from two protruding beams...Great sympathy was felt for the girl, and it was hoped by many that the governor would relent before the sentence had been fulfilled.

The Evening Post, June 1872,[i]

CHAPTER ONE

Southside of Harbour Grace
Thursday, November 23, 1871

Johanna Hamilton lay motionless in bed next to Patrick Geehan, listening to the incessant rattle of his chest. She remained very still, hoping against hope that he would remain asleep. The thought of him putting his hands on her was sickening, knowing his deranged behavior. How could this man, whom she once loved, have committed such atrocities? She quietly rolled her rosary beads through her fingers, hanging on to the thread of faith that God, indeed, was a God of mercy. She prayed that He would hear her prayers, even though she felt that her soul was now condemned to eternal damnation.

During late fall, the morning sun breaks over Harbour Grace South from the highest crest of Feather Point Hill. When it is calm, as it was that morning, the harbour resembled a mirror and the sun's reflection off the water was so brilliant it hid the peaceful and pastoral landscape of the Southside.

As the sun rose a little higher in the sky, the early frost began to disappear, leaving light dew on the grass. About two miles to the west is the quaint community of Riverhead. A road winds its way through Riverhead and begins an ascent over a ridge through a lonely wooded area just before leaving the village. It is the only route leading to the communities at the head of Conception Bay. Soon, it would be busy with horse-carts and foot travelers.

This stretch of rocky road was still hidden from the sun since it was shadowed by the hill to the south. Bill Byrne from the Thicket was driving his horse and dray on this road through Riverhead and towards the Glover Road to cut some firewood. As he neared Michael Sullivan's house he saw that he had arrived at the quarry, where gravel was obtained for repairing the roads in the community.

Feeling the need to answer a call from Mother Nature, he thought this would be as private a place as any to take care of business. After hitching his horse to a nearby tree, he climbed all the way down into the pit, making sure that he was well under the road so as not to be seen.

Much to his astonishment, he saw a pair of black-laced ankle boots protruding out from under the brush at the very bottom of the pit. Compelled by curiosity, he eased his way over to the area and slowly turned back the alders. On exposing the body of a woman, he quickly jumped back, releasing the bushes to cover his grisly find. Shocked and frightened, he began to scramble up the face of the quarry with great dexterity and speed. Every now and then his threadbare boots would cause him to slip, sending stones and gravel cascading back down the slope. The climb seemed endless until he finally reached the road.

Knowing the closest house was that of Michael Sullivan, Bill began to sprint out the road, not pausing until he arrived at Sullivan's gate. Before going into the yard, he paused to catch his breath. Thankfully, someone was awake in the house since smoke was billowing from the chimney. Bill didn't get a chance to knock. Michael opened the back door to greet him, having seen him panting and winded while leaning on his gate.

A crotchety man in his late seventies, Michael stood in the doorway with his pipe clenched in his teeth, giving the appearance of a grin. Bill knew otherwise. He suspected that he had disturbed the old gentleman while he was having his morning tea.

"Good morning, Bill. Is something the matter?" asked Michael.

"Tis that, a good morning indeed." Bill was gasping and blowing, hardly able to get a word out without taking a breath. "But not for the poor woman I found on the Ridge Road just up from your place. It's surely not a good morning for her. I think she's dead. Oh my God, Michael, there's a dead woman in the quarry."

Sullivan was a much cooler and stoic man than Bill. "Come on then, my son, let's go up and see," he said as he quickly donned his coat and cap, snuffing out his pipe by jamming his finger down into the bowl. He poked the pipe and some matches into his top pocket in readiness for his next draw.

The two men hurried back up the road, having to stop on occasion for Michael to take a breather. They quickly descended into the quarry, slipping and sliding on the loose gravel. Occasionally one would grab the other to prevent a fall. Bill led Michael over to the woman's body, turning away and grimacing as he held the bushes back for Michael to see. The woman was lying face down. Michael convinced Bill to turn her over. It was obvious that rigor mortis had set in.

Both these hardened men were horrified by the condition of the woman's bloated and scratched face. Dried saliva covered her lips and chin. Her tongue protruded from her mouth, making it evident she must have struggled to gasp her last breath. It was a sight that would be forever etched in their memories.

The stench of death was sickening. Cupping his mouth and nose with his hand, Bill said, "I think I've seen her at the church in Riverhead." Michael didn't recognize her at all.

The woman was dressed in working clothes, a pair of dark woolen trousers underneath a heavy cloth dress. Her clothing appeared to be in order. A bonnet was tied tightly around her chin.

Though wide-open, her eyes were still and cold. Bill Byrne had shot many animals during his years, but he had never seen an animal, no matter how long it had been dead, appear as horrifying as this poor woman.

The men bowed their heads in a quiet moment of silence. After some discussion, they decided their best course of action. They would go to Harbour Grace and report their finding to Dr. Allan. Michael returned to his house to get a blanket for the corpse. Bill refused to stay down in the quarry by himself. He climbed back up to the road and stood there, waiting anxiously for Michael's return.

Back at his house, Michael got a blanket from the daybed in the kitchen and folded it under his arm.

"I'll be back in an hour or so, Alice," he called out to his wife before exiting the house. He said not a word about what had happened or what he was about to do. "No need to upset the old woman," he mumbled under his breath.

Michael walked back the road to where Bill was waiting and

passed him the blanket. He leaned against Bill's dray for a few minutes rest before they took another trip down into the quarry. Since they weren't dealing with an emergency, there was no need to rush. Because of its rigidity, the woman's body was awkward to fully wrap. The woman's limbs resisted their attempts to cover her completely, having a tendency to push back to the same position in which they were found. Finally, after much struggling, they managed to secure her arms tightly against her body, and then do the same with her legs. Both men knew that the dead had to be respected.

"She's been here for a while," puffed Michael as he wiped his watering nose with his sleeve.

"She's as stiff as a board. Poor woman," commented Bill.

Although it was still early, they knew that Dr. Allan's surgery would be open by the time they got there. Having secured the body at the bottom of the pit off they rode, with Bill pushing his old mare as fast as he deemed wise.

"It's strange nobody found her, considering she must have been there for a while," said Bill.

"She was pretty well hidden under the road and in the bushes. Kind of hard to see. Anyone could have passed by and not seen a thing. And no one has been working in the quarry lately," Michael responded.

"That's true, but she must have walked down into the pit for some reason, because if she had fallen into it she'd be pretty marked up," guessed Bill. "I'd say that she's been there a couple of days. She may have been on her way home, although I never heard tell that anyone had gone missing."

Michael nodded in agreement, but his conservative nature prevented him from speculating. "Poor woman," he said. "I hope she didn't suffer, no matter what happened to her."

The trip to Harbour Grace took about an hour. It was an

uncomfortable ride on a dray, a cart never meant to carry passengers. The wheels seemed to find the worse ruts, constantly jarring both men back and forth. Michael found it especially hard with no place to rest his ailing back. He felt every bump and rock.

"Christ man, we should have gone by way of Water Street," he said, arching his back.

"Well, we're almost here now." Bill was tempted to ask Michael why he had bothered to come. But sensing the old man's crooked disposition he opted not to do so.

Dr. Allan had already begun his surgery for the day. The reception room was filled with waiting patients who looked up curiously as the men came in. Michael walked calmly across the room and bent down to whisper to the young nurse behind the desk.

"We have found the body of a woman," he said, as he nodded at Bill Byrne standing beside him. "He discovered the body on his way down Spaniard's Bay Road about an hour ago and then he came to get me. We didn't know what else to do but come here."

Without any further acknowledgment, the nurse left her chair and went into the doctor's office, closing the door behind her. Almost immediately, Dr. Allan came out of his examination room with his stethoscope wrapped around his neck and his black doctor's bag in hand. It seemed to Michael and Bill that he was ready for business. Michael wanted to say that there was no need for doctoring, but he held back.

"You say the body you found is on the main road to Spaniard's Bay, near the Upper Island Cove turn off?" Dr. Allan asked as he reached for his coat. Michael and Bill both nodded in agreement. "My son is in the next surgery so he'll join me." Dr. W. Allan Junior had just returned from McGill Medical School and taken up practice with his father. "I have to go and get my buggy, gentlemen. I will meet you outside."

Michael and Bill stood near the elder Dr. Allan's house and waited for him and his son to meet them. The doctors came out of the narrow lane beside the house in the buggy. Without stopping his rig, Dr. Allan slowed up. "We will go on ahead," he called. "You go down to the police station and let them know about the body. And tell them that I am on the way to the scene."

Michael and Bill willingly obliged, going directly to the police station on the east end of Water Street. Michael barged in ahead of Bill.

"Dr. Allan sent us," he said as he walked up to the counter without giving the policeman a chance to get up from his desk.

When the officer stood up Michael continued to be the spokesman. "My name is Michael Sullivan from Riverhead and this is Mr. Bill Byrne from the Thicket. He found the body of a poor woman up in Riverhead on Spaniard's Bay Road when he was on his way into the woods this morning. We just left Dr. Allan's and he told us to come here. He and his son are on the way to the scene now."

The tall policeman with glasses positioned on the edge of his nose had an air of authority. He introduced himself as Officer Fallon and asked if the body was still where they had found it.

"That it is, sir. It is right where Bill found her," Michael answered. "The poor woman was face down, so we turned her over and put a blanket around her. Out of respect, you know."

"Do you who know she is? Did you recognize her?"

"Bill thinks he saw her at Church in Riverhead, but he doesn't know her name, sir." Michael continued to speak as if Bill wasn't able to talk.

"Well, I'll send Constables Hutcher and Daley with the police wagon," Fallon dipped his pen into the ink well, scribbling several notes onto the police blotter without asking any more questions. After a few minutes, he looked up. “Hopefully, the police will be there before the doctors leave the scene,” he said. “And they will, I’m sure, be in contact with you.”

As was the case with Dr. Allan, Constable Fallon showed little appreciation for the men’s efforts. There wasn’t even a thank you or a handshake. Not to be deterred, the men returned to Riverhead with a sense of accomplishment for having done some good.

“It will be a sad day for somebody on the Southside when they get the news of that poor woman’s death,” said Michael.

“That it will be a sad day,” agreed Bill, as he once again drove Queen towards Riverhead. “It’s not the news a husband or family will be expecting. There’s nothing worse than seeing a priest coming to your door.”

It took about an hour to arrive back to where they had discovered the woman. Her body was now lying in the police wagon, wrapped in Michael’s blanket. Dr. Allan and his son were just leaving the area in their buggy. Dr. Allan tipped his hat to Bill and Michael as they drove past.

By now, crowds of people, young and old, had gathered out of curiosity. One of the onlookers standing on the road happened to be from the Southside. He was John Fitzgerald, a man known to both Riverhead men.

“The poor woman is from your area, I believe,” Michael said to John as he slowly and stiffly disembarked from the rig. Bill Byrne stayed aboard for he had to continue on home.

John Fitzgerald nodded his head. “Yes, it’s poor Mrs. Jane Geehan,” he said. “She’s Paddy Geehan’s woman. They’re bringing her back home now. I think Pad has been looking for her these past two days. She had a bad heart and was not feeling too well these last couple of years. Poor soul.”

Michael nodded at Bill Byrne. “Bill found her this morning. We just got back from doing the police report. I don’t know Paddy Geehan, but we’ll be having a prayer for him and his missus. Have they any children?”

John shook his head. “No, but she has an older brother who lives with them.”

As the crowd was dispersing, everyone seemed to have some theory as to the woman’s sudden passing. Nobody even guessed that Mrs. Jane Geehan had left this world under felonious circumstances.

CHAPTER TWO

November 4th, 1867
Four Years Earlier

Johanna Hamilton migrated to Newfoundland from County Cork, Ireland, at the age of fifteen, following her older sister's advice. Her sister, Catherine, had earlier come to Riverhead, Harbour Grace, where she married John Drake, a local farmer and fisherman. Catherine and John were now the parents of four children.

The Hamilton girls' father had abandoned Johanna and her mother five years earlier in Cork County, leaving them with a rundown farm. Catherine feared that Johanna and her mother were destined for the poorhouse, and she encouraged Johanna to come to Newfoundland, saying she stood a good chance of getting work as a servant girl. She said their mother could more easily fend for herself back in Cork, not having the burden of Johanna's welfare. Even though Catherine gladly welcomed Johanna to stay with her, times were rough for her and her family. Their living quarters were small and there were many mouths to feed.

Johanna stayed with the Drake family for several months while she searched for work. One day, Catherine got word that the Munns, a well to do merchant family, were hiring young servant girls to work in their mansion on Water Street and she suggested that Johanna go see them. Johanna walked to Harbour Grace and met with John Munn's chief clerk. He was a thin sharp featured man who introduced himself as Fred Apsey.

"I'm sorry," he said, looking at her sadly. "Your sister should never have given you false hope of finding work here. We can offer you very little in the way of work, except for the Labrador fishery, that is." Apsey paused and waited for Johanna's reaction. Seeing none, he continued in hopes that she would be interested. Because of the strenuous work, it was difficult to attract young women to work on the Labrador.

Apsey picked up some papers on his desk and looked at them carefully before he spoke again. "We have two boats going to the coast next spring, and one of our planters will be in need of a cook."

Johanna looked at Apsey and said nothing for a minute. She was homesick. She was penniless. She knew she had to make her own way. She had to get work. She knew nothing at all about Labrador and the fishery there but if there was work available she felt she had little choice but to accept it. She had no idea of the primitive living conditions she would experience working as a servant girl in a fishing hut at Nowlan's Harbour, Labrador.

"I can cook and clean, but I know nothing about fish," she admitted.

"Not to worry," Apsey said briskly. "Patrick Geehan, the skipper, and Garrett Sears, his shareman, will teach you all you need to know. As a matter of fact, Mr. and Mrs. Geehan own a farm on the Southside, and it is possible they may be in need of domestic service during the winter. There may well be a job there for you. My advice would be to go see them."

Feeling dejected since she had her mind set on being a full time maid in the Munn household, Johanna made the long walk back to Riverhead. As soon as he saw her, John Drake could see she hadn't received the news she was hoping for.

"I didn't think you'd be back so soon. I gather you didn't get good news?" John said gently. He was a quiet man, supportive and respectful. Johanna never understood how he and her volatile sister were able to stay together. They were so different. Yet, after five years of marriage, they had already brought four children into the world.

"The Munn family has no work for me," Johanna told her brother-in-law. "Their clerk told me about the Geehans on the Southside. Mr. Apsey said Patrick Geehan and his brother-in-law are looking for a girl for their fishing room on the Labrador, and he said I might get some work at their farm until then."

"Don't go near'em!" yelled Catherine from the backroom. "Patrick Geehan is nothing but a whoremonger and a drunk."

Johanna hated the word "whoremonger." It was the very word her mother had often used to describe her estranged husband. Johanna hadn't seen her father since she was ten, yet her memories of him never seemed to warrant her mother's harsh words.

John looked at Johanna and then yelled at Catherine. "My Jesus, woman. That's something for you to say. You'll be eatin' the rails next week." John was referring to Catherine's practice of receiving Holy Communion each Sunday even though she was so quick to judge the Geehans.

"Well, John Fitzgerald and the others on the Southside will tell you that Paddy Geehan and Jane went for weeks without speaking after that young servant girl named Marshall left.

They say she refused to go to the Labrador with him because of his shenanigans."

By now Catherine was out in the kitchen wagging her finger at John to make sure her opinion was the one upheld. John knew his place and decided not to debate it.

"Johanna, let me tell you. Paddy Geehan saw his way to get himself a good dowry a few years ago so he asked for Jane Sears hand in marriage. Jane is a woman years older than Patrick."

Catherine clearly had the floor by now. She then made the serious gesture of removing her apron and stopping her household duties.

"Grandfather Sears passed away a few years ago and left a beautiful farmhouse, cattle, and plenty of farmland to Jane Sears and her brother Garrett. Aunt Lilly Sears, Jane's mother, had passed away many years before that. Jane is getting up in years, way beyond fertility, and works along with her brother, although they never saw eye to eye either. Poor Garrett didn't go to school and is a little simple, you know."

"How do you know they never saw eye to eye, Catherine?" John interrupted. "You're only going on with what the old chaw bags in the River are saying." John's words were again putting him on dangerous ground.

"John Drake, if you want to live to puff another draw from that pipe, you'd better shut your gob!" Catherine took a moment to stare down her husband. With her hands on her hips, she intended to make sure that John wasn't going to interject again.

She took a deep breath and continued. "A handsome brute he was, a much younger Paddy Geehan, that is. Any woman worth her salt and having a good pair of eyes in her head would love to have him. Dark skinned, muscular and as fit as a fiddle. Sometimes if a man is quiet, it is worth it to ignore his drinking. Especially if he keeps his eyes to himself." Catherine was almost swooning when suddenly she realized she had lost her train of thought. “But that Pat Geehan is a wolf in sheep’s clothing. He can be a bad man when he takes a drop. In fact, he can suck it out of a hen’s arse, as mother used to say about Da. I’ll tell you that.”

“But Catherine, I have little choice. If they have a job for me I should take it,” she said, frowning a little to show she was unappreciative of Catherine’s negative comments about their father. “You and John have been good to me, but it’s time for me to make my own way.”

“Indeed, there’s not much room here this winter with five mouths to feed, and me being sick again with another child, and us with only two rooms,” Catherine said finally. She was starting to realize it would be an added burden on her family if Johanna didn’t take the offer. “Well, maybe you should go and see for yourself. Give it a try. We’ll always make a place here if things don’t work out. You will only be a walk away if you need us.”

“I’ll make a visit tomorrow and see for myself,” concluded Johanna. “Going back home to Cork isn’t something I can do. Work is even scarcer at home than it is here.”

John Drake remained silent, but not because of Catherine’s bullying. He knew if Johanna could make it on her own, it would be the correct course of action for everyone.

CHAPTER THREE

Southside of Harbour Grace
November 5, 1867

Johanna packed her clothes in her mother's old cloth valise. She carried it with her just in case the Geehans wanted her service immediately. Everything she possessed was in that bag. John Drake offered to accompany her, but Johanna decided a fifteen-year-old would demonstrate greater maturity by visiting the Geehans on her own.

It was a cold gray day in November as she made her way down the Southside. The wind was brisk and the breakers licked at the shoreline. Because the tide was high, the heavy sea sprayed salt water over the road. Johanna could feel the dampness of the sea on her face and through her clothes. Gloomy days, such as these, gave her a lonely feeling. She missed her mother terribly. And even though she hadn't seen her father for a long time there was still an ache in her heart for him.

Johanna had never finished her schooling. She'd struggled academically from the start and quit school at the age of eleven to stay home and help her mother with chores around the farm. Her life thus far was one of destitution and poverty since the farm yielded very little harvest. As she grew older, it became evident her lack of education would be compensated for by her looks. She had become a strikingly beautiful young woman. In contrast to most of those of Irish descent, her complexion was dark as was her long thick coal black hair. Her skin was clear and unblemished. Her curvaceous figure and pretty face had already caused many heads to turn as she walked the streets of Harbour Grace. But Johanna seemed unaware of her beauty and innocent of the effect it had on men.

When she saw the Geehan house Johanna remembered Catherine's words and agreed it was indeed beautiful. The structure was not unlike the houses found at home in Ireland. It was a small two-storey peak roofed dwelling. A second story dormer window distinguished it from most other houses of its style. The setting was perfect in every way. The farmhouse stood near neatly constructed barns, sheds and rock walls. Johanna had no way of knowing that the pleasant exterior of the farmhouse was just a facade, hiding great tension and unhappiness.

Patrick Geehan was out in the garden standing in the back of a box cart. Garrett Sears was inside the upper door of the barn hauling the hay in, as Patrick used his pitchfork to bail the straw up to him. Johanna walked up the path to the house and thought it proper to knock on the door, as opposed to interrupting the two men at work. She nervously rapped on the door and waited for someone to respond. She heard the hook on the front door being freed up. A middle-aged woman she thought must be Mrs. Geehan opened the door and nodded at her.

"Good day, young woman," she said to Johanna. "Can I help you with something?"

The woman was wearing a long black dress, plain and unadorned. With her graying hair pinned up in a bun she looked much older than the forty-six years Catherine had said she was. Catherine had also said rightly that Jane Geehan was very stern and serious looking.

"My name is Johanna Hamilton and I've been sent here by the Munns to see if your family might be in need of my services. I'm not sure if I even have the right house. I'm looking for the Geehans," Johanna spoke mostly to the doorstep rather than to Mrs. Geehan.

"Well, you have the right farm, but I didn't know anything about needing any servant girl."

Mrs. Geehan looked annoyed as she asked Johanna to wait on the stoop. Without introducing herself, she abruptly slammed the door in Johanna's face. Johanna could hear the older woman strut through the house and out the back door.

A muffled discussion ensued from out back which was loud enough for Johanna to realize there was some debate going on. The chatter went back and forth between a man and a woman until she heard the back door slam. Finally, after the sound of more footsteps, these being much heavier than those earlier, the front door opened again. This time a very handsome man filled the doorway.

"So you've been sent by the Munns, have you?" he asked with a smile that Johanna couldn't help responding to. "I'm Patrick Geehan and we are very much looking for help next spring when we go to Nowlan's Harbour on the Labrador. You're a bit early for that, though, aren't you?"

"That I am, sir. But Mr. Apsey at Munns said your family might want a servant girl for the winter, as well as help on the Labrador in the spring. I can cook, bake, wash and tend to cattle the same as any man. I can milk cows, shear sheep and scythe hay. You see, I grew up on a farm. When the spring comes, and if you like my work, then I could travel to the Labrador coast with you, if you would be so obliged." Johanna got these words out almost in one breath.

"Well, come in out of the cold and we'll see what we can do. What's your name?" he asked.

"Johanna Hamilton, sir. I am Catherine Drake's sister. She is married to John Drake from Riverhead. She moved here from Cork, Ireland, years ago."

"Cork? That's where my Da was from." Geehan seemed pleased as he reached out and gently shook Johanna's hand. He said nothing about knowing either John Drake or Catherine.

Patrick Geehan was a tall man standing at about six feet. He was broad across the shoulders with black wavy hair and sported a neatly groomed mustache. If she hadn't known his true age to be thirty-nine, Johanna would have thought him to be in his early twenties. She found him to be a splendid looking man. Catherine's earlier description of him was quite accurate.

Mrs. Geehan silently returned to the kitchen. Without saying a word she pulled out a chair and sat down. Geehan continued talking to Johanna but looked mostly at his wife and hardly at her.

"Johanna," he said, "this is my wife, Jane. I think it would be a good idea to have you come work here for the winter and then on the Labrador in the spring. You would be a great help to Jane since this farm can be very busy. And I know we would be glad to have you cooking for us in Nowlan's Harbour."

"Well, you'll be sleeping in the room off the porch. That's the only place I got for you," Jane Geehan said as her husband finished speaking. Those were the only words she uttered. Mrs. Geehan kept her arms folded as she sat at the table and continued to stare out the kitchen window. Her eyes were cold and she looked angry. Obviously, the hiring of a servant girl wasn't her idea.

The back door opened and an older man walked into the kitchen. He went directly over to the fireplace to warm his hands. He didn't look at anyone but Patrick Geehan.

"Are you coming back out, bye, or are you expecting me to finish puttin' in the hay?" he asked, continuing to grumble to himself as he spit his chewing tobacco into the hearth.

Patrick introduced the man to Johanna as Garrett Sears and they shook hands. Garrett was dressed in overalls that had been patched over several times. A gruff looking man, he was unshaven and practically toothless. The corners of his mouth had yellowed with nicotine, and tufts of gray hair protruded out from under his ragged salt and pepper cap. He was the extreme opposite of Patrick Geehan. Johanna thought he seemed unfriendly, much like his sister.

Jane and her brother might not be warm, friendly people, but the kitchen in which Johanna sat was a comforting cozy place. The fireplace, made of local stone and undoubtedly crafted by a very competent stonemason, occupied almost the entire east wall. A deep hearth with two granite props held up a heavy iron mantel. Underneath the mantel a black cauldron and a kettle were hanging on separate pothooks. Lanterns were placed on both sides of the hearth. Shelves with cupboards underneath were on one side of the fireplace. A daybed was situated next to the fireplace, conveniently positioned so that its occupant could reap the full benefits of a fire on a cold day. Mrs. Geehan's rocking chair was placed near the window allowing her a full view of the harbour and the road. The kitchen table was underneath the window, and a full-length sideboard displayed pottery and pewter dishes the likes of which Johanna had never before witnessed. Jane Geehan had inherited quite a collection of tableware from her mother.

"Johanna will be working with us here this winter to give Jane a hand. In the spring she'll be coming with us to Nowlan's Harbour," Patrick said as he tried to get Garrett to focus, but the old man only glanced at Johanna and grunted something inaudible. Johanna felt even more uncomfortable. Patrick, so far, had been the only person to show any friendliness or sign of welcome to her.

The entire evening turned out to be a painful introduction to the Geehan household. Mrs. Geehan prepared supper as if Johanna wasn't in the room. Her offers to help were ignored so she sat quietly at the kitchen table.

She could see that there was a front room off the kitchen and stairs leading from the front room up to the second floor. Feeling ill at ease, she finally excused herself and went out to the backyard to have a look around. She saw Patrick and Garrett hard at work but they paid no attention to her. She finally went back inside and sat at the table again. The men stayed out till dark, continuing their work until they were called in for supper.

The ill will between Patrick Geehan and Jane continued at the supper table. Both would snap at each other occasionally but there was never any civil conversation.

After a while, Patrick stopped eating and began talking to Johanna.

"Tomorrow I'll give you some chores around the farm. We rise at about six and feed the animals before we feed ourselves. I'll do most of those things with you so that you'll have an idea of how to proceed. But as you grew up on a farm I am sure you are not going to have any problems. Farm work is farm work wherever you are."

Johanna smiled at him, relieved to be getting some direction. She always felt that not knowing what to do, even if she had the skill, was nerve wrecking.

Patrick continued. "Mrs. Geehan will get some bed coverings for you and show you to your room. We need early nights so the lamps will be doused at eight-thirty every night during the winter." Patrick had taken on a more authoritarian manner for the first time. Johanna suspected he wanted to show his wife that Johanna was going to be treated like a servant girl and nothing else.

Garrett Sears lay down on the daybed as soon as he finished the meal he had gulped down as if it was his last. Johanna helped Mrs. Geehan with the dishes. She watched where every dish and pot was stored.

"Can you make bread?" Mrs. Geehan asked abruptly.

"I can and I use my mother's recipe," said Johanna proudly. "It's the finest loaf in all of Ireland."

"We'll be making a pan tomorrow and we'll be following my recipe, not your mother's. I'm not much for change."

The words made Johanna feel as though she'd been slapped, but she listened carefully as Mrs. Geehan spoke again. "We'll be wanting potatoes in soak first thing after you are done with the animals. We have potatoes every day, regardless."

At eight-thirty exactly, the Geehans went off to bed followed by Garrett. No one said goodnight. Johanna couldn't believe that three people could exude such negativity. She decided there and then that she would cope no matter what. Surviving these hostilities would take discipline and independence. But she was going to survive!

Johanna got into bed and reached into her mother's valise to pull out a pair of rosary beads. They were ones that had been given to her by her father when she made her First Holy Communion. She rummaged through the valise. Once, twice and then again. Her rosary beads had disappeared. She fingered the crevices of the bag and took out every piece of clothing. Still nothing! She had lost her most cherished possession. Not to be defeated, she closed her eyes and began using her fingers to count the first decade of the Sorrowful Mysteries, "The Agony in the Garden." This prayer always gave her comfort. It recounted how Jesus, by himself, had gained contentment and courage in his final hours.

With her room being adjacent to Patrick and Jane's, she could hear a mumbled dialogue through the wall. The voices soon got louder. Johanna wasn't accustomed to people fighting like this. She grew anxious and scared.

"You had no goddamn business bringing that woman here without my permission," she heard Jane say.

"We need the help, particularly this summer in Nowlan's Harbour," Patrick responded. "But if we wait till then, we mightn't get anyone. Besides, we can spend the time getting her ready."

"You took one look at that young woman and you hired her. If you do anything else she's gone," Jane said harshly. "Garrett and me still own this place and we can put you out pretty quickly. So watch your peepers. I got rid of that young Marshall girl. I can get rid of this one too."

There was silence in the room next to her. Johanna's heartbeat had been racing but it began to slow down as the arguing faded. Jane was a jealous woman and Johanna knew that jealousy was a demon in itself. Her first thought was that Patrick Geehan must be a patient man to allow a woman to jaw him like that. On further thought, maybe Jane Geehan had good reason to be jealous.

Johanna continued her rosary. Not having attended Mass since she left home, she felt this was the only vestige of faith she had left.

CHAPTER FOUR

Southside of Harbour Grace
November 30, 1867

As the fall progressed, darkness set in earlier with each passing day. The Southside of Harbour Grace was largely unsheltered against the easterly gales blowing directly off the water. The winds were the most cutting that Johanna had ever experienced. However, the damp cold weather wasn't nearly as chilly as Jane Geehan.

After a full day of hardly speaking to Johanna, except to snap an order or utter a curse, Jane would spend most of her evenings seated by the fire. She insisted each night that Johanna go early to her room, away from the heat of the kitchen. Many evenings saw Johanna go to bed cold, hungry and fatigued. Her new life was turning out to be one of drudgery and misery. Hope of achieving contentment or self-value was quickly eroding.

"Go out to the barn and pick up a few more splits for the morning before you go to your quarters," ordered Jane one evening as she rocked back and forth in her chair. Occasionally, she would take a pinch of snuff from her tiny snuff-box and then lightly sponge her running nose with her handkerchief.

The splits were stored in the barn in order to keep them dry. Splits were chopped junks of wood that had been "shaved" with a sharp knife to easily enable them to catch fire. They were mostly used to get the morning fire started more quickly. Tonight, though, Jane thought that a couple of splits would give her another blast of heat before going to bed.

Old Garrett was well asleep on the daybed with a blanket pulled up to his chin. Patrick was out visiting his neighbor, Mr. Shugarue. He often did this to pass away the long fall evenings. Johanna suspected his visit was more of a respite from Jane than anything else.

Doing as she was told, Johanna stood up, quickly put on her coat, and grabbed the lantern. This was a job she hated! Going out to the barn, in total darkness, evoked thoughts of spirits and demons in stories she had heard as a child. She was afraid of what she might discover in the blackness of the barn. Once she had sprinted across the back yard and entered the barn, she felt a little safer since she was immediately surrounded by the warmth of the animals. She raised the lamp high above her head so that the light spread out and she could see almost all the interior of the barn.

"Well, you managed to get away from the old bat for a few minutes, did you?" came a voice from the shadows where the light hadn't been able to reach.

Johanna had such a fright she dropped the lamp to the floor. There was complete darkness once again. At first, she groped to find the lamp but then she thought it best to make a run for the door.

'It's only me, Johanna. Don't worry. I didn't mean to frighten you."

She now recognized Patrick's voice and could feel his presence near her.

"Jesus, Mary and Joseph, Mr. Geehan. I didn't know you were out here. I thought you were over to Shugarues. You scared the livin' daylights out of me." She could smell rum as Patrick inched nearer.

A flame erupted as Patrick struck a match allowing Johanna to see his face. After picking up the lamp, he struggled to insert the match into the lantern with drunken dexterity. The barn became fully lit again. Rather than being afraid or threatened, she took comfort in Patrick's presence. She could see him clearly. He held a partially filled bottle of dark rum in one hand while he steadied himself with the other against the horse's stall. Awkwardly, he handed the lamp back to Johanna.

"We don't get a chance to chat much. Not with Garrett and Jane looking over our shoulders. I want to tell you that I really appreciate your work and your being here. You've brightened up the old place, you know." Patrick was slurring his words as he tried to focus on Johanna. She was well accustomed to the mannerisms of the men back home that often had too much to drink so he didn't worry her. Patrick stood a little closer and rested his hand on her shoulder.

"You have certainly proven yourself with us," he said as he squeezed her shoulder. "I've seen you go about your work and you do it well. Since you arrived, our chores out in the yard have been cut in half. And I've never seen the house so clean and warm."

Johanna knew Patrick's intent, but it didn't matter. She hadn't heard a compliment since she'd arrived at the Geehan house and his words were like poetry to her. Even though she knew he was foolish with rum, she welcomed his verbal stroking and hung on to his every word.

"Well, Mr. Geehan, I didn't fancy that you even knew what I did, especially in the house," she responded with a little grin.

"Call me Patrick," he said, as he moved his hand from her shoulder to her back, and put his face very close to hers.

"All right, Patrick it is then. But I don't think Mrs. Geehan will allow it, Patrick," she said. He was making her nervous. "It's getting on; I'd better be getting back into the house with the splits unless you want Mrs. Geehan out here."

Suddenly, she was grabbed and pulled in so closely that Patrick's body pushed fully up against hers. She thought of resisting at first, but the embrace felt so comforting that she closed her eyes and blissfully enjoyed being swept up with passion and desire. Patrick's lips touched hers as they locked together in a prolonged kiss that seemed to last forever. There was no resistance on her part. When he released her from the embrace, he staggered back. He now appeared more lucid, as if he were shocked back to sobriety by what had happened.

All the hatred heaped upon Johanna by Jane Geehan, all the loneliness she had experienced, had now vanished. Not for a minute did she feel guilty or worry that Patrick Geehan was married. She didn't care that he "belonged" to another woman. For this moment, he was hers and hers alone.

Patrick stood up straight. "You'd better get back in the house as fast as you can," he said as he loaded her arms with splits. "You can't say a word about this. She'd go right off her head, and nobody knows what she'd do."

As Johanna was leaving, he pulled the cork out of the bottle for another drink of rum. Left alone in the darkness, he dropped down onto a stool and wondered where all of this was going to lead. He'd craved Johanna since he first saw her at the door and he knew he had to find a way to be with her. She was a fifteen-year-old child in the body of a mature woman. He realized he was playing with fire. Patrick Geehan also he understood that he could not lose what he had gained by making a deal with the devil in taking Jane Geehan's hand in marriage.

"Well you took long enough," snarled Jane when Johanna appeared with an armful of splits. "Throw them behind the stove and put a couple on the ashes. Take your time so you don't stir up any soot. That should keep it warm for a little longer tonight. What in the Christ were you at out there? It took you all night."

"Oh, I gave old Prince a little hay and spent some time with him in the warm," responded Johanna.

"Well, from now on do what you're told more quickly or I'll be holding back a few pence come Christmas. Me and Garrett are here like two lumps of ice and you are out there with a fecking animal." Jane was visibly upset.

"I'm sorry, Mrs. Geehan. It won't happen again," Johanna said politely. But, hopefully, she thought, it would happen again, and sooner rather than later.

CHAPTER FIVE

Southside of Harbour Grace
December, 1867

Since the incident in the barn, Patrick hadn't approached Johanna again. He kept his distance during the month of December leading up to the Christmas season. He went out of his way to avoid her, most times even taking his meals in silence. She was convinced that his behavior wasn't a rejection of her. She recognized that the slightest sign of any attention paid to her would alert Jane of his feelings. Patrick's rejection, in a strange way, caused Johanna to be even more desirous of him.

During the weeks when the people of the Southside were preparing for Christmas, Jane Geehan seemed to grow more hostile towards Johanna. She even restricted her attendance at church on Sundays and other holy days of obligation. Johanna wasn't permitted to partake of any services during the entire Season of Advent.

"We'll be going up to Confession tonight if you'd like to come along," John Fitzgerald, the Geehan's neighbour, called out to Johanna from across the yard one day. "My brother, Patrick, will be with us and we're taking the sleigh so there will be lots of room. You and Jane are quite welcome to ride with us."

Johanna hadn't yet been introduced to Patrick Fitzgerald. All she had heard was that he was unmarried and shy. John Fitzgerald had issued an invitation to Johanna and Mrs. Geehan but he didn't mention Patrick Geehan. Everyone knew Patrick had walked away from the church many years earlier.

"I'm afraid I'll be keeping the fire going tonight as Mrs. Geehan will be going to church with Mr. and Mrs. Shugarue. Thanks kindly anyway. The men are working a bit later than usual with the nets and such. They won't be in for supper until six so I will be busy until late in the evening," explained Johanna.

"Confessions are at five-thirty. If you can see your way clear later, come on over around five," replied Fitzgerald. Johanna knew the futility of making that request to Jane Geehan and decided to keep her mouth shut.

During Christmas, Johanna was given two days off to spend with her sister and her family up in the River. Just before she left, Patrick volunteered to bring her up with the horse and sleigh. It was a clear crisp day as Johanna sat alone, wrapped in a blanket, on the bench directly behind Prince, Patrick's beautiful black stallion.

Patrick stood on the back runners of the sleigh as they left the farm. It was common practice that only married couples joined each other on the bench up front once they got underway. But after they rounded the last turn on the Southside Road and were completely out of sight, Patrick stopped Prince and jumped up on the seat close to Johanna. Snapping the reins, he whistled for his horse to continue.

Johanna had always thought that as soon as Patrick got a chance he would quickly find time to be with her. She had been so patient. And now was her time.

"You must think me a horrible person," he said. "Tryin' to be with a girl so innocent in her youth and me a married man with no hope of anything to come of it."

Patrick's words were spoken as if their encounter in the barn had taken place a few minutes ago. But it was seven weeks ago to the very day that they had kissed in the barn. Johanna wondered how he could have waited so long to approach her again. He continued to stare straight ahead as if a reply wasn't necessary.

"I don't think you're horrible at all," Johanna said. "I think of you as a strong man. A man who is in need of something more than what Jane Geehan has ever offered you. I've seen her put you down. Holding the farm over you. Saying you've got no courage and then laughing at you." The word courage in Newfoundland carried a deeper, more sexual connotation having to do with a man's propensity for making love.

"I have to ask for your forgiveness for having kissed you that night, against your will," said Patrick.

"There'll be no need of forgiveness for it was a beautiful kiss, one that I'll never forget. It wasn't against my will at all."

Johanna was well aware that Patrick was a married man. But her heart told her there was nothing wrong with coming between two people who hated each other. She thought maybe Patrick would leave Jane and the two of them could make a new life together. A happy life. They could have a family, a little boy who looked just like Patrick. A little girl who looked like her. If they had to they could leave Harbour Grace. She knew they could be happy anywhere. She and Patrick loved each other. They were meant for each other. But even as she had those thoughts… somewhere… deep down inside was a little niggle of doubt that she tried hard to suppress.

"I really shouldn't have any desire for you," said Patrick. "I know it's a sin for a married man to turn towards another woman, but Jane never stops jawing me and making little of me. It can get very lonely at times." Johanna could hear the anger and frustration in his voice. "Even worse, I'm more than twice your age."

"I don't mind your age," Johanna responded. "It was torturous for me to be sitting in the kitchen right across from you and not being able to touch you or even talk to you for these last few weeks."

"We'll have to be patient, little one. There's no harm in our spending a little time together, even if it's just to talk. Still, it will be difficult to do even that until we get to Nowlan's Harbour. There, we'll have a little freedom for a while." Patrick reached over to pat her hand.

Johanna held onto his hand. She wanted desperately to say, "Can't you just leave her now? There are no children. We could make a life together somewhere else and start over." However, she couldn't allow herself to utter those words. It was as if she were standing outside her body, watching herself acting in a way she'd never thought possible. A single kiss from someone who was a stranger just a few weeks ago had blossomed into her wanting this man for the rest of her life. She knew she loved Patrick and wanted to be with him forever.

Patrick was silent as he maneuvered the sleigh dangerously close to the Southside cliffs. Johanna felt no fear as she watched the waves break over the ice-covered boulders below. She felt nothing only frustration and disappointment. They finally turned the corner by Mackey's Store, causing the discussion to end.

Patrick left his seat on the bench beside Johanna and returned to the rear of the sleigh as he drove across the River and onto Glover Road. Catherine was peeking through the partially closed curtains in her front room as the sleigh stopped in front of the Drake house. She watched as Patrick came around to the front to assist Johanna. She took note of the length of time he held Johanna's hand as she pushed herself off the sleigh. She felt frustrated that she couldn't hear what Patrick whispered to Johanna before he left.

"I'll miss you, Johanna, during these two days," he'd said. "You'll have to get John Drake to bring you back after the holiday. The old woman will have a fit if I come to get you."

Johanna entered the Drake house with much less excitement than Catherine had anticipated. She'd thought Johanna would be delighted to see the signs of Christmas festivity that were everywhere throughout the house. The tree was up and fully decorated with candles and homemade ornaments. Holly had been placed over the doors and in the windows. The aroma of Catherine's baking permeated the rooms. The children ran to Johanna as soon as they saw her and she was overwhelmed with hugs and kisses. She had no choice but to be swept along by the holiday atmosphere prevalent in the household. After a day of singing carols and having fun with the children, she and the Drakes attended Midnight Mass together. Johanna's decision not to receive Holy Communion sparked Catherine's interest.

"You didn't receive the Blessed Sacrament tonight?" remarked Catherine, finding the right moment to speak to Johanna in private.

"No. You know the old woman wouldn't even give me the time to get to confession."

The Catechism taught Johanna at a very young age that lusting after another woman's husband was a mortal sin. If she died under the pain of sin, she would most certainly be condemned to hell. Not having had a chance to go to confession, she would be committing a sacrilege by receiving communion while in the state of sin.

"You must have done something awful," said Catherine.

Being her inquisitive self, Catherine was boldly pushing Johanna to share the details of her guilty conscience. Johanna had no intention of doing so. What bitter irony, she thought, as she half listened to her sister. Her soul was now stained with mortal sin. Jane Geehan had gone to church to make amends with God while she ordered Johanna to stay behind and mind the fire. The miserable old woman had prevented Johanna from being clean in the eyes of the Lord.

"What a mean hake not to give you time to go to Mass or confession," Catherine was still baiting Johanna.

"Well, I don't mind what Mrs. Geehan does to me," said Johanna. "I do my work and say nothing. But there are times in that house, because of her, that it's not a fit place to live. And she, goin' on her knees to the priest. It seems like there's nothing but one big fight in that house. One of these days, though, she and her brother, old Garrett, will come to blows, I can tell you that."

"You think with him being her only brother and just a poor simpleton she'd appreciate having him around," said Catherine.

"Yes, everyone thinks that, but only those behind closed doors know what goes on," said Johanna. "The two of them fight like cats. I've never seen people hate each other like they do."

"It's a wonder Patrick Geehan allows that to go on, especially if he still takes the rum. Is he still drinkin?"

"He has a drop once in a while. You can't blame him sure. He's got some patience. If she's not nagging him about something, there's a racket going on between Jane and Garrett. Many a night, the old woman got to leave and go over to the Connors to get Mr. Geehan. Old Garrett has either put his foot to the wall or taken a swing at her for some reason or other. Patrick Geehan is an angel for holdin' back. He could break that old man in two, but he holds back because he realizes that Garrett is very childlike."

"What happens to you when this is goin on? You must be petrified half the time?"

"Oh, I go outside and stay in the barn with Prince until everything settles down. It's warm and peaceful out there. Then I come back in and everything is back to normal, or as normal as it gets."

"Normal? How can things be normal if they're fightin' all the time?" Catherine asked.

"Jane Geehan is the divil herself. I've even seen her swing at Garrett and barely miss him. She's done the same to Mr. Geehan." Johanna was being careful not to call him Patrick. "Normal in that house is when all three of them are in the kitchen and no one is speaking. When they are mad and sulkin' at each other that's when it's peaceful. At least then they are not fightin' and bawlin.'"

While Catherine knew of Geehan's drinking and chasing women, she hadn't realized what a house of horrors the farmhouse was. She was becoming more and more upset as Johanna spoke.

"Why don't you give it up, girl?" she said. "It's not worth your getting hurt. Come back here with us and we'll make do."

Johanna looked at her sister with gratitude even as she shook her head and said, "Not with you like you are, sick with a child and all. You've got a house full and John is finding it hard enough. Besides, Mr. Geehan is as good as gold to me. I'm sure if things got really bad between Garrett and the old woman, he would step in."

"Has Geehan bothered you at all?" persisted Catherine.

Johanna knew what Catherine meant. "No. He doesn't come near me. He must be turned from the likes of us."

"But there can't be anything between him and his wife. You never know what's on his mind. With her being crooked and so much older than him. Especially where she's on the change and all. God knows what will happen if he gets on the shine. He is still in his prime and must be wanting his way with a woman. You make sure to watch yourself around him."

Johanna kept her face blank. "Well, he can drink what shine he wants," she said. "I'm not the woman for him, a man with two dozen or more years on me. No. I'll be waiting for the right man, Catherine. You can depend on that."

On the morning of December 27, John Drake and his eldest child escorted Johanna back to the Geehan farm. It was a beautiful day as they rode down past the Morrisseys and the Connors. The snow had piled higher over the past two days and the temperature had dropped. Johanna accepted that winter had settled in. As she walked up the freshly shoveled path towards the Geehan house, she saw Patrick. He acknowledged her by waving his hand and then turned his back to continue his chores. Johanna noticed that the wind had become more cutting. She felt sure that this was going to be a long cold winter.

CHAPTER SIX

The Vestibule of the Cathedral of St. John The Baptist, 1895
St. John's, Newfoundland

"You know something? You look more beautiful than this magnificent structure," John Coombs whispered in Sarah Keough's ear. He and Sarah were standing in the vestibule of the Roman Catholic cathedral in St. John's, a splendid building which had taken fourteen years to complete after its foundation was laid by Bishop Michael Fleming in 1841.

They had arrived at one o'clock, a full hour before the ceremony. The cathedral was located on the highest ridge overlooking the city of St. John's. With time to spare they had stood outside in the churchyard looking at a stunning view which included the city spread at their feet as well as St. John's harbour and out to the Narrows, the only way into the harbour. The huge entrance doors of the cathedral were propped open and a cool breeze off the harbour filled the interior with fresh air. There weren't many warm days in this city, but July 1, 1895, was unusually hot.

Sarah was in her twenties and wearing a pale green dress which enhanced her light complexion and clung to her trim, well-proportioned figure in all the right places. Her hair was dark and wavy and her eyes were blue. She had one of those faces that too easily gave away her feelings. Her nose wrinkled before she laughed, and the corners of her mouth turned down if she had a sad thought. There was no question she could easily attract almost any man she desired. But the only one she wanted was standing right there with her.

"Are you sure you're ready for this?" she asked John.

"I really don't know," he answered. "If my prayers are being answered, I should be fine." Due to habit more so than prayer, he nervously scrolled through the rosary beads in his pants pocket.

The young couple stood in the vestibule of the ornate structure, both dressed in formal attire and holding hands. It would appear to anyone observing them that they were about to get married, but such wasn't the case. John was about to go to the altar to make his final vows as a priest.

"I know we talked about this over and over again. God chose me; I didn't choose Him," John looked at Sarah as he repeated the words that Bishop Thomas Power had used when he spoke about vocations to the Church. "I've always had a need for somebody or something. It's a want that I've never been able to satisfy. No matter who I'm with, I have never felt fully connected. It's like my heart is always searching for where I belong. Even though my parents love me very much there is an emptiness or void inside me which they could never seem to fill. The Holy Spirit, on the other hand, I believe, has been calling me. I hope that I'll find the bond I want through the Church."

Sarah said nothing as he looked searchingly at her. The hour had arrived! Her heart and mind burned to ask him why she couldn't be the one to fill the void, the emptiness that he felt inside. What had begun long ago as a friendship had become something else for Sarah over the years she and John had known each other. But never once had he given her any indication that she was anything more than his very good friend.

"You seem to understand me more than anyone," he said to her now. But his words brought no consolation. Since he had chosen the Church over her, Sarah had been devastated. Her prayers for the last couple of years had been for John, not for him to be a priest, but for him to be her husband.

John Michael Coombs had been baptized on September 18, 1872, in this very church. He grew up on Prescott Street and was taught by Irish Christian Brothers. In 1875, the Brothers had accepted an invitation from the Benevolent Irish Society (BIS) to come to Newfoundland and assume responsibility for Roman Catholic education in St. John's. The Christian Brothers Schools opened in January 1876 and attendance quickly shot up from 66 students at the former Orphan Asylum Schools in November to 300 students, the full limit of the space available.

Under normal circumstances, John would never have been able to gain entrance to an elite institution which catered to the more affluent upper crust of the St. John's Catholic population. But his parents, although not wealthy, were both in positions that gave him an advantage in gaining admittance. His father, Mark Coombs, had been a caretaker at the Orphan Asylum Schools and then at the Christian Brothers Schools, up until he took up duties at Mount St. Francis Monastery, the newly opened residence of the Irish Christian Brothers on Merrymeeting Road. John's mother, Theresa, was a cook for Bishop Thomas Power and worked in the kitchen of the presbytery that annexed the cathedral.

John was the only child of Mark and Theresa Coombs. He eventually went on to study and graduate from St. Bonaventure's College where he excelled in all academic areas. Although schooled amidst the elite, John preferred not to draw attention to himself. He gravitated towards events where he could blend within the crowd, despite the Christian Brothers' attempts to make him more social. His shyness lingered as he grew older. The fear of rejection, the root of all bashfulness, never allowed him to establish significant relationships, other than his long and abiding friendship with Sarah Keough.

Sarah was raised by her grandparents after her mother died in childbirth and her father passed away shortly afterwards. There was something almost mystical about her lifelong friendship with John. Understanding his feelings of emptiness, of not being connected, of not knowing where he belonged may have been the unifying factor in their relationship. She felt her circumstances of not knowing her parents had evoked similar feelings of emptiness in her as well.

The only person, besides John, that Sarah felt close to was her grandmother. Her grandmother was a health care assistant at the Forest Road Hospital and Sarah took great satisfaction in doing volunteer work with her. Attending to the sick, helping feed the aged, and giving comfort to the dying helped fill the emptiness in Sarah's heart. It was by giving that she was able to deflect the negative feelings of being alone.

John Coombs, on the other hand, had struggled to find something to give meaning to his life and had never seemed to understand that Sarah was able to find purpose and satisfaction in helping others. She wondered if John was blinded to her feelings for him because of that. In any event, he had rejected her many attempts to attract his interest. Though his ordination as a priest was now imminent, she had to leave the door cracked just a little. She had to say something to let him know how she felt.

"John," she said softly. "When you returned from the Seminary each year we were always able to resume our friendship and you seemed so happy to be home with me. Is there anything between you and me that could ease your sense of being alone? It's still not too late. All we have to do is walk away from here."

John turned away to stare at the portrait of Bishop Mullock, who had succeeded Fleming following the latter's death in 1850. Sarah's words had shaken his resolve, but his gesture told everything. His final decision had been made. The bells from the tower of the east belfry began ringing out with such reverberation that words, if there had been any, would no longer be heard. While the bells marked an invitation for all to come and celebrate Father John's marriage to the Roman Catholic Church, they also signaled the end of Sarah's hope that John would be hers.

They were both in tears as they held each other. Sarah finally broke away. This great edifice, the Cathedral of St. John, symbolized love and devotion for those who entered. It dominated the landscape for miles around and served as a beacon for those trying to find their way in from treacherous seas. For Sarah, this glorious house of God represented sadness and disappointment. Why couldn't God, the God of love, share this man with her?

John made his way into the sanctuary to put on his cassock. Today he would begin a quest, a spiritual journey, to find his place in this world. Michael Francis Howley, the newly appointed Bishop of St. John's, was set to perform his first ordination in the Diocese.

CHAPTER SEVEN

Southside of Harbour Grace
March, 1868

"This is how you do it, Johanna. You stir and punch the net down into the bark until it is completely covered. Keep moving the twine around until it's ready to come out," said Patrick. "It must be completely blackened."

The heat from the fire underneath the huge barking drum was almost unbearable but Johanna continued to stir the net around the cauldron, trying to get the method of barking perfected. It was late March and getting the fishing gear ready for the Labrador had become a priority.

"Okay, Johanna, now lift the twine out very gradually with the pitchfork, and let it rest on the edge of the barrel while the bark drains off. The net has to be almost dry before it leaves the tub."

Patrick took the pitchfork and demonstrated the process as he talked. "Garrett and I will pull the twine along the yard as you play it out until it is completely stretched. We'll get as far as the cellar with this first trawl. After that one is done, we'll haul the next one over to the barn."

Even the cold March winds weren't able to cool Johanna's face as the heat from the fire scorched her skin. Plumes of smoke continued to baffle up relentlessly. With every breath, she ingested the harsh fumes. They filled her nose and lungs until she went into a fit of coughing.

"Great work, Johanna," shouted Patrick, raising his voice so that he could be heard above her coughing. Suddenly, Johanna felt light-headed. She sat down in the snow in order to keep from falling into the hot cauldron.

"Are you all right?" asked Patrick, as she continued to cough, finally bending over to spew up black-like phlegm. Exhausted, she slumped to her knees and lay down on the cold snow.

"Jesus Christ," yelled Patrick, as he knelt down beside her. "Garrett, come over here. Hurry. Let's get her into the house and send for the doctor."

Patrick attempted to pick her up but Johanna resisted. "I'll be alright. Give me a minute," she said, as she continued to cough. But at the same time she managed to unbutton her coat and loosen the scarf she'd wound around her neck.

"I'll get her a drink," Garrett said as he raced off to fetch a dipper of water from the back house. "I'll be right back."

"Johanna, you should have stopped and taken a break. You should have said you weren't feeling well," said Patrick. His face was creased with worry.

"I couldn't stop with you driving me like a horse," Johanna's voice was sharp. This was the first time she had been able to interact with Patrick after a long three months of his acting very cool towards her. Anger was now taking the place of her physical weakness. His aloofness during the winter months had demoralized her. His indifference was even worse than the abuse she suffered from Jane Geehan. Damm Patrick Geehan anyway, she thought.

"I'm sorry, Johanna," Patrick said as he sat on the snow beside her. And then as he looked at the expression on her face he frowned. "My god, girl, we haven't got to go through all that again, have we? We've talked it to death. You know we can't have anything together."

"That's your choice and not mine." She could no longer hold back the tears. She wiped her eyes as tears trickled down her face. "I'll be leaving tomorrow."

"You can't go," Patrick looked shocked at her words. He was now impassioned. Johanna, on the other hand, was physically and mentally distraught. She had to make herself face the awful fact that nothing would become of her love for him.

They fell silent as Garrett returned with a dipper of water. Johanna gulped it down much too quickly for Garrett's liking. "Slow down, girl. Sip on it slowly. You are pushing it too hard. You'll make yourself sick," he said, displaying the first sign of empathy she'd seen in him since she arrived at the Geehan farm. He wasn't as simple as people believed, she thought.

Patrick got up and helped Johanna to her feet. "Go in and lie down on the daybed for a while," he said. "Garrett and I will finish the nets and you'll be fine tomorrow."

"I'll see how I feel a little later," Johanna said.

Patrick breathed a sigh of relief with the hint that Johanna had cooled down and maybe changed her mind about leaving. He hoped her talk of leaving was just a threat. He would be hard-pressed if she left now. It would be impossible to find a girl to go to Nowlan's Harbour with only a few weeks left before sailing for Labrador.

Patrick took Johanna by the arm and led her to the house. She insisted on finding her own way as she staggered through the back door and towards the kitchen.

“What’s the matter, girl, not feeling well?” asked Jane as she watched Johanna enter the house. Jane didn’t bother to get out of her chair to assist the visibly sick girl.

“I’ll be fine. I am just a little overcome from the smoke. I need a few minutes rest,” replied Johanna as she lay down on the daybed.

“Don’t close your peepers for too long. The men will be wanting their supper soon enough,” snapped Jane.

Johanna said nothing as she closed her eyes. She felt better lying down.

Outside in the yard, Patrick was visibly shaken. His plans for the coast would be crushed if Johanna didn’t go. It wasn’t only the absence of her cooking and washing. Patrick had other plans for her. He was more than willing to forget that she was only fifteen years old.

CHAPTER EIGHT

The Wharf on the Southside of Harbour Grace
May 29, 1868

"Have you got everything?" shouted Jane as she pulled the cart up next to Patrick and Garrett. She negotiated the horse and cart masterfully around piles of nets, wooden boxes, grapnels and cages containing small livestock. The *S.S. Vanguard* was tied up at the wharf and lifting cargo aboard as she and Johanna arrived. Jane stayed aboard the cart while Johanna eagerly jumped down. She was looking forward to her first trip to Labrador.

"Well, if I haven't got everything, I'll have to appeal to our neighbours," Patrick said as he looked up and grinned at Jane.

The Fitzgeralds and the Hearns were within earshot of the Geehans and could hear the talk. All three families had fishing rooms in Nowlan's Harbour and traded with John Munn. Munn and Company, the largest fisheries supply and general trade firm in outport Newfoundland, had provided supplies to the three crews in return for their season's catch of fish, along with their accumulation of cod liver oil. Throughout the summer, Munns would send a collector boat to pick up the product from time to time. On occasion, there'd be a bottle of rum among the supplies as a sign of old Mr. Munn's appreciation. Patrick Geehan made sure that his provision of rum came with each visit.

Now, John Fitzgerald came over towards the Geehans and shouted to Jane above the voices of the many people there to bid farewell to the crews heading for Labrador.

"Don't worry, Jane," he yelled. "We'll look after them. We won't let them go hungry. And in no time at all, we'll be back on the wharf and you'll be here to meet us all."

The Fitzgeralds moved up the wharf and away from Jane. There they shared their private thoughts about the Geehans. "This is the third season with her not going down there with her man," said John. "I wonder if everything is good with them."

"I envy her, not having to face that long trip. I wish I could stay home and tend to the garden. We really don't know what's ahead of us when we head out, do we?" John's wife, Catherine, said.

"True enough," said John. "But, you know, it makes me wonder. It's a long time without your woman on the Labrador, and him with that young Irish girl. It's a wonder Jane allowed that. He and Jane mightn't even get a letter to each other, with the mail boat hardly getting into the harbour."

"You know Patrick Geehan," responded Catherine. "It's only when he gets on the drink that he's been known to get a bit wild for a woman. It's unlikely he's got much rum with him on this trip."

Patrick Fitzgerald, John's brother, opted not to comment. He was a shy man of few words. He kept his thoughts to himself. But it was obvious to John that his brother admired Johanna Hamilton.

"I can see why Patrick Geehan would want his way with her,"

John said to his brother, after Catherine had moved away and he knew she couldn't hear him. "That young Johanna would make a great woman for you." John laughed when he saw Patrick blush.

"You'll love it in Nowlan's Harbour, my child," said Mrs. Hearn. She was standing next to Johanna aft of the mainsail as the ship left the wharf. Catherine Hearn was a good friend as well as a relative of Jane Geehan.

"I hope so," replied Johanna. She already felt befriended by Catherine, who lived with her family in Bryant's Cove.

"We'll be there in three or four days, depending on the wind." Catherine said as she offered Johanna a piece of homemade candy. "Did you enjoy your work on the farm this winter?"

"Yes, I loved it. It's hard, you know, keeping up with two men. There's so much to be done." Johanna knew she had to watch her words when chatting with Catherine Hearn. Patrick had warned her that everything said to Catherine Hearn would go back to Jane Geehan.

The trip to Labrador wasn't the horrific voyage that it had been made out to be by Jane Geehan. There were no mountainous waves washing people overboard. In fact, their journey up the north coast of Newfoundland and across the Strait of Belle Isle was quite peaceful. Aboard the ship, women and men were quartered in the steerage with each family or crew having a designated area. Families had to carry everything with them in order to live for fourteen or fifteen weeks in isolation down on the Labrador.

The *S.S. Vanguard* had been recently built by John Munn and was designed especially for the seal hunt. This spring Munn had decided to use the ship to transport his crews to the Labrador coast. In 1868, the *Vanguard* was considered to be one of the most seaworthy three-mast schooners in Newfoundland waters. Powered by both wind and steam, she was able to move all of Munn's planters up to Labrador quickly. At this point in time, John Munn had over two thousand fishermen working somewhere in his business.

After four nights, the *Vanguard* anchored off Nowlan's Harbour and the men began the process of tendering their supplies into their respective landings. This was no easy task for the man using the winch, who had to carefully off-load the supplies into small dories with the precision of threading a needle. One misplaced pallet or misguided box could easily capsize a dory.

In the absence of his wife, Patrick was able to relax around Johanna. People on the coast were in their own little huts and they kept to themselves. Competition among crews in getting the greater catch increased the isolation between families. Except for Sundays, when nobody fished, families seldom visited or communicated with each other.

When Johanna saw the Geehan shack she was dismayed. It was old. It had been passed down to the Sears family by the Nowlans of Brigus. The Nowlans first fished from Nowlan's Harbour for Thomas Ridley and Son back as early as 1830. Now it was 1868 and the one room shanty had barely withstood the test of time.

Garrett pulled the boards off the only window, enabling daylight to fill the damp musky area for the first time since last summer. Patrick pried open the door and stepped aside to allow Johanna to be the first to enter. The building was no more than twelve feet square, standing to a height of about eight feet. It had a flat sagging roof and leaned to the north, no doubt because of the prevailing winds. The hut had been poorly cobbed, a process of using a mixture of straw, mud and water to create a smooth floor covering. The cob had broken up and shrunk back from the walls so that rodents of various sorts had been able to get inside. Johanna began to make a mental list of projects needing her immediate attention. It made little sense to clean the dust and dirt without first re-cobbing the floor.

A rusty pot-bellied stove, which may at one time been some rich man's source of heating and cooking, stood in the corner. Hanging on a hook behind the stove Johanna spied a set of off-white rosary beads. She took the beads off the hook and saw that each bead was shaped differently, indicating that they had been hand-crafted. A small ivory crucifix hung at the end of the five decades of the rosary.

"Who owns these rosary beads?" she asked, as she gently rubbed her fingers over each bead.

"They have been here ever since the Nowlans left," said Garrett. "Father always said that they were made from whalebone. Mother often used them to say the rosary but she would always leave them hanging there at the end of each summer. They haven't been used since she passed away."

"They are lovely," said Johanna. "If no one wants them, I would love to have them."

"They're all yours," said Garrett. "Da always said they were likely given to the Nowlans by the Eskimos visiting here from up north."

Johanna quickly pocketed the rosary beads and was pleased that she now would have something to help her with her prayers, something to use to count her prayers. She'd greatly missed the rosary beads that had gone missing, the ones her father had given her.

There were only two wooden bunks in the one room shanty,

which left Johanna wondering where all three of them would sleep.

"Where will I be puttin' my head?" she asked.

Patrick pointed to an opening in the rear wall which was not visible from the front and was covered with a wooden hatch. Reaching down, he opened the hatch and showed Johanna a very tiny linhay. This was a small room built-on specifically to enable one more person to sleep. It was accessible only by crawling into the very cramped space. Johanna peered in to see a wooden bunk, not unlike the one she had slept in on the ship.

"Tight quarters," she said, half joking. "A woman needs more of a berth than that."

"That's not for you, Johanna. Your bunk is here," he pointed at one of the two bunks in the larger room. "Garrett will take the linhay. He never seems to mind." He looked towards Garrett. "You stayed in the linhay last year and you found it all right, didn't you?"

"It's only a place to put me head. We'll be so tired every night that we'll be able to sleep on a rock," Garrett responded. He too looked more relaxed and seemed more at ease without Jane around, thought Johanna.

"You take that bunk and I will take this one," Patrick said to Johanna, pointing at the one he meant. "I'll put up a curtain we can use for privacy. As Garrett says, it's only at night that we'll be spending time in here anyway."

Johanna spent the next few days trying to get the place in some kind of order. The old stove served its purpose although Johanna had misgivings about its safety and preferred the fire be put out by bedtime. The men didn't worry about cleanliness. Food was their priority, as they needed the energy to row out to their fishing berth, do their trawling and return with their catch. Each trip would result in their having to gut, split and salt as many as four to six hundred pounds of cod fish.

Johanna was called into action to slit the throats of each cod so they would bleed out before the process of gutting the fish began.

"You're a great cutthroat," said Patrick one day.

"You're the one I learned from," Johanna laughed. She was comfortable being at the cutting table with the men. Although she was busy, she found that she had no problem handling the work.

The waterhorses, or stacks of split fish, were getting higher and more numerous as the fish were added daily to the many piles. As the stacks got higher, the weight forced the water to drain from the fish. Every few days the temporary stacks of salted fish would be dismantled. The fish would then be individually laid out on the flakes for drying. It was then that Johanna's work got very strenuous, for laying the fish out was an almost non-stop activity. The flakes were roughly built on the beach, just far enough away from the tide, requiring Johanna to constantly bend over as she worked. As the days passed, the skin on her hands began to crack open and bleed because of the salt.

The summer days were long, but the time was going by very quickly. Teamwork and fine weather combined to help shape up what was going to be to be an excellent summer. Patrick and Johanna had grown closer and more comfortable with each other as the fishing season progressed. Although they talked together often, neither of them ever spoke of their past encounter. This wasn't because Johanna didn't think about Patrick in a romantic way. She was still very much infatuated. It just so happened that Patrick never spoke of what had happened in the barn.

One cool Sunday in early August, Johanna decided to take the path over to the Hearns. She was running low on salt, and while the men were sleeping she decided to visit Catherine Hearn to see if she had any to spare. With only about five weeks to go she could make do, but it was better if she didn't run out.

"Good morning, Mrs. Hearn," Johanna called when she reached the house.

Mrs. Hearn seemed very pleased to see her. "And good day to you, Johanna. How are you doin' with the chores and all? Are you getting used to it?"

Johanna laughed. "Well, every day there's something new to learn, especially with the fish and all."

They continued with some small talk and Johanna borrowed enough salt to do her for the rest of the summer.

"Fine man, that Patrick Geehan, and a great worker," said Mrs. Hearn. She finished her comment as if she were waiting for Johanna's opinion.

"He is that," she responded. "Of course we've all got to pull our weight around here, haven't we?"

"He is lucky to have a young peppy girl like you around. Jane will be happy to hear you're looking after her menfolk so well. She'll have to show you a bit of respect, now that you have proven yourself."

"Thanks, Mrs. Hearn. I appreciate your kind words," said Johanna.

"Sure, call me Catherine now. You're just like family."

Johanna bid farewell and returned to the Geehan hut where both men were getting their much needed rest. That night, guessing that Patrick was still awake, Johanna whispered from behind the curtain that separated them, "Patrick, you're right. Mrs. Hearn was definitely looking for information to bring back to Mrs. Geehan."

There was silence for a few seconds and she assumed Patrick

was asleep and hadn't heard her. Then the curtain was slowly drawn back and he crept into her section of the cabin.

"I told you so," he whispered, as he crouched down by her bunk and gently touched her arm. "She's just waiting to go home and say things to torment Jane." He stroked her arm and then lifted her fingers to his lips and softly kissed them. "You will be back home in a few weeks and be able to have a break with your sister. I can tell you are very tired," he said.

She could smell rum on his breath. It was the same smell she remembered from the barn that night last fall. This was the first time she'd been aware of his drinking on the coast. All the while here, she had never observed him take a drop.

"I'm going to see to it that you will be happy with your share from this trip," said Patrick. "You have done the work of two men here. With Garrett getting on in age, I wouldn't know what to do without you."

He stood up as if to leave. Johanna looked at him but didn't say anything. Although a little nervous, she was disappointed at his quick departure. And then, very gently, using one knee, he knelt on her bed, as though waiting for her to accept his invitation. She remained motionless. Then she reached up and held his hand to guide him completely into her bunk.

Through the open window, waves could be heard breaking in on the beach just below the hut. Millions of pebbles were being carried back and forth over the beach in a never-ending rhythm. Such action enabled the ocean to erode the rocks until there was no more friction between them. Now they were moving in unison, rolling gently, one against the other, until the sea finally allowed them to rest.

Johanna awoke to a new day. She was alone in her bunk. The morning sun shone brightly in through the window, creating warmth that she hadn't experienced since arriving on the coast.

The sea had calmed enough that she could hear Garrett and Patrick bickering as they began their row out to the fishing grounds. The men had let her sleep in for the first time since coming to Labrador. Johanna wished with all her heart that she and Patrick could remain in this harbour paradise forever. Last night had been perfect.

CHAPTER NINE

The Cathedral Palace for the Diocese of St. John's
July 3, 1895

Father John Coombs was summoned to meet with Bishop Michael Howley on July 3, 1895, at the Cathedral Palace. Howley had been appointed Bishop of St. John's in 1893. He was the first native born Bishop of St. John's, all his predecessors having been born in Ireland. He had requested this meeting in order to become acquainted with the new priest.

Father Harold Cooney, secretary to the Bishop, walked into the library where Father John was waiting. Having served several summers in the St. John's Diocese while home from the seminary, John was quite familiar with Father Cooney.

"His Excellency will be in shortly," Father Cooney said as he reached out his hand to welcome Father John. "No need to be nervous. He's a fine man and just wants to get to know you and talk about your first appointment."

Without warning, the huge oak door swung open and the Bishop marched into the room. Beaming from ear to ear, he walked around the large table and embraced Father John.

"Welcome, my son," he said. Bishop Howley was very youthful looking and, although dressed in full cassock, seemed informal and inviting. "Are you all settled in at the presbytery?"

"Yes, Your Excellency. I'm very comfortable and anxious to take my charge."

"That's wonderful. We'll need you to work out of St. Patrick's Parish." Father John and Father Cooney waited for the Bishop to be seated before they took their places. Cooney opened a notebook, ready to take any orders that might be issued. "As a curate, you'll be under the direction of Monsignor Morrissey," said Howley. "They have a very busy church at St. Patrick's. A lot of issues with the congregation, you know. You've worked with Monsignor before, I take it?"

"I have. And I look forward to it once again," Father John said. He was relieved he wasn't being sent outside of St. John's for his first assignment.

Bishop Howley smiled at him. "That's good. You'll be here with us, though, until they have room for you at the presbytery at St. Patrick's. Monsignor would like you to take these next few months to be a chaplain at Her Majesty's Penitentiary. I know that might be a difficult assignment and not how you want to begin your ministry, but the old Monsignor isn't well and can't keep up his schedule at the prison. And St. Patrick's Church has assumed the chaplaincy for this year again. You'll do the 8:30 masses at St. Patrick's during the weekdays. Monsignor will chat with you about the rest of your duties."

Father John was disappointed to hear he was going to be the chaplain at the prison since he really wanted to work with the people of the parish, to build relationships, and assist them in worship. Being in the company of convicts would be his last choice. The Bishop read his expression. "Don't worry, my son. I haven't given you a life sentence. It will be only for a short time, and I'm sure the other parishes will be soon coming after me for your services."

Following protocol, it wasn't until after Bishop Howley stood up that Father Cooney and Father John did the same. Again, Bishop Howley shook Father John's hand. "Welcome to our family, young man. Together, we have an awesome burden and I'll pray that God will give you the strength to carry on with your duties."

The Bishop nodded to Father Cooney, "We have an appointment up the street in the white house, Joe, so we'd better get moving." Father John knew he was referring to the Colonial Building and a meeting most likely with William Whiteway, Prime Minister of Newfoundland. The meeting ended as abruptly as it had started.

Father John took a couple of days to rest and to be with his parents. Not being excited about his new posting, he took some consolation that after a few months he would be away from the prison. He could then start working directly with the parishioners of St. Patrick's.

One very foggy morning in July, Father John rose at six and began his Divine Office before breakfast. It was his first scheduled day as a Roman Catholic priest. The morning began with the half hour of reading and meditation required by Catholic priests each day, otherwise known as the Breviary. He had great trouble concentrating on his prayers since this was his first trip to the prison, a place he had never entered.

Deep in thought, he was totally oblivious of his surroundings as he walked up Military Road and onto Forest Road, continuing until he reached Her Majesty's Penitentiary. Thick fog camouflaged the huge stone church-like building. He had arrived at his destination without even realizing it. He walked up the steep cobblestone steps and neared the guard house on the front landing.

"A new fellow today, is it?" said the uniformed warden standing by the outside gate as he eyed the young priest's collar.

"Yes, I'm Father John Coombs. I'm the new chaplain from St. Patrick's."

"Sister is here waiting to meet you," said the guard. "Hold on a second." He slid open a tiny shutter and shouted. "Open the gate. We have a visitor."

The sound of an iron clang could be heard as another warden unbolted the door from inside. There was an ominous squeaking sound as the big door slowly swung back. Another wall of iron bars prevented the priest from going very far inside the centre cell block. This caged foyer had to be unlocked to allow him complete access.

"Welcome, Father. I'm Captain Foster," said the uniformed man who approached. Sensing his anxiety, Foster joked, "You'll be out in ten years. Follow me."

Father John forced a smile as Captain Foster continued, "Sister Madonna is in the guards' room. She's anxious to get started. I never saw the likes of her in my life. She's pretty strict with the inmates and lets them know she's no pansy. She deals mostly with the women, unless they especially request a priest. Her and Monsignor never saw eye to eye, you know. There were times when I thought that I would have to send one of the boys in to settle them down."

Captain Foster stopped to explain the prison layout. "You're not to go over there unless one of the boys is with you. That's death row. It consists of five jail cells on the first floor directly across from the guard station. Feel free to talk or mix with any of the prisoners in the other cells. Go to their cells and introduce yourself. Some will invite you to sit and talk. Others won't care to see you. If they do request your presence, you'll call out for a guard to let you in. We'll decide if going in with that particular prisoner is safe." Foster removed his cap and wiped his head as he began to walk towards the guards' room.

Opened less than forty years ago, Her Majesty's Penitentiary had a dark and dingy appearance. Very little sunlight could enter the building except through three tall windows in the centre block itself. None of the cells had windows.

The centre block was a huge open rectangular room with a high-pitched roof. The ceiling was constructed with large wooden beams, crisscrossing and butting together to support the roof. The roof trusts resembled huge crosses. Completely surrounding the centre block were three floors of jail cells. The entire cellblock had been designed so that all the prisoners were always in full view. Father John looked at them. Some lay in their bunks, while others stood with their hands on the bars of their cell and stared at him.

The exterior walls of the prison were constructed of stone block. Prisoners weren't able to get a glimpse of daylight unless they were out in the yard for recreational purposes. A musky aroma greeted Father John and Captain Foster as they walked down a damp corridor leading away from the cellblock towards the guards' room and the kitchen. Sister Madonna was waiting in the guards' room. She nodded a greeting when she saw Father John.

Like all Mercy Sisters, Sister Madonna's garb was as intimidating as her disposition. From her throat to her feet, she wore a black-twilled woolen habit. Around her waist was a two-inch wide leather belt, fastened on the side with an iron ring. Another long leather strap was sewn to the belt at her side. A large pair of black prayer beads were strung through the iron ring and woven around a steel chain stretching down to the floor. A veil of white calico was wrapped tightly around her head leaving just her face exposed.

The young priest was not aware that Sister Madonna knew more about him than he realized. She had been in the convent a long time. She had, in fact, been privy to his family from the day he was born. However, the circumstances of his birth didn't permit her to have a relationship with either him or his family. Sister Madonna, through the Congregation of Mercy Sisters, had made it a point to follow his progress in life with the Coombs family. Mark and Theresa Coombs, because of their work with the Bishop and the Christian Brothers, were close to the Sisters of Mercy.

"Good day, Sister Madonna. I'm Father John and I guess we'll be working together," Father John said as he and the nun reached out and barely touched each other's hands.

"We're already a little behind," she said abruptly. "You've got three visits to do this morning. Did you bring Communion?"

Feeling embarrassed, Father John felt at a loss for not being prepared. And he hated being put off guard, especially by a woman. "Sorry, Sister. I wasn't informed specifically about my duties. I thought our initial meeting would help me to prepare," he said, speaking briskly.

"I'm not the one who needs your apology," she said. "There's a man in cell number eight waiting for Holy Communion for three weeks. He's not well and Monsignor hasn't been here since June. Maybe you can see him first." She turned her back to walk away.

"What's his name?" Father John asked.

She continued to walk. Without turning around she called back to him. "He'll tell you himself. No need to see the guard. His cell door is open. It's been that way for over fifteen years."

Father John reached into his pocket and pulled out a small prayer book. He realized this wasn't a good beginning with

Sister Madonna.

Eyeing the cell with the open door, he earnestly began his first act of mercy.

He saw an older man lying on a wooden bunk with a blanket pulled up to his chin despite the humidity. The priest tapped on the iron bars with his prayer book.

"Are you up for a visit, sir? I'm Father John."

The man turned over, slowly sat up and eased his legs down to the floor. He was thin and frail looking. He had to squint to see Father John.

"I've been looking to receive Holy Communion, Father," he said in a raspy voice.

"Have you gone to confession? If you want, I can hear your confession today and bring you communion on Tuesday."

"Yes, Father. I would like to go to confession. That would be good."

The priest put his hand on the man's shoulder and sat on his bunk. Because of the lack of privacy, they felt obliged to whisper.

"Go ahead with your confession," said Father John. "Are you sorry for your sins?"

The man nodded. "Yes, Father, I am. I have been a terrible sinner."

"Would you like to share your sins with me and God the Father Almighty?" asked Father John. The old man hung his head in silence. When he looked up at the priest, his eyes had filled with tears.

"I'm here because of my past, Father," he said.

"Yes, go on," said the priest.

"I have been asking for forgiveness for many years, but I don't think Our Lord will ever forgive me," continued the man.

"So you have confessed this sin before, to other priests?"

"Yes, Father. But I can't get peace of mind. I haven't been able to, not with any priest."

"Why do you think that our Lord wouldn't forgive you? He is a God of mercy," Father John said, trying to reassure him.

"Many years ago I helped a woman, whom I loved very much, bury the body of a man," said the prisoner. "If his body had been discovered she would have been blamed for killing him. In actual fact, it appeared he had been killed by another man whom she feared very much."

Father John nodded as he encouraged him to continue.

"The killer had buried the man in a shallow pit," the man looked off in space as he spoke. "During the night, while the killer was drunk and asleep, this woman heard a noise at the door. Checking the back yard, she found that the grave was now empty. She called me from my bed to help her find him. We discovered him in a drain by the road; by now I thought him to be most certainly dead. At her insistence, I carried him back to the original burial site and began to re-bury him. Before finishing the deed, unbeknownst to her, I struck the poor man with a rock to make certain of his death. For sure, I thought, this woman trusted and loved me. I did it for her and for the sake of the poor dead man."

Father John touched the man's hand. "So you are feeling guilty, thinking that you may have killed this man?" he said.

"Yes, Father, but it gets more complicated. Later that week, before she and the killer were arrested, she refused any of my attempts to show her my love." The prisoner looked at the priest as he readied himself to confess the real basis of his guilt.

"I was angry with her, Father. I was mad because she rejected me. And my anger spurred me to lie in court about her character," he continued in his raspy voice. "My false testimony and that of others went against her. She was found guilty and sentenced to hang. While she awaited the death sentence, it was discovered that she was pregnant. She was permitted time to have the child and it was then taken away from her."

"Do you think you are the father of that child?" asked Father John.

"I really don't know," answered the man. "She had been with the killer for many months before she and I had relations."

"Are you here in prison because of that action?" asked the priest.

The man shook his head. "No," he said. "Back then, the Court had been given some information which could have revealed my evil deed. During a Coroner's Inquest of the man I buried my action was almost uncovered by another witness. He claimed he had seen the ghost of the dead man I had buried. However, nobody believed the man. The slain man would have to have crawled out of a grave or come back from the dead for such information to be deemed credible. The witness's testimony was dismissed. But, if truth be told, he most probably did see the man I later buried."

"So if your action was not discovered why were you jailed?"

The man sighed and continued, "It's hard to live with yourself if you can't change a wrong you caused. I tried moving away from home to see if that would quiet my conscience. I found odd jobs here in St. John's. After several years, my drunken actions caught up with me. My mind became twisted. One night, during a barroom brawl, I beat the life out of another man on Water Street. I had no reason to do it. Only rage. Rage brought on by drunkenness and guilt. I had inflicted great pain on that poor woman. No mother should have to bear the grief of losing her child, maybe my child."

"Let's get on our knees together and pray for your forgiveness," said Father John.

The priest and the convict knelt down together by the wooden bunk with their heads buried in their hands. The priest said the prayers of absolution in Latin. After his blessing, Father John said, "God in his mercy has forgiven you. And now that you are forgiven, you are to pray the five Sorrowful Mysteries of the rosary for your penance."

They both bowed their heads in silence for a few minutes and then the convict began the rosary. While they were both kneeling down, Father John had noticed a note etched into the bunk. Scratched into the wood were the words: *Johanna Hamilton, June 29th, 1872. God have mercy on such an innocent soul.*

Father John thought it ironic that twenty-three years ago somebody had claimed innocence in this very cell. Now this man, who had accepted his guilt, was finding it difficult to find forgiveness.

Father John finally got to his feet and laid his hand on the man's head. "May the peace of Christ be with you," he said.

"And with you too, Father. God bless you and thank you."

"May I ask where your home community is?" asked the priest.

"I grew up on the Southside of Harbour Grace and that was my home until I came here to St. John's. My name is Patrick Fitzgerald."

"It was very nice to meet you, Patrick. I'll return with Holy Communion on Tuesday."

Father John went on to make the rest of his visits. While he was waiting at the main gate for a prison warden to let him exit, he saw Sister Madonna visiting with a female prisoner in one of the cells on the third floor. She was holding the woman's hand and engrossed in conversation.

He had judged the Sister to be a cold and curt woman. In fact, he was a little annoyed with her and intended to share his feelings with Monsignor. Father John Coombs was a man of the cloth in the eyes of Our Lord, given the power and authority to forgive sins. He was ordained to say Mass and given the power to carry out all His sacraments. Sister Madonna was a lowly nun, unable to carry out any of these duties. How dare a Sister of Mercy have that attitude towards a priest!

"Ready to leave now, are you, Father?" asked the warden and John saw it was Captain Foster who had let him in earlier. Foster noticed that the priest was looking towards Sister Madonna.

"She is a fine woman," he said, his eyes following Father John's. "She's a saint as far as everyone around here is concerned." It was as if Foster had read his mind and had come to the nun's defense. "She's been here for twenty-five years. There are times when she has taken people from the depths of hell and given them a purpose to live. She's done a much better job than any of the other religious people we've had around here."

Father John felt as though he had been rebuked. "I'll be back on Tuesday morning, a little earlier this time," he told Captain Foster. As he walked back to the presbytery, Father John's mind was much clearer, but his conscience was a little guiltier.

CHAPTER TEN

Nowlan's Harbour, 1871

For Patrick and Johanna, the next three years were paradoxically idyllic and trying. Each season at Nowlan's Harbour facilitated the renewal of their love affair with greater intensity. On the other hand, during the winters, Jane Geehan's presence caused their relationship to go dormant. For Johanna, the winters were excruciating. She longed for spring when hers and Patrick's love would again be free to blossom.

"I am finding it harder and harder for us to return and be apart again. We'll never be able to be together, Johanna," Patrick said as they lay quietly in Johanna's bed one night during August of 1871. "Captain Stone will be coming to take us home in a few weeks. Then it's back to a life that neither of us wants."

Johanna and Patrick had the same conversation many times before and a solution didn't seem to be in their grasp. Frustration was building.

Patrick continued, "You are still quite young, only eighteen. You have your full life ahead of you. Not like me, a man of forty-one. We really haven't a future together. Maybe it's time for us to make a move."

"Where would we go?" asked Johanna.

"I don't know. She'll have everything if I leave and we'll be penniless. You know, she and I haven't had relations for three years. There's nothing left between us. She has never once shown any concern about my lack of intimacy with her. Ours is a marriage in name only."

Without kissing Johanna good night, Patrick got up off the bunk and crept back to his own bed. He seemed angrier and more out of sorts tonight. As Johanna lay quietly in her bed, she listened to him gulp another drink of rum. She'd noticed that he always did his drinking at night. She'd also observed that his consumption of rum had increased this summer. This worried her because she was seeing his behavior changing. Ordinarily, he would never have spoken to her about his marriage. And this was the first time he had left her bed without showing some sign of affection. As a result, Johanna had a restless night.

The next day was routine. The men worked throughout the day, first on the water and then preparing the fish for transport. They didn't have time for dinner. Johanna could hear them bickering as they worked.

"Jesus, man, you can't even lift a barrow of fish. Put some muscle into it, bye," said Patrick, as he and Garrett were carrying a barrow of fish down over the wharf to the dory in readiness for the next collector boat.

"I'm doin' what I can Paddy, my son. You got way too much loaded on this."

Patrick was unapologetic. "Next summer, I've got to get someone else here with me. You can't even haul the feckin' oars for any length of time. I do all the work. You're getting too old for this, bye."

The sounds of quarreling continued as Johanna prepared supper and she couldn't believe that Patrick was being so cruel to Garrett. And then she heard Garrett say, "Well, don't you forget who owns this fishing room, Paddy. If I tells her what's goin' on here, you'll be the one who won't be back here next year."

Johanna now worried about what Garrett might be telling Jane Geehan. She peered out the window and could see that he and Patrick had made it to the stage head with the barrow of fish. They continued to grumble and were still within range for her to hear what they were saying. She saw Garrett make a gesture as though he were taking a drink.

"You're not much good yourself in the morning after suckin' that down," he said to Patrick.

Maybe, Johanna thought, it was Patrick's drinking that Garrett was threatening to report to his sister. Maybe it was nothing at all about her and Patrick. The arguing between the men went on all evening. Johanna had to cover her ears as she tried to get some rest for they had an early rise the following day. With just a few weeks left on the coast, she hoped that Patrick and Garrett's feuding wouldn't escalate.

The next day was cold, wet and windy. Four Sundays from today they would be leaving for home. At about ten o'clock in the morning, while all three of them were resting, Johanna heard the sound of men's voices outside the hut.

"Hello in there!" a man called out. When Johanna got up and went to the door she saw John Hearn and Patrick Fitzgerald standing by the woodpile.

"Good day to you," said a frustrated sounding John Hearn. "We were wonderin' if Paddy and Garrett had a few minutes. We've got a small leak around the drain plug of our dory and we need a hand to lift it out of the water so that we can get at it. We're going to cork it as best we can until we get back home."

"Johanna," called Patrick on hearing the men talking to her. "Tell the byes to come in while we get ready."

Hearing this, John Hearn and Patrick Fitzgerald entered and stood on Johanna's side of the room. Patrick and Garrett readied themselves to leave the house before pulling back the curtain and revealing their side of the room. Johanna noticed the two visitors taking a good look at everything.

"You are doing a great job of keepin' the house, ma'am," said John Hearn.

"Thank you, Mr. Hearn," replied Johanna.

She caught Patrick Fitzgerald looking at her; gazing at her in a manner she had seen other men do. Once he realized Johanna was aware of his staring, he became embarrassed and began to blush.

While exiting the hut, Patrick Geehan said to John Hearn, "I'll give ya all I got when lifting, but I don't want Garrett to put too much strain into it for he is prone to a very bad back. We'll have to watch him. This is not the place for a man to get sick."

Johanna couldn't believe what she had just heard. Patrick was either putting on an act of being truly considerate of Garrett, or else he was worried that Garrett was going to return and cause Patrick great trouble with Jane.

Since the men were going over to see to John Hearn's boat, she thought it might be a good time for her to drop in on Catherine Hearn. She had grown fond of Catherine and appreciated her advice.

Johanna and Catherine stood at the front door as the men grunted and called out orders to each other, hauling the boat up out of the water on a makeshift launch. The Hearn's servant girl, who had come to the coast with them for the first time this season, sat at the kitchen table within earshot of Johanna and Catherine.

"She can be a difficult woman when she wants to be," said Catherine. Johanna wondered if she was talking about Maureen, the young girl in the hut.

"Maybe Maureen needs a little time or even another season to get used to it here," replied Johanna.

"No, I'm talking about Jane Sears." The local people never gave up on using the family name of the wife instead of her married name. "She's my cousin, you know," continued Catherine.

"I didn't realize that," said Johanna.

"Her father spoiled her and gave her everything. We all love her, but I know she has been difficult with you. She can be a hard woman to get along with."

Johanna was aware of Patrick's warning about not saying anything to anyone. She had been told to keep things to herself. However, she didn't often get an opportunity to talk to other women and Catherine Hearn seemed to genuinely care about her. Johanna found her to be trustworthy.

"Times were tough over the last number of years, but I got good pay and a roof over my head. I'm thankful for that," she said.

"I hear that Jane is sick this summer," said Catherine.

Johanna nodded. "Yes, we got news of that on the last mail boat," she said.

Catherine stood up and put the kettle on to boil before continuing, "It's bad enough that she is not well, but to have people talking about her and Patrick behind their backs is terrible. You know, they are saying all kinds of things about what Patrick is doing with an old hake like Jane."

Johanna was recalling some of the gossip her sister had shared with her over the winter. Feeling comfortable talking to Catherine she said with a grin, "If you listen to what everyone is saying I'll be taking Jane's place by Christmas. And then it will be Aunt Johanna and not Aunt Jane."

"There might be some thinking that, but Jane is a very fit woman. She has bounced back to good health more than once," stated Catherine.

"That's for sure." Johanna made certain that she agreed.

Catherine made tea and brought out a tin of ginger cookies and she and Johanna and Maureen chatted about this and that until the men showed up, having finally managed to get the dory up on the launch so that John Hearn and Patrick Fitzgerald could get to work on her stern.

Patrick Geehan suddenly appeared in the doorway. "Come on, Johanna, we'll be needing a good supper after that," he beckoned to her.

Catherine stood next to her husband watching Johanna leave with Patrick.

"He said that like he was married to her," Catherine's sharp eyes followed Johanna and Patrick as they walked back to the Geehan place. John Hearn nodded his head in agreement. But he had learned a long time ago to mind his own business. Patrick Fitzgerald was also watching Patrick and Johanna. His eyes were focused more on Johanna.

Throughout the next four weeks, Johanna saw Patrick and Garrett continuing to quarrel and argue on matters of little significance. This season was concluding very differently than the last three. In the past, Patrick and Johanna had taken the time to cherish their final days together. Bliss had now turned to anxiety for Johanna. She saw that there had been a major shift in Patrick's personality.

CHAPTER ELEVEN

Southside of Harbour Grace
Saturday, November 18, 1871

At the end of each season, Patrick Geehan was true to his word, and Johanna received almost as much money as Garrett for her work on the coast. Jane Geehan wasn't pleased.

The fall and winter evenings were getting painfully long. The drudgery of living at the Geehan household never became routine for Johanna. On this particular evening, Jane resumed her rocking and knitting while reciting a litany of chores to be carried out the next day, mostly by Johanna.

"Johanna, tomorrow we'll have to transfer the potatoes from the upper house to the cellar. We'll be getting heavy frost soon and the men are too busy to be at it. We'll use the blue cart. It's lower and Prince finds it easier to turn."

"Yes ma'am," agreed Johanna.

Patrick had just come in and hung the kettle over the fire. Without looking up, Jane continued her knitting and her talking.

"We'll be taking an extra three pounds off your compensation this month," she said. "It was a hard year and we've all got to live." She had waited for Patrick to appear before she delivered the news to Johanna.

"You certainly are not taking three pounds away from Johanna," Patrick said as he glared at Jane. "That girl worked hard this year and she'll continue to be paid in full as promised."

"That she won't," said Jane. "Garrett got nothing this year compared to last."

Jane stood up and threw her knitting on the floor. She and Patrick were now nose to nose. Jane was becoming increasingly flushed. In a rage beyond what Johanna had ever witnessed, she reached up and grabbed Patrick by the face as she said, "You'll do as I say!"

"Stop it, stop it, please," Johanna cried out while using her body to push Jane back, and forcing her to release her hold on Patrick whose face was scratched and bleeding. Without warning, Jane swung her hand in an attempt to slap Patrick. Instead, she connected with Johanna. A hard stinging blow knocked Johanna to the floor. Patrick and Jane stood in shock as Johanna struggled to get to her feet.

Patrick wheeled around and left the kitchen immediately, slamming the back door so hard on the way out that its latch wasn't able to hold it shut. In tears, Jane ran out of the kitchen and upstairs, leaving Johanna lying on the floor.

Johanna had expected Jane to run away from such a calamity, but she'd thought better of Patrick. Yes, he had stood up to Jane on her behalf regarding the money. But after what had happened he hadn't stayed to see how she was. He hadn't asked if she was hurt. Johanna was now beginning to wonder if he had any real manhood at all.

She stood up and managed to reach Jane's rocking chair and

she did exactly what Jane would do: she rocked back and forth, trying to gain some solace. It wasn't so much the pain of being smacked in the face that had upset her, it was the trauma of the physical altercation. She eased herself up from the chair and went out to the back house to look at herself in the mirror. There was some swelling around her right eye. As she looked at her reflection, she knew it was time to take a long hard look at her situation with the Geehans.

Johanna pulled on her coat and boots, deciding that she needed some time away from the confines of the house. Maybe if she visited the Fitzgeralds just across the garden, she would find somebody to talk to and so ease her mind. She didn't have to mention the fight.

Patrick Fitzgerald answered her knock. She hadn't spoken to him since Nowlan's Harbour. "Hi, Johanna," he said, looking pleased to see her. "Please come in."

"Thank you. Is your sister-in-law at home? I was looking for some red wool. I'm knitting a pair of cuffs for my nieces and nephew for Christmas," Johanna had found it difficult to knock on the Fitzgerald's door without a valid reason. She had plenty of wool at the Geehans but she wanted to provide a reason for her visit.

"I'm afraid she and John are playing cards with the Connors tonight. But come in out of the cold for a few minutes. I'll put on some tea." Patrick had been waiting for an opportunity to meet Johanna on a more personal basis. He was very taken with her and thought this might be his chance to get to know her.

The Fitzgerald house had a pleasant and welcoming atmosphere and Johanna felt comfortable and safe in Patrick's presence. "A cup of tea would be nice. I can't stay long as I have an early rise. Tomorrow is Sunday and Mrs. Geehan will be getting up early for church."

Patrick Fitzgerald was a single, attractive man. He immediately threw a few logs in the hearth. The wood instantly ignited the simmering ashes into a raging flame. He and Johanna settled down on the couch by the fireplace as they waited for the tea to steep. The tea and the conversation were a welcome respite from the misery of living next door.

Patrick sensed Johanna's distress. He was more observant than she realized. He could see her face more clearly with the light of the fire. "Your eye is swollen," he said as she turned her head. "Did you have an accident or is it none of my business?"

Johanna tried not to cry, but hard as she tried salty tears rolled down her cheeks.

"It's been a terrible fall, Patrick," she said. "Mrs. Geehan has been a tyrant to me these last few years and Garrett and Patrick have been at each other ever since I moved into the house. Tonight things got really bad between Patrick Geehan and Mrs. Geehan. It came to a head with a fight between Mrs. Geehan and Patrick. I tried to stop her from hitting Patrick and she smacked me by mistake."

Johanna went on to describe some of the ways she had been mistreated at the Geehan house. Patrick listened attentively, upset to find out about her life with the people next door. He and his family had lived by them all this time but they never really knew what went on behind closed doors.

"I heard Garrett and Patrick fighting nearly all summer on the Labrador," he said. "But I had no idea you were having such a hard time."

Johanna wiped away her tears. "I'll be leaving soon. I want to find something else. I really hate fighting. I wasn't brought up with it."

"Fighting is awful. It's not something we are used to in this household either," Patrick said. Thinking that Johanna would benefit from something a little stronger than tea to settle her anxiety he asked, "Would you like a glass of my sister-in-law's sherry? It might help you sleep tonight."

Her visit became an extended one, a visit that neither of them would easily forget. One glass of sherry led to another. After a couple of hours, he put his arm around her and felt her relax. She cuddled close and put her head on his shoulder.

Johanna craved some tenderness tonight and Patrick Fitzgerald happened to be there. Over the course of the evening, passionate kissing and fondling turned into sexual intimacy. This was the second man Johanna had been with in this way. It was never her intention to go that far with Patrick Fitzgerald, but one thing led to another and she found the experience very pleasurable. She hadn't resisted, and he hadn't forced the encounter. But she wasn't in love with this man, wonderful as the evening had been.

Johanna stood up abruptly and straightened her clothes. "It's getting on. I have to get back," she said.

For Patrick, what they had done together was an act of love, the start of something wonderful between him and Johanna. He was a man of few words but he felt his actions had spoken volumes. He didn't know it but he had wrongly sensed her need for compassion as desire for him.

"I'm here if you need anything," he said as Johanna shut the door, not allowing him to accompany her back across the yard. As she looked back at the Fitzgerald house, she took comfort in being able to see the light in his bedroom window. She hoped he understood there was nothing between them beyond what had just happened. Patrick Fitzgerald was a wonderful man, but for better or for worse her heart belonged to Patrick Geehan.

The bruise on Johanna's face was very evident the next morning. As was her duty, she arose early and fed the animals.

Jane Geehan came down to breakfast and took no notice of any injury to Johanna and made no apology to her. There wasn't even a word of good morning.

"I'm off to Mass in Riverhead with the Shugarues. Please put the salt meat on at ten and I'll cook the vegetables when I get back," Jane said, as she reached up over the gun rack to the shelf where she always stored her Mass book. Johanna recalled Jane saying at one point, "There's no better place to put this prayer book for protection. Poor Ma put this very book over Da's gun for forty-eight years."

Patrick and Garrett were out in the barn but they finally came into the kitchen. Patrick's hair was in complete disarray; he was unshaven and wearing the same clothes as the day before. Garrett nodded to Johanna before he lay down on the daybed. Patrick couldn't look her in the face. She saw his bloodshot eyes and noticed that his hands were shaking, likely from the drinking he'd done the night before. He took a glass from the cupboard and shuffled out to the back house for some water. He didn't come back to the kitchen. Johanna was now convinced it was time to leave. She would go back to her sister and her family until she could find some other work. She had to get away from this house.

For Johanna, it was another long day of silence and tension. In bed that night, she didn't hear the usual muffled conversation between Patrick and Jane before they went to sleep. Tonight there was stillness.

Johanna had already made her plans. She intended to secretly pack her clothes the following morning and then wait until everyone had settled down after supper before walking up to the River. She knew that Patrick Geehan would try to convince her to stay if he knew that she was about to leave. She had to be the one strong enough to bring an end to this unholy liaison.

CHAPTER TWELVE

Southside of Harbour Grace
Monday, November 20, 1871

After breakfast, on Monday morning, November 20, Johanna put the potatoes in water and continued on with her usual duties. It would take a full day to bring all of the vegetables into the cellar after Jane Geehan got out of bed and had her breakfast. Johanna thought she would get started by going to the barn, tackling Prince and hitching him up to the cart. With that done, she managed to get several loads of vegetables hauled and stored in the cellar before nine. The day couldn't pass quickly enough for her. She would be leaving at day's end.

Jane finally came out the back door and approached Johanna, who was in the process of carrying pails of potatoes out and dumping them into the cart.

"Try rolling them into the cart rather than dumping them from the pail," said Jane. "You'll do less harm that way." Johanna was going to argue that potatoes don't easily damage. Instead, she didn't say a word, realizing that her time with the Geehans was limited. She and Jane continued to transport the vegetables to the cellar without any further dialogue.

"Could one of you please come down here and give me a hand with the twine for a few minutes," Patrick Geehan called. He'd cupped his hands around his mouth so that his voice would carry.

"I'll be back in a minute," Jane said, as she passed Johanna the reins of the horse and climbed down from the cart. "Carry on till I get back."

Jane moved swiftly toward Patrick seeing that he was in a hurry to pull the tangled twine off the fence. To Johanna's surprise, after only a few minutes of helping Patrick, Jane began walking back towards the house.

"A goddamn drunk. That's all you are. A good for nothing," she bellowed as she waved a rum bottle at her husband. "You won't be drinking any more of this today." Johanna saw that Jane was swinging a rum bottle back and forth as she marched towards the house.

Patrick dropped the net and began to chase Jane up to the house, leaving Garrett to hold his end of the twine. "Come back with that bottle; there's only a noggin left for tonight," demanded Patrick.

He and Jane entered the house. Patrick closed the door behind them. It appeared to Johanna that he didn't want anyone to hear what he was about to say. Garrett continued his work, seemingly oblivious to the disturbance. Jane could hear shouting and crying but decided that she wasn't getting between Patrick and Jane Geehan ever again.

The fighting went on for about half an hour. Johanna made a couple of more trips to the cellar, occasionally stopping to see if peace had yet befallen the farmhouse. On her last trip to the cellar, she stopped the horse and listened and realized that all was calm. At one point she saw Patrick Geehan standing out in the porch. The storm had abated, the fight was over. It was now eleven o'clock and time to put the potatoes on the fire to boil for dinner.

She unhitched Prince and led him into the barn for a well-deserved rest. Johanna was very fond of Prince. She had spent many lonely moments in the barn with him, sponging him down and chatting to him. It was as if the animal could understand her. Sometimes, Prince had been Johanna's only refuge.

While Garrett continued to work on the twine by the rock wall, Johanna made her way to the house. If they wanted to eat by 2:00 o'clock she couldn't delay dinner any longer. She cracked open the door to alert the Geehans of her presence.

Upon entering, she saw Patrick Geehan sitting in the rocking chair with his face buried in his hands and his elbows resting on his knees. There was no sign of Jane.

Johanna hung the potatoes on the fire and threw some more wood on the ashes. She noticed that the door to the front room was shut. She thought that was odd. She wondered if Jane had gone into the room to be by herself.

"Will I get the table ready or will the Mrs. be taking care of that?" she asked.

Patrick took his hands away from his face as he lifted his head and sat up in the chair. There were fresh scratches on his face and traces of blood trickled down his cheeks. His hands and shirt were also stained red.

"She won't be getting anything ready anymore," he answered in a flat monotone. "Her way and her manners are after putting an end to her."

"What have you done, Patrick?" Johanna's voice rose in fear.

He nodded towards the closed front door. "I wouldn't advise you to look."

"Patrick, is she…is she dead?" Johanna whispered. She could hardly get the words out, and she couldn't believe it when

Patrick nodded.

She lifted her apron to her face to muffle her scream. Every muscle in her body locked with tension. Suddenly, she began to run back and forth from the kitchen to the porch, not knowing where to turn or what to do. She felt sheer panic. Putting her hand on the latch, she thought to escape the house, but Patrick restrained her and pinned her against the wall.

He put his hand over her mouth. "Shush! Shush! It was an accident. Listen. She was sitting in the chair. I grabbed her by the shoulders and tried to shake some sense into her. I let her go and she just sat there on the chair with a queer colour. I left for a minute and she must have had a heart attack. When I came back into the room, she had fallen to the floor. She'd hit her head on the table."

Johanna began shaking her head. "No! My good Jesus. No! The Lord praise us and forgive us! What have you done? I'll call the women. I'll get Mrs. Shugarue and Mrs. Fitzgerald. We'll lay her out. Let me go," she screamed. "Let me go!"

"I'll let you go, but you've got to settle down. You can't go for the women. They'll think I killed her. You know I wouldn't do that. You know I wouldn't kill Jane," Patrick said as he continued to hold her against the wall.

"Please, Patrick. The doctor will come and straighten it all out." Johanna started to cry again.

He shook his head. "No, I'll have no chance," he said. "They'll think you were involved too just because you are here. Ever since Jane drove that young Marshall girl away people are talking. They'll believe Jane was killed. You know that. I'll have to make sure that when she's discovered people will believe she died on her own."

The pupils of Patrick's eyes had widened. Sweat was beading on his brow. His breathing was getting heavier as the minutes wore on. He looked crazy. Johanna thought she had no choice but to go along with him.

"Let me go. I can't think like this," she pleaded.

"Let me handle everything," he said, as he released his grip on her burning wrists. "Go get cleaned up. If Garrett sees you like this he'll know you were crying and realize something must have happened. Just continue to make dinner, and let me know when it's ready before you call him. Don't worry. I'll explain."

Patrick left the house and headed to the barn, leaving her alone in the kitchen. She closed the kitchen door to make sure she wasn't able to see Jane's body. Fearing for her own life, she realized that Patrick had slipped into total madness. Anxiety, fear and confusion combined to create a cocktail of uncontrollable emotions. Johanna was also worried sick that she would be implicated in the death of Jane Geehan.

Mindlessly, she walked out to the wash stand and splashed her face in the cold water left in the basin. She pulled a comb through her hair and began to set the table. From the kitchen window, she could see Garrett out by the twine, busily working on the net. She doubted that Patrick would ever be able to convince Garrett that his sister had died of natural causes.

"Patrick, dinner is ready. Will I call Garrett now?" she called from the back door. She was surprised at how normal her voice sounded.

"Yes, call him and go back in the house to take it up," Patrick answered.

She went to the front door and called, "Dinner is on the table, Garrett."

Before she returned to the kitchen, she saw Garrett drop the twine and began his walk towards the rear of the house. As she lifted the pot off the fire, Johanna heard three gunshots coming from behind the house. She recognized the sound immediately.

"Oh my God! Pad! Pad! What are you doing?" came a loud shriek.

She quickly put the pot back on the fire and ran to the back house and pushed open the door. She saw with horror that Garrett lay face down with the upper half of his body hidden underneath the horse's cart. Blood was splattered all over the cart's wheel and tailboard.

Patrick Geehan stood on the back step holding a shotgun by the barrel. He was rubbing his fingers through his hair and talking to himself.

"He'd never have believed me," he was saying. "I had to do it. Now it's over. No one saw it, no one heard and now we're safe."

"My God, Patrick! Patrick. What have you done?" cried Johanna as she quickly pulled the door shut, fearing that she would be next. Within seconds, she pushed the lock through the latch, preventing Patrick's entrance.

"I did it for us, Johanna. Let me in!" Patrick hammered and kicked on the door to no avail.

She decided to make a dash for it. She could go out the front door and run to the Fitzgerald's for help. She raced out into the hall hoping to reach the front door, but Patrick Geehan had beaten her to it. He was already inside the house. He put his hand across the narrow hallway to stop her from escaping.

"You can't be leaving now," he said in a very low voice, speaking as calmly as if nothing had happened. "If the crowners come, you'll be as guilty as me."

"I don't know what you mean. I didn't touch either one of them," Johanna screamed. "I didn't do anything."

"I know that's true. But the law will never believe you," he paused for a moment and then grabbed her by her shoulders. "Listen, we can get through this. Jane has been sick for years. It would come as no surprise to anybody that she died. And I had to get rid of Garrett for his word would send us to jail. You know what he saw on the Labrador. You and I would hang if we got blamed for killing Jane. Don't you see? It had to be this way."

Johanna's mind was in turmoil. The police should be called. Patrick should have reported Jane's death and not gone as far as he did. Unfortunately, though, he was now correct in saying that she would be linked to the killings. What could she do? What could she do?

"We'll find a way to put this behind us," said Patrick, still speaking in that low calm voice. "I'll get Garrett out to the barn and cover him with hay until I get a grave dug out in the pit tonight. I'll get Jane moved out to the backroom where you sleep and you can stay with me tonight. I know you fear the dead. But you'll be with me until we get this all worked out."

"I can't do this, Patrick. I'm leaving," said Johanna. "I am already packed and ready to go. I am going to my sister's."

"You'll not leave me now, Johanna," Patrick reached towards her but she shrank away from his touch. "This is our chance to be together. I did this for you and me to be together. That's what you wanted, isn't it?"

Johanna knew she was trapped. What could she do? Where could she go? If she persisted in leaving, would Patrick Geehan completely lose control and make her his next victim? She hadn't done anything wrong but people would undoubtedly label her guilty.

Patrick took her hand. "Let's take the next few hours to think and plan. I promise that if the truth comes out I'll clear your name. If I get my plan to work, we'll have our lives together. It's what we've wanted all along."

Johanna sat in the rocking chair and nodded her head in apparent agreement. She felt she had little choice but to agree with all that the madman was saying.

CHAPTER THIRTEEN

Southside of Harbour Grace
November 20, 1871

Johanna remained in the house for the rest of the afternoon while Patrick dug Garrett's grave. She made sure that she had every door to the kitchen barred tight. The neighbours to the east were the only ones able to see Patrick dig the grave, so he rigged up a sail to the eastern side of the pit to hide his efforts. A foot or so would be deep enough for the body, especially with the frost coming on this winter.

After several hours of toiling, Patrick finally dismantled the sail. He came into the house just as it was getting dark. Johanna was curled upon the day bed with a blanket over her when Patrick entered. It had been a drizzly gray afternoon. Now a heavy rain began to pound down on the roof of the farmhouse.

With mud up to his knees, Patrick's face was dirtied from wiping it with his soiled hands. He now had the appearance of a crazed lunatic. Walking over to the cupboard, he rummaged around to find a full bottle of rum. Pulling the cork out with his teeth, he tipped the bottle and guzzled down two or three swigs. He wiped his mouth in his sleeve and said, "We have a long night ahead of us, woman."

"I won't be touching the dead, if that's what you're talking about." Johanna dared to respond.

"Well, Johanna, either you'll do as I say, or we'll both be hanging by the neck in a few weeks," he continued to speak in that eerily calm voice as he removed and threw his dirty clothing out in the porch.

No discussion took place after that remark. While talking aloud to himself, Patrick paced the floor for nearly three hours, only stopping long enough to fill his pipe and have a shot of rum.

Johanna pretended to be sleeping, hoping he would ignore her. All this time she was saying the rosary with the beads from Nowlan's Harbour, asking the Blessed Mother for the strength to get through this quagmire.

"Don't you know when a man is hungry?" Patrick sounded aggressive again.

Without uttering a word, she got up and got him some bread and tea. Maybe his madness would subside if she tried to behave normally. He was on the cusp of insanity, and Johanna very much feared for her life. At about midnight, Patrick started putting on his oilskins.

"I'll just need you to carry one end of the barrow so that I can place Garrett down in the hole. You haven't even got to look."

"That I won't do it. I'll not be goin' out there," Johanna responded.

Patrick slowly walked over to the daybed with both fists clenched. In one move, he ripped the blanket from her and smacked her across the face with the back of his hand. Blood ran down over her mouth and over her chin.

"Get up off the goddamn couch and come with me," he yelled as he pulled her up off the daybed. Johanna knew she had to do as he insisted, or God only knew what he would do to her.

He reached for a lantern as they exited through the back door. She grabbed Jane's overcoat before they stumbled across the back yard and out into the rain and the darkness. On reaching the barn, Patrick didn't light the lamp until they were inside with the door closed.

Johanna tried not to look, but she saw Garrett under the straw in the pig pound. Three pigs were pawing at his body, which was facing down. One pig had already chewed his right ear completely off, leaving only the white clean flesh where his ear used to be. She heard a moan. It had to be a noise from one of the animals; a man couldn't survive an assault like the one on Garrett Sears.

"Jesus, the pigs are eating him, Patrick!" she screamed.

"Shush, be quiet." He slapped her across the face, driving her up against the pound. "If you don't stop shouting, I'll let you have it again!"

Patrick grabbed the pitchfork and began to prod the pigs, driving them away from the body. Missing the pigs as he attempted to clear them away, he stabbed the body by accident. The body appeared to jump with each jab of the pitchfork. Johanna noticed that part of Garrett's right hand had also been gnawed off.

"Go over there and stand by the barrow facing the door so you won't have to look at him. I'll load him aboard," said Patrick.

Johanna heard Patrick grunt and swear as he rolled Garrett onto the handbarrow.

"Now lift up the barrow and kick open the door. We'll leave the light on in the barn. I'll keep the door open until I get him down the hole." The rain seemed to get even heavier as they struggled to the pit with their gruesome load.

"Now tip him over so that he'll just slide off," Patrick ordered. Johanna heard a plopping sound as Garrett's body splashed into the shallow grave which was now flooded with water. "Go on inside now while I cover him over."

Johanna obeyed. Drenched and cold, she was glad when she got to the house and was able to towel off. It was now two in the morning and she had to get some sleep. When she got into her bed, she pulled the clothes up over her head, hoping that daylight would soon arrive. Shortly afterwards, she heard Patrick come into the kitchen. He stayed on the daybed.

Around three o'clock in the morning she heard the distinctive sound of the back door latch. She edged her way slowly out of bed, carrying a candle to show her the way through the kitchen. Patrick Geehan snored loudly as he slept in a drunken stupor on the daybed.

Johanna had to see what had rattled the latch. After lighting the lantern, she pulled on her boots and made her way to the back yard. As she got closer, she could see that either the grave had been tampered with or Patrick Geehan hadn't done a great job of covering it up. As she peered into the hole she saw that Garrett's body had gone missing. Horror swept over her! There was no evidence that animals had been near the site and dragged the body out of the pit. Johanna knew immediately what she had to do.

Trudging through the mud, she made it across the field and got to the Fitzgerald's farm. She now had to take a chance. Reaching up to try the latch on the storm door, her heart beat rapidly. The door wasn't bolted. She pulled off her boots.

Once inside, she crept through the kitchen and found Patrick Fitzgerald's bedroom. As she remembered his promise of helping her in need, she knew that this would be a tall order.

Gently and quietly, she turned the knob. She entered his room and closed the door behind her. She then eased her way towards his bed. Patrick was sleeping soundly. Getting down close to his ear, she gently covered his mouth with her hand.

"Patrick, shush, it's me, Johanna. You have to help me. Patrick and Garrett have had a terrible fight." Patrick was startled at first. He then sat up in bed.

"You have to help me," pleaded Johanna. "Come quickly! We have to find Garrett." She didn't mention that Garrett had escaped from his grave.

Patrick Fitzgerald, without questioning Johanna, pulled on his clothes and followed her in silence. Using Johanna's lantern, they spied Garrett lying in the drain just down the road from the Geehan farm. Patrick felt for a pulse but there was nothing. He carried Garrett back to the farm. By now Garrett was a muddy mangled corpse, dripping with blood and soaked with water. Patrick placed him in the same hole he'd been in and quickly covered him with earth.

Standing in the darkness of the night and now being fully drenched, Johanna and Patrick finally had a chance to speak. He readily accepted Johanna's explanation that Patrick Geehan had shot and killed Garrett as a result of an ongoing disagreement.

"It came to a head today when Garrett said he intended to tell Jane that Patrick and I were intimate in Nowlan's Harbour," she explained. "Patrick Geehan forced me to help him bury Garrett. He wanted to conceal what he had done. He threatened to implicate me in Garrett's death. He told me that people were spreading rumours about him and me. He smacked me across the face several times when I said I wouldn't help him. He said he would tell everyone we were lovers. I had no choice but to help him. When we carried Garrett from the barn, I thought for sure he was dead. But he must have been unconscious to get out of the pit like he did."

"Where was Jane Geehan when all this was going on?" asked a puzzled Patrick Fitzgerald.

"As you know, they hadn't been getting along either. She wanted to go to Turk's Gut to see her sister. On Monday morning, after Patrick refused to take her, she left to walk there on her own. He gave her five pounds before she left and we haven't heard from her since."

Fitzgerald, blinded by his affection for Johanna and seeing the marks on her face, accepted her explanation. "Why don't you stay at our house tonight?" he suggested. "Old Paddy Geehan may hurt you again."

"No, I'm getting out of here tomorrow, as soon as I get a chance. I'll be going up to John Drake's for a while. I can't be implicated in the killing of Garrett Sears. It will be Patrick Geehan's problem when I'm long gone."

Patrick Fitzgerald wasn't upset about news of her impending departure. He was thinking that if she left, her farthest destination might be Riverhead. He didn't know that she wanted to travel a much greater distance than that.

On Tuesday morning, the sun was brilliant. The roosters were making their usual sounds mixed in with the calling of the seagulls. How a beautiful peaceful morning could contrast with such a miserable night, Johanna thought as she listened for Patrick Geehan. Thankfully, he hadn't come to her room during the night. Not hearing him, she got out of bed and dressed and went out to the kitchen.

"Ah, you're awake," said Patrick Geehan. He walked over and

gave her a kiss on the cheek. He was a different man than he had been last night. "I'm very sorry about last night. I mean smacking you like I did. Your screaming would have awakened the Fitzgeralds or the Shugarues. I slept on the daybed. I'll make the breakfast today. You sit to the table and relax. You had a hard day yesterday."

A fire had made the kitchen warm and cozy. Johanna reflected that Jane Geehan was far from being warm as she lay dead in the front parlour, while Garrett was buried in the back yard. How could Patrick Geehan act as if everything was normal?

"We have to make the day seem as if everything is fine," said Patrick. "You understand? Later, you need to go over to the Fitzgeralds, while I make my way to the Shugarues. Pretend you need to borrow something and let them know you are worried about Jane not returning. Make sure you tell them that she left with Garrett. Explain to them that he caught the boat at Brigus and is sailing to St. John's to get his feet fixed. They know about his bad feet and his intention to get them cured. Let them know that Jane was thinking about visiting her aunt at Turk's Gut. You can say that it is my intention to take the horse and go look for her later today."

Johanna was too deep in the plot to turn back now. She'd have to collaborate with Patrick Geehan in order to keep herself out of trouble.

Suddenly, a loud knock came on the door. They stared at each other as if somebody had already discovered their conspiracy. Patrick Geehan opened the door. She hoped it wasn't Patrick Fitzgerald.

Standing in the doorway was Thomas Morrissey. Mr. Morrissey lived about three houses down from the Geehans. In his seventies, he was still able to chop wood, plow ground and cut hay with any man on the Southside half his age. He had a reputation of being a drinker himself. Being the local accordion player and singer, Thomas was often the centre of many a kitchen party.

"How's Garrett?" he asked.

"Garrett?" said Patrick. "Why do you ask that?"

"Well, I saw him on my way home from Jack Doolan's early this morning. He looked to be in awful way. I didn't mind the rain because I had borrowed some oilskins from Jack. And then out of nowhere came this figure limping down the road just past your place. As I got closer I saw it was Garrett in his overalls. Blood was pouring down his face. He was soaking wet and he was full of mud and dirt. 'Garrett,' I says, 'Are you all right?' He didn't answer. He just kept walking."

"It wasn't Garrett," snapped Patrick. "If it was, it was his fetch or ghost. We haven't seen him since Monday when he left for St. John's."

"Oh, I must have been mistaken then. It had to be somebody else." Morrissey could see the consternation in Patrick Geehan's face and he wasn't about to argue.

"Well, have a good day, Thomas. Thanks for your concern. I hope whoever it was made it back home all right," said Patrick.

"I'm sure he did. We would have heard about it already if he hadn't," assured Thomas.

Patrick Geehan watched Thomas walk down through the garden and away from the property.

"No, there's no way," he cried. "What he said was crazy."

"It's impossible," agreed Johanna.

They hurried though the door and out to the hole. The ground had been covered just as Patrick Geehan had left it. Morrissey, in his opinion, had been drunk again.

Johanna managed to eat breakfast, but she had no appetite for a conversation with Patrick Geehan. Later in the morning, she readied herself for her visit to the Fitzgeralds. Her reason for the earlier call in search of wool was a good excuse for this occasion.

"Good day, Mrs. Fitzgerald. I'm back again, looking for some wool. I'm sure Patrick mentioned my earlier visit," Johanna said, as she stood on the back step of the Fitzgerald house.

"Yes, come in. I have plenty of red wool," said Mrs. Fitzgerald, who was always a pleasant woman. "You'll not have much time to knit many pairs of mittens between now and Christmas. Didn't Jane have any wool left? I'm surprised that she ran short, especially at this time of the year."

"Well, she and Garrett left on Monday to go to Brigus. Garrett is catching the boat for St. John's to have his feet looked at. Jane hasn't returned so Mr. Geehan is planning on going to Turk's Gut to get her. He figures that she stayed on with her sister. I wouldn't want to take any of her wool because I'm not sure what she has planned for it."

"My goodness, what happened to your face, my darling?"

Johanna grimaced. "That's what happens when you try to do things too quickly. Last night, I didn't bother with the lamp when I went out to the barn to get some wood. While I was poking around in the blackness, I hit my face on the pigs' stall."

"Poor thing. You are such a pretty girl. You don't need a mark like that. Do you need anything to put on it?" Mrs. Fitzgerald looked concerned.

"No. I'll be fine. I'm sure I'll find something at the house."

Everything went as planned at the Fitzgeralds, she thought. As she was leaving, Johanna sensed that Catherine Fitzgerald was now convinced Jane had gone to the boat with Garrett.

"Thanks for the wool. I'll make sure that it is returned when I make my next trip over to Harbour Grace," Johanna called out as she left the Fitzgerald house. She trusted that Patrick

Fitzgerald would keep quiet about what had happened last night. He seemed to understand why she had to hide Garrett's death.

Patrick Fitzgerald listened to Johanna's story from his bedroom. He knew exactly where Garrett was. However, Johanna had told him that Jane had gone on her own to Turk's Gut. He wondered why Johanna would now have Jane travelling with Garrett. That reasoning would certainly complicate things when Jane got back home. He wondered why Johanna hadn't left the Geehan household as she had said she was going to. He lay back on his bed, and it suddenly occurred to him that he too had now been dragged into a killing.

His infatuation for Johanna helped soothe away his concerns. He chose to remain silent because of his feelings for her. Patrick Fitzgerald was unaware that Johanna didn't have the same feelings for him as he had for her.

At about noon on Tuesday, Johanna saw the Shugarue's servant girl, Mary Vokey, approaching Patrick Geehan, having entered the garden through the rear gate. Again, Patrick had the sail erected on the east side of the pit so that he could conceal his work. He was raking over the soil where he had buried Garrett.

Geehan was so intent on his work that he didn't hear Mary approaching.

"Excuse me, Mr. Geehan," she said, as she tapped him on the back.

Patrick jumped. "Dyin' Jesus, girl. You frightened me to death."

"I'm sorry to have scared you, sir. Mr. Shugarue wants to know if you can kill a pig for him sometime today or tomorrow, if you are not too busy."

"That I can," Patrick answered. "I just put some squid in the ground and I'm raking them in so that my vegetables will come better next year. Did you do that in Ireland?" Mary Vokey had just arrived from Ireland and immediately went to work for the Shugarues.

"Yes, sir. We used all kinds of fish and sometimes kelp in the ground."

"No, I meant are you in the habit of creeping up on people and frightening them like that?"

"No, sir. I'm sorry," Mary looked down at her boots.

"When does Mr. Shugarue want me?"

"I think he can use your help whenever you are ready, sir."

"Tell him I'll be over today since I've got to go and get Mrs. Geehan tomorrow."

Johanna saw Patrick put his rake in the barn. When he came out, he was sharpening a huge butcher's knife by rubbing it back and forth over a stone. He was known locally for his skill in butchering animals.

It was a welcome break for Johanna when she didn't see Patrick Geehan until about nine o'clock that evening. He entered the house, trying to walk without staggering. He mumbled something unintelligible. She decided not to ask him to repeat it. He began to fill his pipe as he slumped down in the rocking chair.

"I'll be needing you one more time tonight, Johanna," he said, and this time she was able to understand his slurred speech. She realized he had been given more than a little something to drink by Daniel Shugarue.

"In what way will you be needing me?" she asked cautiously.

Patrick looked at her. "I put the dray in the barn this morning. I used some brim and rope to wrap the wheels so that we wouldn't make any noise tonight as we carry Jane up to the ridge to drop her down in the quarry."

Johanna was shocked to realize that she was being once again unwillingly called into action.

"We'll leave around four-thirty in the morning while it's the darkest hour. I've got her all ready. I'll lay her on the dray and just let her slide off into the quarry." Patrick stopped talking for a moment in order to refocus his thinking. For some reason, when he was drunk he always waved his finger as he spoke. "When she is found, it will look like she fell there."

"What if we are seen?" asked Johanna.

"It will be very dark. Even if we were seen, it wouldn't be light enough to notice the wheels have been covered or to see the body. Who'll see us at four thirty in the morning anyway?"

Johanna knew that the risk was much greater than Patrick Geehan was trying to make it appear. With every action Patrick was taking, she was falling deeper into the abyss of an unwanted conspiracy. She went to her room but wasn't able to sleep as she thought about what she and Patrick Geehan were about to do. When the clock struck four, Geehan appeared at the door.

"I have the dray out by the back door. We'd better get moving." A few hours' sleep had restored Patrick's sobriety but not his sanity. While Johanna got dressed, he dragged the body, now draped in a sheet of canvas, to the back porch. Johanna was repulsed when she encountered the noxious smell of death. Patrick struggled to lift one end of the body onto the dray.

"I'll get up and drag her up towards the front. Hold her so she doesn't slip back to the ground," he ordered.

It was dark, cold and windy in the early morning hour of November 21. After the grisly cargo was secured with rope, they headed up to Spaniard's Bay Road, neither one of them choosing to speak. It was surreal as they rode on the dray since the covered wheels were making no noise whatsoever. Only the sound of Prince's hoofs could be heard as Patrick had the horse trotting at a brisk pace.

When they arrived at the quarry, Patrick pulled the rig close to the cliff. He handed the reins to Johanna, pulled on the brake, and climbed to the rear of the wagon. He rolled Jane's body off the dray and it fell into the darkness. Jumping off the dray, he grabbed the lantern and disappeared down over the hill. Johanna knew he was at the bottom, unfurling the tarp and positioning the body.

There were no lights except for Patrick's lantern down in the distance below her. She wondered how he managed to get down to the bottom of the quarry without falling, and then remembered that he knew this quarry very well for he often came here for topsoil. Desperation was now his motivation, and he had to gamble that nothing would go wrong.

"Okay. Let's go," he whispered, appearing out of the darkness with the lantern now extinguished. They made the turn to begin the trip back to the Southside.

Patrick Geehan was breathing easier. "It will be a while before someone finds her. Now we just have to wait. This plan has to work, Johanna. It's fail-proof. Jane's ill-health these past couple of years and people thinking that Garrett has gone missing to St. John's should keep us from being discovered. It wouldn't be unusual to expect somebody as simple as Garrett to disappear."

Johanna wasn't as confident. She was quietly considering her options. Maybe she should visit the police. At least, she hadn't killed anybody. Would her side of the story be taken as the truth or had she gone too far in assisting Patrick Geehan?

There was another wrinkle in the whole affair now, about which Patrick Geehan didn't know. The circle of deception had widened, for Johanna had now included Patrick Fitzgerald.

CHAPTER FOURTEEN

St. John's
January, 1896

Father John Coombs was beginning to settle in as curate to Monsignor Morrissey. It was Monsignor's desire that Father John take over more duties in St. Patrick's Parish. There were two other priests living at the presbytery and sharing duties with him, but being the newest member of the parish team he found that he was subject to most everyone else. As well, he had retained responsibility for Her Majesty's Penitentiary. This certainly was not how he had envisioned his role.

It was at two o'clock in the early hours of January 23 when Father John woke up to the sound of the doorbell. It was odd that the housemaid hadn't gone to answer the persistent ringing.

"I've got it Father! I've got it!" yelled Mrs. Donahue as she rushed to the front door while still tying her robe. "I'm sorry, Father. I was sleeping like a log."

When she unlatched the door, a strong gust of wind suddenly and unexpectedly blew it completely wide open. Snow piled up in the entrance and Father John could see that St. John's was in the midst of a major storm.

There was a lone figure covered in wet snow from head to foot at the door, a woman standing out on the step with a scarf wrapped around her face and a knitted stocking cap pulled down over her head.

"Come in. Come in!" said Father John.

Mrs. Donahue quickly shut the door behind the woman. When the woman uncovered her face, Father John couldn't believe what he was seeing. Sarah Keough rushed towards him with open arms as she wept uncontrollably. Father John held her in his arms and waited for her to regain her composure. While he had constantly thought about her, he hadn't seen her since the day of his ordination.

"You have to come and see Pop. I think he's dying, John. I think he's dying," she cried.

Mrs. Donahue, taken by total surprise, was astonished. "Let me put the tea on, my darling. Take off that wet coat. You'll catch your death."

"No. We haven't time. He's been calling for a priest." Sarah looked towards Father John. "Can you come?"

He released her from their embrace. "I'll come with you right away. Let me get my case." As did all priests, Father John had a small leather kit in which he carried anointing oil, which was used for the Last Rites of the church, as well as the Blessed Sacrament.

He pulled on his heavy overcoat and fur hat and returned for Sarah. They didn't have far to walk, across LeMarchant Road and up over the hill to Campbell Avenue. Holding on to each other, they struggled through the blizzard-like conditions to reach Sarah's grandparents' house.

Mrs. Keough was sitting on the bed in the backroom of the small one-storey house, clasping her prayer book. A lone candle cast flickering shadows over the walls as Father John and Sarah entered the bedroom. Mr. Keough lay very still in the bed and his eyes were shut. Father John opened his case to retrieve the blessed oils with which he would anoint the dying man.

"In nomine Patris et Filii et Spiritus Sancti. Amen," he began, losing no time initiating the Latin ritual after seeing the man's condition.

Sarah and her grandmother knelt down as the priest administered the Last Rites. Father John then knelt beside them and took out his beads to begin the rosary. Within minutes, Mr. Keough had passed away. Mrs. Keough stood up to give her husband one last kiss. Sarah did the same.

The next door neighbor, a woman named Martha Hollett who was a close friend of Mrs. Keough, knocked softly on the bedroom door before coming in to join them. She gave Mrs. Keough and Sarah a quick hug and then knelt beside them.

Father John pulled the sheet up over Mr. Keough's face and blew out the candle. He led everyone out of the room, shutting the door behind them. Father John knew that his place was with Sarah and her family till morning.

Martha Hollett had summoned the undertakers early that morning and they all waited in the kitchen while the two black clad men completed their work. Except for putting out suitable clothing, Sarah and her grandmother had little to do while Mr. Caul and his assistant prepared the body for the wake. After the undertakers left, they sat in the parlour and Mrs. Keough talked about how she met her husband and the life they had enjoyed together. After assuring them that he would drop back later, Father John left to attend to his other parish duties. Sarah accompanied him to the outside porch.

"What have you been doing these last few months?" John asked her.

"I have begun working at the General Hospital on Forest Road," she replied.

"I'm glad for you. It's a noble thing to do, serving the weakest of our society."

"We'll be forever grateful, John," she said, resisting the idea of addressing him as "Father." It was an awkward moment for John as she reached up and kissed him on the cheek. They held each other for a few seconds and he suddenly remembered how much he had missed her gentle touch.

"Sarah, I often think about the day in the Cathedral and how upset you were. I felt that it would just complicate matters to contact you again." John felt an explanation was necessary, but he wasn't sure if this was the appropriate moment for it. "It would have achieved nothing but prolong any sadness we were both feeling."

"I still feel that sadness, John," said Sarah. "I don't think I am able to get over missing you. You should know that there's been nobody in my life since then, and I have no interest in anyone else."

John was surprised but not saddened to hear Sarah's words. He truly thought that Sarah had moved on. While he was disappointed in the role he had in the church thus far, he really couldn't express his feelings to her. It was still early in his vocation and he had to give the religious life a chance. He had taken a vow of celibacy for life, and it was too soon to write off his relationship with God. A conversation with Sarah about his feelings might be a step on the slippery slope to sinfulness.

"Sarah, my heart aches, too," he said. Hearing those words, Sarah was elated. What she heard next, however, crushed her sense of optimism. “But we have to pray to the saints to take away any temptation we may be encountering.”

Her hopes were dashed again! Never could she pray that they would be apart. Her finding him at St. Patrick’s presbytery last night was a sure sign for her that they were meant to be together. She had no idea that John Coombs would be the one who would comfort her and her grandmother during this very sad time. She didn’t even know that he was at St. Patrick’s Parish.

“I’ll see who Monsignor wants to do the funeral Mass. I’ll assist with the celebration of the Mass in any event,” he said. In reality, the Liturgy was far from his mind.

“Thank you, John. We’ll see you later.” She quickly closed the door, leaving him standing outside in the doorway. John sensed her frustration. This was not how he wanted the conversation to end.

The snowstorm had subsided and people were again moving along the downtown streets as he walked back to the presbytery. But another storm had been churned up in John’s head. Sarah Keough was on his mind, and he agonized that he might have made a terrible mistake. Maybe he should have left the Cathedral with her on the day before his ordination. Maybe he had made a mistake.

CHAPTER FIFTEEN

Southside of Harbour Grace
Thursday, November 23, 1871

Four days after the death of Jane Geehan, on Thursday at noon, November 23, Patrick Geehan was tossing some straw in the horse's pound. It had been three long nights alone with Johanna. She had grown cold towards him. Although she came to his bed he could sense her rejection. Stopping his drinking and treating her kindly in every way possible didn't seem to bring her closer to him. The events of this past week had wiped out all that they had together.

From the distance, he thought he heard the sound of a woman wailing. It was Johanna! He threw down his pitchfork and bolted as quickly as he could to the back door.

"You can't go any further, Mr. Geehan, I'm sorry," said Officer Daley. His strong imposing figure filled the doorway. "The priest is here to see you."

Father O'Quinn stepped out from behind the policeman. "Patrick, my son, Jane was found up in the River this morning at around eight o'clock. I'm so sorry to tell you that she passed away suddenly."

"Oh, Jesus, Mary and Joseph. What happened? Can I see her?"

"I'm afraid you can't. We have just put her body in the front room and Dr. Allan and his son are there trying to determine the cause of death. You'll have to wait."

"Can I go into the kitchen then?"

"Of course," said the priest. "We'll get the housemaid to hang the kettle on the fire. We'll get a cup of tea."

Patrick walked into the kitchen and found Johanna sitting on the daybed using her handkerchief to dry her tears. Standing up, she reached towards him. With neither saying a word, he briefly held her and then sat at the table. She remained on the daybed. Officer Daley and Father O'Quinn soon joined them, sitting at the table with Patrick.

"I have a few questions, sir. I apologize for having to do this even before you see your wife. It will be part of the Coroner's Inquest for tomorrow. It's very routine," said the policeman.

"I was expecting her back yesterday," Patrick told the policeman, who was already making notes. "I intended to leave today with the horse to see if she needed a ride back. You know. Where she has been sick these last few months."

"When did she leave and where was she going?" asked the policeman.

"I haven't seen her since Monday past. Her brother, Garrett Sears, was taking the boat from Brigus on Tuesday afternoon to go to St. John's to get his feet cured. He lives here with us. Jane has family in Turk's Gut, just beyond Brigus, and was accompanying him as far as the boat. Her intention was to spend a couple of days with her aunt."

"So she left that morning with her brother?" asked Daley.

"Yes, very early, before sunrise. Garrett had bad toes from

frostbite many years ago and he was finally getting them done."

Dr. Allan and his son opened the kitchen door. "I'm sorry for your loss, Mr. Geehan," said the younger Dr. Allan, "When I saw your wife last summer, she was complaining about her breathing. It was most probably her heart."

Patrick made no comment to the doctor but directed his attention to the policeman. "Where did they find her?" he asked.

"About two miles up on Spaniard's Bay Road. It appears she tumbled down into the quarry. She had been there for some time," said Daley.

"That makes sense, Patrick," said the elder Dr. Allan. "As I was examining Mrs. Geehan I thought I overheard you say she was returning from up the bay? She may have left there some days ago and took sick while walking down over the ridge. When we got there we could tell she had fallen in such a manner that she was well concealed, sort of under the cliff, in the bushes and below the road. It was unlikely anyone could have seen her."

"Do you think she suffered?" Patrick asked the doctor. Johanna was astonished by his performance. He truly appeared shocked and distraught.

"I don't think so. Except for the cut on her head from the fall, there were no other signs of trauma," consoled the doctor.

"Can we see her now?" asked Patrick again.

Everyone followed him and Johanna into the front room where Jane had been placed upon the couch. A white sheet covered her from head to toe. Dr. Allan slowly turned back the cover to allow Patrick and Johanna to see her face.

"Dear Father in heaven, have mercy on her soul," said Patrick, as he reached out to hold Johanna's hand. Johanna suddenly felt weak and fainted into Patrick's arms. Officer Daley had no trouble lifting Johanna and carrying her out of the front room. Placing her gently on the daybed, he went to fetch some water.

The priest then administered the Last Rites to Jane Geehan's lifeless body, and everyone knelt until the short prayer had been concluded.

"Patrick," said the younger Dr. Allan, "I suggest that you call some of the women nearby to lay Mrs. Geehan out and begin the wake as soon as possible. We'll be going by Mr. Parsons on our way back to the surgery and we can send him over with a coffin. By the time he gets here, she'll be ready, and he will look after everything from there. I urge you not to keep her open for more than tonight and have the funeral as early as you can." Dr. Allan didn't have to say why.

The house began to fill with people as soon as the doctor and the rest of the company left. John and Catherine Fitzgerald were the first to arrive.

"We just got the news, Patrick. We are so sorry," said Catherine.

Patrick Fitzgerald filed into the kitchen behind Mr. and Mrs. Shugarue. He was pale and visibly upset.

"What do you think happened?" Patrick Fitzgerald directed his question to Patrick Geehan.

"Dr. Allan believes it was her heart. She's been complaining for months now," replied Patrick Geehan.

"Who found her, I wonder?" Patrick Fitzgerald asked. He had more than a vested interest in the answer.

"A man from the River. She must have been there for a while according to the doctor. I'd say as soon as she saw Garrett off at Brigus, she left to walk home instead of going to her aunt's house."

Patrick Geehan had his face buried in his hands as he sat at the table. He appeared to be in tears. It was apparent to most of those in the kitchen that he had become too emotional to talk. Johanna knew the difference! She saw the look on Patrick Fitzgerald's face. He wasn't fooled either.

The wake would begin as soon as Mr. Parsons arrived to lay

Mrs. Geehan out. It was common that the local people would keep a vigil throughout the day and night. It served to give the relatives some company during the wake.

While the undertaker and the women did their work in the house, the men gathered around the back yard. Clouds of smoke encircled their heads as they puffed on their pipes and remained mostly silent out of respect for Jane Geehan.

"It's really strange," said John Fitzgerald to Patrick Geehan. "I thought I heard Garrett calling out to you on Monday around noon."

"No, bye, you couldn't have. You didn't hear Garrett."

"I heard a couple of gunshots and saw a plume of smoke right over here, near your back door," insisted John. "Then I thought I heard Garrett sing out, 'Paddy! Paddy!' It sounded like he wanted to show you something."

"That must have been Johanna," said Patrick. "We had a hawk hanging around here after our chicken and hens. On Monday I had the gun laid on the step, loaded and all, just waiting for him to pitch somewhere. Sure enough, I heard Johanna call me, saying that she saw the hawk. I went out and saw the hawk with a hen in his craw trying to get flight. I grabbed the gun and fired twice. I hit the bastard but didn't kill him. He dropped the hen and took off."

"Ok, Patrick," interrupted Mr. Parsons, in a very serious and somber tone of voice. "I think it best if you come see your wife now."

When Patrick Geehan came into the house, Parsons quietly whispered to him, "I think we'll have to close the casket after you say your goodbye. We'll get Father Quinn to bury her on Saturday morning."

Patrick walked into the parlour and knelt at the coffin for a few minutes. He then came out and advised Mr. Parsons to shut the coffin.

CHAPTER SIXTEEN

Southside of Harbour Grace
November 25th, 1871

Jane Geehan's wake was held on Thursday and Friday. She was buried on Saturday, November 25. Many local people came to the farm during the wake. In keeping with the traditions of an Irish wake, several stayed overnight at the Geehan house and gathered in the kitchen or the parlour. Nobody slept. During the night, some people played cards while others occupied their time telling stories, doing recitations or playing a musical instrument. A bottle of rum was opened and drained by the men before morning. It was by no means a solemn affair.

Johanna decided that once she got beyond the funeral, she would be leaving Patrick Geehan and the Southside forever. Her brief rendezvous with Patrick Fitzgerald would have to be curtailed even though he had done her a great service. She knew he would never talk, since he would incriminate himself by doing so. As soon as the funeral was over, she would have to be clear with Patrick Fitzgerald that there was no longer anything between them.

Every effort had to be made to ensure that Jane Geehan was buried without alerting any suspicions. Johanna thought the best approach was to totally immerse herself into her role as the servant girl she was hired to be. Trying her best to be hospitable and friendly, she made sandwiches, served tea and even offered the ladies some of Jane's sherry. Her behavior, though, was to be interpreted differently.

"Did you contact Garrett, the poor thing?" Mrs. Hearn asked Johanna on Thursday after supper.

"No, I leave that stuff to Mr. Geehan," answered Johanna. "Who knows where he is anyway?"

"A telegraph could be sent to the hospital, I suppose," suggested Mrs. Hearn.

"That it could, but I don't know if Mr. Geehan even wants Garrett here. How would Garrett react if he knew that his sister died after escorting him all the way to Brigus? Can you imagine the strain that was on her heart?" Johanna wanted to reinforce the idea of Jane's natural death. "Given Garrett's state of mind, nobody knows how he would take her death, especially if he felt some blame."

Patrick Geehan and John Fitzgerald were standing out by the pit where Garrett had been buried. "It will be a lonely place for you now, Paddy," said John. "You are lucky to have the young girl here with you. Garrett will most likely be laid up with the operation and won't be able to do much this winter."

Patrick Fitzgerald gazed at the pit and listened to his brother and Patrick Geehan. He only now comprehended the magnitude of what had happened on this farm these past few days. He was now suspicious of Jane Geehan's death. Johanna's lie about Jane escorting Garrett to the boat, as told to his sister-in-law, was making sense.

“Indeed I am lucky to have Johanna. I’ll miss Jane terribly. She was such a good woman,” stated Patrick Geehan. “I’ve got her clothes put aside for the women. She’d want me to do that. Jane was a person who didn’t believe in wasting anything.”

John Fitzgerald hid his surprise at Patrick Geehan’s quick decision to rid himself of Jane’s clothes.

“Johanna can do the work of any man,” said Patrick Geehan. ”We’ll have to make do for now. Garrett will be fine by the time April comes around.”

John spoke up. “I was over to the Coroner’s Inquest this morning, as you asked. The only two witnesses called were Bill Byrne from the Thicket and Dr. Allan. There were only six in the jury and a handful of onlookers. Bill Byrne had to recount where he found Jane. Dr. Allan had to give the cause of death. The whole thing only took about fifteen minutes. The judge expressed his sincere condolences.”

“Thanks for doing that, John,” said Patrick.

As the day of the funeral drew near much talk was being circulated about some peculiarities surrounding Jane’s death and the wake. People began looking for an edge to catch so that they could pull open the well-wrapped package of untold secrets. There was nothing normal about this whole situation. The gossip began.

“I can’t believe that he didn’t get in touch with her only brother. He didn’t even try,” said Catherine Hearn.

“Look at the way Johanna is acting. It’s like she owns the place. Jane would never allow her to take over like that. John Fitzgerald told me that they’ve even got Jane’s clothes packed up and ready to be given away. Just imagine. Treating her like that before she’s even laid to rest,” said Catherine Fitzgerald.

After the funeral mass on Saturday, some of the neighbours

followed the hearse and the funeral cortege to the cemetery. Uncharacteristically for the people of the Southside, many opted not to do so.

"It was a beautiful service," said Daniel Shugarue, as he and his wife rode their buggy down the Southside Road. "But not many went to Harbour Grace. I found that strange. Most times there's a huge procession."

"I'm not one bit surprised. There wasn't much sadness in that house with Jane's death. At the church, Patrick Geehan never even shed a tear," said Mrs. Shugarue. "Then that Johanna, with no shame at all, sat right down by him. Up in the front pew by the coffin and all. How brazen!"

Daniel Shugarue wasn't a man to gossip. Alice Shugarue, on the other hand, didn't need prompting. "From the stories I heard about their living quarters on the coast and how close they seemed to be, I can tell you she was more than a servant girl. Some say Patrick and Johanna were different people in the summer than they were at home in the winter." Alice looked disgusted.

That's enough talk!" said Daniel. "There's no doubt that the man has some troubles ahead of him. We'll be minding our own business." They continued their ride in silence.

Saturday was one of the longest days Johanna had ever experienced. After the funeral, she and Patrick Geehan returned home together driven by Johanna's sister, Catherine, and her brother–in-law, John Drake. The Drakes had accompanied Johanna and Patrick to the church service and drove them to the cemetery. The Immaculate Conception Church Cemetery was a four-mile ride from the church. The entire event, including the funeral procession, took about five hours.

"Come in and get some tea," offered Patrick on their arrival back at the Geehan farm. "I'll go in and get the fire going."

John Drake stayed outside, and while filling his pipe he called out to Patrick, "I'm going to stretch my legs and take a walk around the yard." Gesturing to Johanna to wait with him, John bent down close to her ear and whispered, "You'll have to leave here as soon as you can. If not, you'll be implicated in Garrett's disappearance."

"What have you heard?" Johanna was concerned that her worst fear had come to pass.

"People are wondering where Garrett is. Him not being here for his sister's funeral is very odd. Patrick Geehan seems removed and he's acting strange, even about Jane's death. I'm telling you, it's only a matter of time before the crowners come here to ask a few questions."

"I'll be leaving here on Monday," said Johanna. "My intention is to go early in the morning before he gets up. He won't like me going and leaving him here to fend for himself."

"Do you want me to come get you?" asked John.

"No. I think it will be less fuss if I just left. If it's all right with Catherine, I'll stay with you for a few days. I hope to get to the States as soon as I can get a passage. We have some family in Boston. I have their addresses and we've had a few letters back and forth."

"You can stay with us as long as you want. But get out of here as fast as you can," John said firmly.

"The kettle is boiling," interrupted Patrick from the back porch.

They filed into the house. It was dark by the time Catherine and John rode back to the River. Johanna realized that she couldn't go to her old room and leave Patrick Geehan to sleep alone. It would be like waving a red flag announcing her departure. She had to make it appear that she had every intention of staying. Any hint of her rejection of him could be dangerous.

It was uncomfortable as they both lay in the bed where Patrick and Jane had spent so many nights. Johanna finally turned down the lantern until there was total darkness. Without saying anything, Patrick moved closer and stroked her hair. She didn't move. He then tried holding her gently. She remained motionless and continued to face the wall. At last he pleaded, "Is there anything I can do to regain your love? You've been through so much because of me. I'm so sorry to have put you through this."

She waited for what seemed to be a long time before responding. "I'll need time," she said. "You'll have to be patient with me." She hoped her response would serve to placate him. Finally he released his embrace and turned over. Within seconds, he was snoring. Now she could rest.

On Monday morning, Johanna woke much earlier than Patrick Geehan. She began to have second thoughts about leaving so quickly. Might this be a greater reason for people to be even more suspicious? She decided to stay a little longer. Maybe a week or two would give her enough time to make arrangements to leave the area entirely. She would contact John Drake and have him book a passage to Boston. In a few days, she would be away from Newfoundland and Harbour Grace forever.

When Patrick came downstairs, Johanna had the fire started.

"Patrick," she said. "This is a difficult time for me. I know that you must feel alone, especially with me pushing you away. But I need time. Maybe I'll go back to my room for a while until I feel more comfortable."

"I'll not hear of it," said Patrick. "We're in this together. Johanna. We'll get through this. Don't leave my bed. We've come this far. I'll give you all the time you need, and I promise to wait for you to come to me when you are ready. I need you now more than ever."

Johanna concluded that she had to remain despite how repulsed she felt. She had to plan her exodus in a quiet, nonintrusive manner. She had to be on a ship before Patrick Geehan knew the difference. At least, as of now, he never expected anything from her beyond her lying in the bed with him. It was just a place to sleep. It was her intention never to have relations with Patrick Geehan again.

They both continued to work hard as they did their chores on the farm. Johanna thought it odd that for the next few days nobody came to visit. It was as if people suspected further trouble.

As she anticipated, Patrick Fitzgerald came over one day while she was drawing water from the well behind the upper shed. He made sure that Patrick Geehan was nowhere in sight. She suspected he wanted to continue the relationship they had begun.

Patrick Fitzgerald had done her a huge service and he had great expectations. But her life was too complicated to carry on with him in the manner he wished. A relationship with Patrick Fitzgerald would only drag him into a situation he didn't need. She had to be cold and decisive so that he knew she wanted an absolute end to anything they had begun.

"Patrick," she said, "I can't begin to tell you how much I am indebted to you, but you must know that we can't continue to see each other. I'm leaving here as soon as I can. With Jane's death and the circumstances surrounding Garrett it's best we have nothing to do with each other. I'm sorry."

Patrick Fitzgerald was devastated. "But what about what we have together? I risked my reputation for you the other night. You led me to believe that you loved me."

"Never once did I say that, Patrick." She turned to walk away, fearing that Patrick Geehan would see them.

"You used me?" Patrick Fitzgerald sounded shocked and hurt.

"No. I didn't mean to. You should know that our not seeing each other is for your own good, even more so than mine. Patrick, if you've got a grain of sense, leave me be and go on with your life. I'll just drag you into a heap of trouble."

He could see her determination, but he couldn't believe how heartless she was. Maybe it was possible for her to walk away unscathed by their short-lived relationship, but for him her rejection of him was a life changing moment. If he couldn't have her, why should anybody else?

CHAPTER SEVENTEEN

Southside of Harbour Grace
December 5, 1871

December 5 was a very cold day. Almost two weeks had passed since Jane Geehan's funeral. Johanna, through John Drake, had made some inquiries about a passage to Boston. To date nothing for certain had transpired, but John advised her that she should hear something within two or three days.

There had been a light dusting of snow that morning. Patrick Geehan wanted to get the last of the wood stored in the shed, so the day before he and Johanna had spent the entire day hand-barrowing junks of wood to the shed. By bedtime, they were both exhausted. It had been a long and difficult two weeks. On this particular Monday morning they had overslept.

Johanna lay motionless in bed next to Patrick Geehan, listening to the incessant rattle of his chest. She remained very still, hoping against hope that he would remain asleep. The thought of him putting his hands on her was sickening, knowing his deranged behavior. How could this man, whom she once loved, have committed such atrocities? She quietly rolled her rosary beads through her fingers, hanging on to the thread of faith that God, indeed, was a God of mercy. She prayed that He would hear her prayers, even though she felt that her soul was now condemned to eternal damnation.

Three thunderous bangs on the front door jarred Patrick awake. Johanna knew the neighbours would have come to the back door, not the front. It had to be a stranger. Patrick stumbled out of bed, trying to find the clock. It was always laid on the dresser next to his side of the bed but this morning it wasn't there.

"Where's the goddamn clock?" he asked aloud, even though he was questioning himself more than Johanna.

There were more knocks, louder than before, and then a voice said, "Open up. It's the police."

Patrick jumped up and drew his pants up over his long underwear. He put his arms out through his braces and hopped out the door as he struggled awkwardly to pull on his socks. "I'm coming! I'm coming," he shouted.

Johanna heard him run downstairs and then began to dress as quickly as she could. She grabbed the dress she'd worn to Jane's funeral out of the closet. Quickly, she tied an apron around her waist to give the appearance she had been up and at work. Taking a glance in the mirror, she hastily brushed her hair into place as best she could.

When she arrived downstairs, two policemen were standing at the back door. Patrick had been restricted from exiting the house and was now sitting at the table with his hands on his forehead.

"Sit down, Miss. We are doing an investigation as to the whereabouts of Garrett Sears," said Constable Daley.

"I told you. He's in St. John's," said Patrick. "Mother of Jesus, can't you let a man mourn his wife?"

"We're just taking a look, sir. Mr. Sears has been gone for quite a few days and nobody has heard from him. Somebody reported you were out behind the house doing a lot of work in one particular area. They said you seemed to be concealing something. We have to follow up. It won't take us long. I'm sorry about this."

The back door was left open and Johanna could see Inspector Foley prodding the pit with a ramrod. Justice of the Peace James Lilly and another policeman stood with Foley while he jabbed the soil at random.

Soon others from the community began to arrive behind the house. Patrick and John Fitzgerald were the first. Then Daniel Shugarue wandered in through the backyard gate.

Suddenly there was a shout. "I think I have something," Inspector Foley announced as he kept poking the rod into the same piece of ground. "Pass me the shovel."

"I'll do it, sir," said the constable. He picked up a spade and began to clear away the dirt. "It's a body," he said in alarm, abruptly stopping and standing back from what he had discovered. "My god, I can see the arm and hand."

The Inspector took control. "Gentlemen, it would expedite matters if you would get your shovels to help uncover the remains. Constable Hutcher will supervise."

When the men left to get their tools, the constable took a rope and cordoned off a section around where he approximated the body had been buried. The men returned with their shovels and within minutes they had fully exposed the corpse of Garrett Sears. They then carefully, as if Garrett was only mortally injured, lifted his body out of the pit. Only one man standing there knew this was Garrett's second time exiting from that grave. Garrett was covered in mud, bloodied and mutilated. There was no doubt he had experienced a violent death.

The constable walked back to the police wagon and returned

with a sheet to cover the deceased while Inspector Foley entered the house. With the policemen by his side, Foley began the legal process, which Patrick Geehan thought he had avoided.

"Patrick Geehan and Johanna Hamilton, you are being taken into the custody of the Terra Nova Police and charged with the murder of Garrett Sears," Foley spoke slowly and solemnly.

Constables Daley and Hutcher proceeded to shackle both prisoners with leg chains and handcuffs. Foley had come prepared, having the police bring along the paddy wagon. He must have thought his suspicions would be validated.

Johanna and Patrick Geehand were assisted into the wagon with the two police officers and so began the trip to the Harbour Grace Courthouse.

"Johanna, I didn't mean…" Patrick Geehan began to say as they headed towards Harbour Grace.

"There's to be no conversation between you," interrupted the policeman. "Any further communication between you will be done through a judge by court order."

When they arrived at the Harbour Grace Courthouse, they were escorted to separate rooms in the basement of the building. Impeded by their restraints, they scuffed by several empty jail cells until they reached the other end of the building.

Inspector Foley and Justice Lilly made a decision to give them fifteen minutes alone. After the two men finished a cup of tea in the galley of the courthouse, they approached Patrick Geehan.

"Well, Mr. Geehan, I don't have to remind you of the charge against you. I am asking for your statement which Justice Lilly will write down. I will then ask you to read, sign and validate what you have said. Do you understand my request?"

"Yes, sir. I am ready," replied Geehan. He seemed very confident. He spoke as if once he made his statement he would be let free.

He said calmly, "I was watching for the hawk as Johanna went for Garrett to come for dinner. Garrett came down. He went in the back house. I was still watching for a hawk, and as I came around the house I saw that the hawk had pitched on the cart. I crept around the house to fire at the hawk. As I drew the trigger, Garrett popped out of the back house. I stood and looked. He fell and the gun fell out of my hands. I went over and caught hold of him and he commenced bawling. Johanna ran out. 'We will be hung,' she said. 'The people will hear him bawling.' There was a pitchfork alongside. I said, 'He is dead now.' Still he was bawling so I struck him with the pitchfork. That put an end to him. I was very sorry for him certainly but when it was done it could not be helped. It was accidentally done in the first place. The two of us put him away for the night and at about midnight we buried him. I knew he would be found in the loose earth."[ii]

"Is there anything else?" asked Foley.

"No, sir, except to say that Garrett looks in much worse shape than when he died. The pigs got after him and we didn't know it until we went to bury him."

"So that's all you have to say?" asked Foley.

"Nothing else except to say that Garrett was near death, seconds away. Johanna's encouragement gave me the will to put him out of his pain.

Inspector Foley had Patrick Geehan sign and date his statement.

"Now we'll go and see what the young Hamilton girl has to say," said Foley.

The interrogation room where they kept Johanna was a cold place with gray concrete walls and no windows. Water was leaking in through one of the cracks in the wall and pooled on the concrete floor. A musky smell of dampness permeated.

Inspector Foley greeted Johanna in the same manner as he

had Patrick Geehan.

"Well, Miss Hamilton, you know the charge against you. Please give us your statement and Justice Lilly will write it down. You'll then be requested to read, sign and validate what you have said. Do you understand?"

"I do, sir. And I will do it to the best of my ability," she answered.

Johanna's voice trembled as she told her story: "Many a time Garrett tormented the skipper and gave him a scalded heart, but I never saw him raise a hand to him until that day. When I went out in the yard I saw Garrett was already lying dead, and I don't know how it happened. Mrs. Geehan's death was caused by fright. She was in a room when she heard me bawling. When I said that her brother Garrett was shot she fell down and hit her head on the corner of a box and then fell face and eyes onto the floor. I went back and shook her and could not get any life in her. I went to the dresser for some holy water to rub on her to see if I could bring her to. I could find none on the dresser, but I found a gin bottle with a noggin in it. Maybe she had gin taken before and that caused her to fall and hit her head on the box."

Johanna didn't know that Patrick Geehan had earlier implicated her in his statement. Nor did she know that he hadn't mentioned Jane Geehan's death. She had lied to the police in an attempt to free Patrick. Her lying now worked against her, exposing the fact that Jane Geehan's death wasn't as it had been perceived.

Inspector Foley read Patrick Geehan's statement to her. She was distraught at what she heard.

"I didn't see a pitchfork," she cried in alarm. "Garrett was dead on the ground. I didn't help Patrick lug him to the barn. They are lies, all lies!"

"Have you been sleeping in the same room with Patrick

Geehan since Jane Geehan was buried?" Foley asked the question, knowing that his investigators had found evidence of her presence in the bedroom.

"Yes, but it was to keep him company. He was bordering on losing his mind. He told me that I had to do as he said or he'd kill me."

Johanna's protests fell on deaf ears. Foley had enough evidence to send the matter to the Supreme Court in St. John's where both she and Patrick would stand trial for the murder of Garrett Sears. There would be an investigation into Garrett's death, as well as into the suspicious death of Mrs. Jane Geehan.

The Coroner's Inquest on Garrett Sears' death was a formality. Public notice was posted to allow people to come forward and give evidence. Judge Peters presided at the Harbour Grace Court, with the shackled prisoners seated in the box.

Many local people attended the inquest out of curiosity. Inspector Foley read all reports and statements, including the postmortem report from Dr. Allan. A ruling of criminal death was just about to be proclaimed when Thomas Morrissey stood up.

"Your Worship, my name is Thomas Morrissey from the Southside of Harbour Grace and I would like to make a statement about the matter put before you," he shouted at the top of his voice:

Thomas was well known for his ability to dance, sing and often take a little too much to drink. There were a few muffled giggles in the courtroom when he spoke.

"Silence," ordered Judge Peters. "Let's hear Mr. Morrissey's statement. Would the clerk continue to record, please?"

Thomas spoke out loudly and clearly. "I would like the Court to know that I saw Garrett Sears at four o'clock last Tuesday morning walking down the Southside about a hundred yards from his house in a bloodied and dirty condition. He wouldn't answer me when I offered help. Yet this Court is saying that he was killed on Monday. When I went to see Patrick Geehan the next morning, he told me that I likely had seen a ghost or a fetch."

Judge Peters looked at Patrick's statement and realized there was some discrepancy. According to police records, Garrett was shot around noon and buried that night.

"Mr. Morrissey, where were you coming from at that hour?" asked the judge.

There was more laughter in the courtroom.

"I was at a 'time' until about four in the morning. I can swear that while I had a bit to drink, I wasn't too drunk to see a dead man walking," countered Morrissey. He glared around at those who had mocked him. "If Paddy Geehan had killed and buried him then it must have been Garrett's ghost I saw."

The Court erupted in laughter again. Johanna remained expressionless. This could work for her or against her. Maybe Patrick Fitzgerald would come to her assistance at the Supreme Court.

"The Court will take Mr. Morrissey's statement into account. Thank you, sir," Judge Peters said as he dismissed Thomas. Because of his reputation for exaggerating and drinking, nobody believed him.

On December 8, 1871, Johanna and Patrick Geehan were to be conveyed by the police prison wagon to Her Majesty's Penitentiary in St. John's. They would be held there until their trial late in the month of May. Johanna's sister, Catherine Drake, was the only visitor allowed to see her before she left Harbour Grace.

Johanna stood up as Catherine entered the visitor's room. Still shackled by chains around her ankles and wrists, Johanna reached out for her sister. They were both in tears.

"You have five minutes, Miss," said the prison guard who was standing by at attention.

The sisters held each other, cherishing every moment. They were both in tears.

"Johanna, you know I love you very much and will support whatever you say," said Catherine.

"I didn't do anything wrong, Catherine. My only sin was to have loved the man who is now betraying me."

"They are taking you away tomorrow."

"I know. Please pray for me. I should have listened to you years ago. He is a bad man and what I did was unforgivable, taking another woman's bed. But, Catherine, I swear, I didn't kill anyone or help Patrick Geehan take Garrett or Jane's life. That is the absolute truth."

Catherine brushed her sister's hair back from her forehead. "I brought some things over for you. The policemen let me into the house to get your personal effects. Here, I brought this for you." Catherine pulled the rosary that Johanna had brought from Nowlan's Harbour out of her pocket and gently wound it around her sister's wrists, next to the chains.

Johanna looked at the rosary and kissed her sister's cheek. "I'll pray these beads daily and ask the Blessed Mother to help me. Please do the same, Catherine," she asked.

"I will," promised Catherine. "I'll pray for you and I will be in court when you appear. They'll find you innocent, I know."

"Miss Hamilton, it's time to go," ordered the guard. He picked up Johanna's suitcase, the same valise she had carried down to the Geehan farm four years ago. Johanna and the guard left the room and Catherine was left alone, sobbing her heart out in the visitors' room.

CHAPTER EIGHTEEN

St. John's
September 18, 1896

"Good morning, Father," said Mrs. Donahue. "Your toast will soon be ready. I know you are in a hurry to get down to the prison today with this being your last day and all. Young Father Walsh is a little nervous about going there. I told him that you'll fill him in on everything." Mrs. Donahue knew the intricacies of the priests' daily affairs at St. Patrick's since she had been there for so long.

"You know?" said Father John. "I think the prison has grown on me a little bit. But it will be good to be able to visit the sick and the shut-ins around here. Before I go to the prison today, though, I'll be taking my parents up to the west end. Dad loves going by the new railway terminus to see all the changes. I never get a chance to take them out anymore."

Father John took the parish horse and buggy, which was usually reserved for Monsignor, along LeMarchant Road. He never tired of the view of the harbour as he rode along the street towards Military Road and then onto Prescott Street. It was a clear sunny morning. The water at the Narrows was flat calm as the fishing boats were returning to the Battery carrying their morning catch. Each boat left a wake as it steamed up to its wharf.

His parents were dressed in their Sunday best, proud to ride along with their son. Mark Coombs had threatened many times to tell John how lucky they felt to have him as their son, but Theresa always felt that the truth of his birth might drive a wedge between them. It was too late now, they felt. It was better to let matters rest. As far as they were concerned, John was their son.

"Dad, can you believe this huge building and the actual railway lines have all been built on pilings?" Father John was referring to the new Reid Railway Terminal and train tracks now built out over the harbour's edge. "You would think that something as huge as this, constructed on such a flimsy foundation, would just slide right out into the water?"

Father John returned his parents to their house at around 10:30 and realized that he was late for the prison. Sister Madonna was accustomed to his tardiness and accepted the young priest with all his faults. Over the past few months, they had built a mutually respectful relationship. He saw her engage the prisoners with her tough love and gentle touch.

Patrick Fitzgerald was first on his list to visit today and he made sure that he had his Holy Communion case with him.

"So what's your excuse today, Father?" asked Sister Madonna when she saw him enter the prison gate. She, too, was soon leaving the service of Her Majesty's Penitentiary. Her twenty-seven years of being at the prison every day were finally coming to an end. A well-deserved retirement was in order; the Convent needed her domestic skills at the Mother House.

"Would you accept my taking care of my poor aged parents as

being a good enough reason for coming late, Sister?" Father John knew she couldn't counter that.

"There's always a good excuse, Father. The fact that they are the same age as me and you are calling them old doesn't soften my resolve to make you more responsible." Sister Madonna knew Father John's parents very well. Years ago she and they had all worked closely with Bishop Power and the Christian Brothers. But she had never met young John until his first day at the prison. Although she heard much about the Coombs from the other nuns she had lost contact with the family.

"I'm on my way now," Father John grinned at her. "How's Patrick today?"

Sister Madonna looked at him. She knew he had worked hard with Patrick Fitzgerald throughout these past few months.

"Patrick is over at the General Hospital, Father John. He's not very well. I think that he may have had a stroke," she said.

Father John was aware of the man's ill-health. Patrick, on occasion, had even hinted of his being ready to leave this world. But the news of him in hospital was upsetting for he had grown fond of the broken man. He especially enjoyed Patrick's stories about Labrador and a place called Nowlan's Harbour.

Patrick would forget about all his cares, his guilt, and his shame when Labrador came up for discussion. Father John was amazed at how hard the man had worked, but his hardships had been balanced by the other joys of his life. The rugged beauty of the Labrador coast, the family relationships that blossomed out of isolation, and the young love that he encountered were subjects he often described to Father John in vivid detail.

Father John, in some sense, felt akin to Patrick, a man who had struggled with a lost love and knew that it would be impossible to regain it. There was a hole in Patrick's life which couldn't be filled. Patrick, too, had become spiritual; connecting with God had become his mission. Like Father John, he wanted to bond with a higher power. It was for this reason that Father John wanted to be there for Patrick in his last hours.

"I'll do my rounds and then run over across the road to the hospital and see how he is doing."

"Well, I'm afraid, John, he won't be back here." Sister Madonna wanted to prepare the young priest for the worst. "I don't think he'll make it. His breathing was quite heavy when they took him away."

Father John finished his calls and hurried out the prison gate dispensing with the usual pleasantries he normally afforded the guards at the exit. They assumed he must have an emergency at the hospital since he left the horse and buggy hitched up at the prison gate. He rushed directly across the road. The old military hospital was a rundown building badly in need of repair. A new modern building was being planned. This would be the government's first large scale attempt to care for the sick and the aged.

"May I help you?" asked a woman dressed in a similar manner to a nun, except that her garb was white. She was wearing a cap pinned tightly to her head instead of a veil. This was the first time he had seen a nurse. Men, also dressed in white, wheeled around stretchers. Some of the stretchers were empty and others had people on them. The place was a beehive of activity. Workers carried loads of bed sheets and towels while others had trays of food. Medical attendants called out orders and directions. With all the commotion, it was impossible for Father John to hear the lady who was greeting him. She beckoned him to follow her to a place where she could be heard. They left the open area and walked onto a more peaceful, larger room which she called a ward. There were about ten beds on each side of the room. All the beds were occupied. A couple of the beds had screens around them.

"I'm sorry, Father," she said. "We'll be able to talk in here." She closed the door and shut out most of the noise. "What can we do for you?"

"I'm Father John Coombs. Patrick Fitzgerald was brought here yesterday from the prison. May I see him?"

"Yes. Come with me. We keep the prisoners in a separate room."

He followed the nurse. Down another corridor, he saw an open door. She entered first. It was a small room with a window having bars on the outside. The only furniture was an iron bed. Father John could see someone lying flat on his back with a white sheet pulled up to his neck. Patrick Fitzgerald lay motionless. The scene was eerily reminiscent of the first time he'd seen him.

"He's right here," said the nurse. "I'm afraid he hasn't spoken since he arrived."

"May I say a prayer with him?" asked Father John.

"Of course. I'll leave you with him. Take as long as you need."

Patrick's eyes were closed as John reached under the sheet to take his frail hand. Father John took out his rosary beads and began to pray. After a few minutes of prayer, he saw Patrick's eyes open ever so slightly. His breathing grew shallower.

"Squeeze my hand, Patrick, if you can hear me," Father John said, and felt a faint tightening as he leaned over the dying man.

"Thank you for being here. Keep with God. She'll find you one day," Patrick managed to whisper.

"What do you mean? Who will find me? Who is she?" Father John asked as Patrick's eyes went still and he let go his grip.

At the age of forty-seven, Patrick Fitzgerald took his last breath. Father John stared at the peaceful face of a man who died well before his time. Patrick looked all of eighty years old, and perhaps he felt he had endured that many.

Unexpectedly, a gentle hand was placed on Father John's shoulder. He turned his head to see Sarah Keough.

"I'm sorry for your loss. I can see that you were close to him," she said, and as he looked up at her he remembered she'd said she worked at the General Hospital.

"Yes, he was a dear friend. This was a man who once took the life of another. Yet I know of no other person who died feeling so close to God." John gave Patrick the final rites of the church as Sarah remained in the room with her head bowed. He finally covered Patrick's face with the bed sheet.

Sister Madonna arrived too late to say her goodbye to Patrick. Seeing his body covered with a sheet, she immediately reached out to Father John and hugged him, a surprising move for her.

"I'm very sorry, Father," she said. "You filled this man's heart. You'll be rewarded in heaven."

"Sister Madonna Lynch, this is my lifelong friend, Sarah Keough." John introduced the two women. Sarah hadn't met Sister Madonna until now, but she could tell that she and Father John were good friends.

"I'm pleased to meet you. I wish we were meeting under happier circumstances," said Sarah.

"Well, I'm sure that Patrick is in a far better place. Let's not forget that," Sister Madonna said as she shook Sarah's hand. "Father, I'll be in touch with you later about the funeral arrangements, but right now I have to get back to work as soon as I can. The hospital staff is familiar with our people and knows the procedures when they pass away. Don't worry, they'll take care of Patrick until we know what his wishes were."

Sister Madonna left as quickly as she had entered. Sarah and John looked at each other. Then, as if by instinct, they knew they needed each other and they embraced.

"It seems we meet at the most sensitive and unusual times, at times when we both need support," said Father John, as he held Sarah. This time it was he who couldn't easily let go.

Sarah said nothing. She had given up on opening herself to him. He was dedicated to God and not to her.

Father John believed in miracles. He wondered if Patrick Fitzgerald's last words were about Sarah. Was she the one who would find him one day? It was inevitable that a day would come when Sarah would find somebody else. Would he be sorry then that he had resisted her love? He hoped and prayed he had made the right decision when he agreed to leave everything in God's hands. Thy will be done, he thought now. In total mental turmoil, Father John again made the decision to leave Sarah. He gently disengaged from their embrace and walked out the door, leaving her standing alone.

CHAPTER NINETEEN

Her Majesty's Penitentiary, St. John's
May 29, 1872

This morning, as she did every morning, Johanna Hamilton was kneeling on the hard cold floor in her cell saying her rosary in full view of the entire cell block. She was one of only three women in the prison, and she wore a long yellow dress made of a heavy coarse material, layered over by a full-length apron. On her head was a white frilly bonnet which covered her cropped hair.

Sister Madonna made sure that Johanna had finished her prayers before she stopped by her cell to speak to her. The nun noticed that her bowl of oatmeal was still untouched and couldn't help seeing that Johanna had lost a worrisome amount of weight this winter.

"Good morning, Johanna. This is an important day. We've arranged for a place where you can get ready in private before we go to the courthouse. His Honour, Judge Robinson, is set to address the jury at ten o'clock. The wardens must have you in the prisoner's box by nine forty-five."

"Don't tell me I have to be in the same place with him," exclaimed Johanna. Although she had come to terms with her own wrongdoing, she couldn't get beyond Patrick Geehan's attempts to involve her in the killings.

"No. Indeed not. You will be in your own space and have a guard assigned to you," assured Sister Madonna. "However, you will be able to see him."

"I'd rather not." Johanna feared not being able to control her emotions when placed in the same room with Patrick Geehan.

It was common practice that male prisoners were called out into the yard to work, while the women mostly stayed inside their cells. Johanna felt that she was in solitary confinement when compared to the male prisoners since there was little for the women to do, bar the sewing required of them from time to time. Except for the nuns, there was nobody to talk to. Her only possessions were her prayer book, her hymnbook and her rosary beads.

"We'll have to put these on for the walk to the room where you can wash and dress," said Sister Madonna, as the guard pinched Johanna's leg restraints together.

When they arrived in the preparation room where Johanna was to dress, she looked in a full-length mirror for the first time since December 1871. She had undergone a radical physical transformation. Her hair was cropped close to her head. Her skeletal face was drawn and her swollen eyes had dark circles. The Penitentiary had taken its toll.

Johanna began to weep. "My God. How will I get through this?"

Suddenly, without warning she began to urge and looked for a bucket to throw up in. Sister Madonna managed to provide a pail. Johanna had to take a seat for a few moments after she got sick. The nun put a cold cloth on Johanna's head. "Breathe slowly and deeply, my child. It will help you relax and feel better."

Sister Madonna cradled Johanna. She rocked her back and forth and rubbed her hand up and down her back. "I'll be there with you all the way," she promised.

Johanna finally composed herself. She pulled on an old dark dress, now much too big for her. On went the restraints again, and off she shuffled to the prisoner's wagon. Two wardens and Sister Madonna joined her for the ride down Duckworth Street to the Supreme Court.

It was a beautiful sunny day and Johanna could hear the birds chirping in the trees. She could see the bustle of the crowd through the iron bars of the wagon as it weaved through the traffic. The sound of people's voices, horses neighing, and the general buzz of the city was music to her ears. She longed for a freedom that she might never experience again.

Johanna was hustled down over the steps from Duckworth Street to Water Street. It was customary to take the prisoners in through the front doors on the first day of court so that the media and the general public could see them. While being escorted through throngs of people outside, Johanna could hear someone shouting, "Hang them for what they did! Treat them as they treated that poor old man!"

She almost stumbled on several occasions but didn't fall because the crowd was so crammed together. Once inside the courtroom, the huge doors slammed shut. Except for the people shouting outside in the street, there was a subdued calm in the room, tranquility, one would normally experience on entering a church. Johanna was guided to a prisoner's box next to the stall Patrick Geehan would occupy. It was empty at the moment.

The courtroom was stately and ornate, with very high ceilings and towering windows. Its enormous pillars and decorative facings were symbols of power and strength. The morning sunlight spilled into the room through the many windows, creating brightness at odds with the sense of doom which everyone anticipated.

The room was designed so that the judge's bench was pivotal to whatever was to take place in the room. When the clerk walked down the aisle between the seats, the echo of his footsteps resonated throughout the room. After taking his chair, he unfolded his briefcase, took out his papers, and put on his spectacles.

The doors suddenly opened again and the quiet atmosphere of the room was shattered by voices asking questions and making rude comments.

"Did you kill your wife, Geehan? Are you still in love with that young Hamilton girl?" Johanna heard someone ask.

The noise stopped with the closing of the doors. Johanna didn't turn around as Patrick Geehan was ushered along directly in front of her by two burly guards. This was the first time she had laid eyes on him since they were put in jail.

"Are you all right, Johanna?" Patrick asked as he turned his head to look back at her. She looked straight ahead and refused to reply or to look at him.

Geehan wore his Sunday best suit, the same one he had worn to his wife's funeral. He took his seat and then pushed back his hair and straightened his jacket. He looked confident and strong. A guard took his place beside him.

From behind her, Johanna heard a voice calling her name. "Johanna, it's me. I'm here" When Johanna turned, she saw her sister seated two rows back. "They wouldn't let me in to see you," said Catherine. "I've been in St. John's since yesterday and I tried to see you but couldn't get permission. The prison has a package for you from all of us. I'll be here until the trial is over and hopefully, I will get permission to see you." Johanna was pleased to see her sister. How she wished she could sit by her, could hold her and talk to her.

Two defense counsels entered the room and took their seats next to their clients. Richard Raftus was a young inexperienced but very smart lawyer who had met with Patrick Geehan on several occasions to plot out his defense. Michael Emerson was Johanna's defense counsel. He too was an ambitious lawyer eager to prove himself. He had every intention of having the Court find Johanna not guilty.

F.T.B. Carter, Q.C., the Attorney General, entered the room with his assistant. He threw his case on the table in front of the judge's bench without acknowledging anyone. He pulled his chair up to the table desk and removed his files, looking at the order in which they might be used. He was robed in black and resembled a minister of the cloth more so than a lawyer. He looked much more authoritative than the lawyers for the accused.

"All rise," called the clerk. "His Worship Judge Byron Robinson will take the bench." Everyone stood as the clerk welcomed the presiding judge. "The jury has been sworn and may assume their role. All have been accounted for," said the clerk.

"I will hear the opening statements. Is the Crown ready to begin?" asked the judge without looking up.

"The Crown is, Your Worship," said Carter. "The Court will prove that Patrick Geehan and Johanna Hamilton conspired to murder Garrett Sears for the reasons of criminal intimacy coupled with the greed to obtain the farm of his deceased wife and her estate. The Crown will call several witnesses who will testify showing motives and actions proving such a charge."

Carter went on to summarize for the Court the following series of events and facts as presented to the Crown by Inspector Foley: "Your Honour, about two miles from Harbour

Grace on the Southside, Patrick Geehan, who seems to be about forty years of age, resided on a small farm with his wife Jane, who was considerably older, her brother Garrett Sears, an elderly man, and their servant girl Johanna Hamilton. Geehan, Sears, and the servant girl Hamilton went to the Labrador fishery at the usual time. Mrs. Geehan remained at home to manage the farm and care for the cows, which she did very industriously, being an active thrifty woman.

"Early in the fall, Geehan, Sears and the servant girl Hamilton came home from Labrador. On the Friday and Sunday proceeding November 20 it was stated to two or three people that Garrett Sears was going to Brigus to take passage by the steamer to St. John's in order to go into the hospital to get his feet seen to. Geehan and Hamilton told their neighbours that Mrs. Geehan was going to Turks Gut, and that she was escorting her brother, Garrett Sears, on the way.

"On Monday, November 20, one of the neighbours heard a gun discharge at Geehan's farm at around noon. On the twenty-third, Mrs. Geehan was brought to the Geehan farm having been found deceased on a road leading to the community of Riverhead, Harbour Grace. A coroner's inquiry found that Mrs. Geehan died of accelerating causes. The Crown officers became suspicious when it was reported that Garrett Sears was missing. A search resulted in the body of Garrett Sears being discovered buried in a shallow pit behind the Geehan house by Inspector Foley. Dr. Allan's report on Sears's body and a revisited report on Mrs. Geehan's body will be entered as evidence." [iii]

Carter put his hands in his pockets and strolled over to the jury. He paused for a few seconds and put his finger against his chin. He seemed to be gathering his thoughts for his opening verbal assault. Looking at each of the jurors individually, while pointing back to Geehan and Johanna, he emphatically stated,

"We will prove that Patrick Geehan and Johanna Hamilton conspired to kill Garrett Sears in cold blood. Their motive was to continue their love affair unencumbered by Garrett Sears, since Mrs. Geehan had been conspicuously taken out of the picture."

Johanna squirmed as she heard his words. She wanted to jump up and say, "No, it wasn't like that." But she knew she couldn't do that. Her defense counsel was the one who had to bring out the truth.

Carter continued his attack. Reaching for his notes, he quoted directly from them as he read the rambling statement Patrick Geehan had given to Inspector Foley on December 6, 1872, the day of his arrest.

Johanna heard again the lies about Patrick's shooting at the hawk and about his accidently injuring Garrett. Holding up Patrick Geehan's confession, Carter looked directly at the jury.

"It was at the insistence of Johanna Hamilton that Patrick Geehan took Garrett Sears' life with a pitchfork," he said. The Attorney General then thundered directly into the statement: "Johanna said, 'We will be hung. The people will hear him bawling.'"

The Crown had fired an opening volley that seemed to silence the entire room. It was a theatrical performance with great substance. Frederick Carter had an impressive voice and a confident manner which enabled him to control the very atmosphere of the courtroom. Carter pointed out that Geehan had also lied about not wanting to upset his wife, Jane Geehan, who hadn't arrived home as of yet. This time Carter picked up Johanna's statement and waved it around as he continued his oration.

"Johanna Hamilton, in her statement to Inspector Foley, demonstrated that Patrick Geehan knew that Jane Geehan had already gone to her Maker. Mr. Geehan knew, as did Johanna, that she wasn't coming back!"

The Attorney General was effectively using Patrick Geehan's own statement as evidence against him. It was, after all, his admission of guilt.

As he took his seat, Carter looked confident. He looked like a man who was going to win his case, a man who would help the Crown win its case. Johanna's hope began to fade as she realized F.T.B. Carter was a formidable opponent.

"Mr. Raftus, are you ready to address the Court?" Judge Robinson asked.

"Yes, Your Honour," said Raftus. In his eagerness, Raftus had stood up before Carter sat down. "We will show the Court that Patrick Geehan did, in fact, try to shoot a hawk and that it was by accident that Sears was mortally injured and subsequently died. Patrick Geehan would never have put Garrett Sears out of his misery except that he was in such an emotional state, Your Honour. Garrett Sears was on death's door, a few seconds away from expiry, and suffering terribly."

Raftus walked over to Patrick Geehan and laid his hand on his shoulder. "At the assertion of Miss Hamilton, this man acted with mercy and logic. His deed only hastened the inevitable." Looking directly at Geehan, Raftus continued, "My client, Patrick Geehan, was a man on the cusp of going completely out of his mind and, in his moment of madness, compassionately made it possible for his beloved brother-in-law to pass away. He then had no choice but to bury the man and conceal his death."

Suddenly Raftus stopped and turned to look at Johanna. "My client, Patrick Geehan, knew that there would be false perceptions about his relationship with Johanna Hamilton," he said. "It is also understandable that Johanna Hamilton was thinking that people would think the worst of them. Is it any wonder that she encouraged Patrick to take the action he did?"

Johanna was shocked and perplexed to see Raftus take such an approach. She felt that she was handicapped from the beginning; she had to fight the Crown as well as Patrick Geehan's defense counsel.

Raftus knew that Geehan had admitted his guilt by making his statement at Harbour Grace. His logic now was cruel, but ingenious. His tactic was not only to demonstrate that Geehan acted out of mercy, but also to twist the blame to Johanna. Maybe such an approach would result in a lesser sentence, or even a not guilty verdict against Geehan.

"Where's this going?" Johanna whispered to Emerson.

"Well, we have an admission of guilt both from the Crown and Raftus," said Emerson. "I think we are right on target."

"I beg to differ, Mr. Emerson. They are making me look guiltier than Patrick Geehan." Johanna was becoming more and more perturbed. "I didn't hand him a pitchfork. I didn't say we would hang. They are making me appear as a cold hearted conspirator who remained calm and counseled Patrick to kill Garrett. Aren't you going to question them?"

"Are you ready to address the Court, Mr. Emerson?" asked Judge Robinson.

"Yes, Your Honour. I would like to address the Court."

Emerson paused to regain his composure. He seemed to be out of breath as he began to speak. "Your Honour, without intending to insult the Crown, I see this as a simple cut and dried case. It is impossible to convict Johanna Hamilton. She was not a party to the killing of Garrett Sears. She was not present for the killing of Mr. Garrett Sears. I dare to challenge the Court to prove she was present when Garrett Sears died. It wasn't physically possible to urge Patrick Geehan on to commit this evil deed as my esteemed colleague has inferred.

"Patrick Geehan had been influencing and controlling this

poor young immigrant servant girl since the delicate age of fifteen," he continued. "Yes, they had been in a relationship for three summers on the Labrador. Yes, she probably thought that she loved a man more than twice her age. However, I ask the jury to consider who really influenced who? A mere child in her teenage years, destitute and with little or no family support, or a forty-one year old well-to-do master who controlled her very life."

Emerson walked over to Patrick Geehan's prison box and laid his hand on the rail.

"Patrick Geehan was a man who was able to lord it over this young girl at all times," he said, as he looked at the jury. "The Court must also note that nobody was present when Geehan allegedly killed Garrett Sears. There were no witnesses. We have only Patrick Geehan's word. That is heresy, something which isn't strong enough on which to base a conviction against my client, Johanna Hamilton. Furthermore, we will prove that Geehan lied, and we will show that he dragged Johanna Hamilton into the whole affair by putting the blame on her."

Johanna settled down after hearing her lawyer's strong opening statement. The next few days would be significant. Her neighbours now had the opportunity to come to her aid. Or, and this thought was too black to even contemplate, they could send her to the gallows. She glanced back at Sister Madonna who nodded her head and smiled. She then looked over at Catherine who waved and smiled. There was finally a glimmer of hope.

Johanna was pleased to have Sister Madonna with her during this desolate time. The nun's loyalty never wavered. Sister Madonna gave her much needed support. Catherine, her sister, showed Johanna her unconditional love.

CHAPTER TWENTY

St. Patrick's Parish House, St. John's, September 19, 1896

The morning after Patrick Fitzgerald's death, Sister Madonna had to make a special trip to see Father John at St. Patrick's Parish presbytery. He was glad to see her.

"Well, my goodness. You are out of bed anyway," she said. "Are you going to invite me in or let me stand out here all day in the rain?"

"Come in, Sister. Mrs. Donahue is off today so I'll have to do the honours of getting you a cup of tea myself."

"Oh, don't be bothered. I'll not be staying long." The nun looked tired and was beginning to show her age. She was very congested this evening and a persistent cough caused her to hold a handkerchief to her mouth for her entire visit.

Father John also noticed for the first time that she had a slight tremor in her hands as she grasped a small tin box. He was concerned about her having walked all this distance. She must be feeling quite ill. Sister Madonna was never one to admit to having any kind of ailment. She thought it showed weakness.

"Father, most prisoners don't have anything to bequeath. Patrick Fitzgerald was one of those who had nothing except a few personal effects which he wanted to keep in a safe place while he was incarcerated. Patrick must have known his death was close at hand because he asked me to safeguard his things. When I opened his personal effects I found that he had everything planned. Just a few weeks ago he willed his personal belongings to you. There isn't much there. However, he left you a letter too." She held out the small tin box, which was dented and worn, showing its years of usage.

Father John accepted the box from Sister Madonna's hands solemnly, nodding as is if he were receiving a sacred article. When he opened the box he found Patrick's old Latin Mass Book, several yellowed pages of newspaper clippings dated May 29 to May 31, 1872, and a letter addressed to him.

Father John asked Sister Madonna to wait while he read the letter. He read it aloud knowing that she was integral in his relationship with Patrick.

To Father John Coombs,

By the time you read this I will have met my maker. Hopefully, my pain will have ended. If you can get permission, I would be grateful for your assistance at my burial. I have arranged for a burial place with my family at the cemetery in Harbour Grace. The parish will have had correspondence from the Superintendent of the Penitentiary. A telegram will be sent to the Parish of the Immaculate Conception, Harbour Grace, on the day of my death announcing the same. St. Joseph's Church in Riverhead, where I was baptized and confirmed, is where my funeral mass will take place. I am requesting the presence of our prison chaplain at the mass, and your participation if approved.

Patrick Fitzgerald

An accompanying note read: *"His body will be transported tomorrow on the train to Riverhead, Harbour Grace. It will be sent to the care of the local undertaker, a Mr. Maxwell Parsons. Last evening, the Superintendent of the Penitentiary telegraphed Father Falcanio, the Administrator to the Bishop of the Diocese of Harbour Grace. This morning, he replied that the funeral mass will take place the day after tomorrow at St. Joseph's Church, Riverhead. You have been invited to celebrate the Requiem Mass with Father Falcanio on that day, at 10:30, if it is your wish."*

After he finished reading the letter and the note he looked at Sister Madonna who cleared her throat and said, "As you know, Father John, you truly have no choice in the matter. You have to go and help celebrate the mass. I can follow that up with a return telegram and let the Immaculate Conception parish know."

"Of course," said Father John. "I'll travel with the body on the train tomorrow. Please accept my thanks as I'm sure Patrick appreciated your work."

"I'll be praying for you and Patrick throughout the next few days," said Sister Madonna as she eased herself up off the sofa.

"I'll get the carriage to drop you back," insisted Father John.

"No thanks, I have my umbrella. I'll be fine." Sister Madonna departed as unceremoniously as she had entered.

The trip the next day was long and arduous. The scenery was magnificent but the many stops along the route turned a three-hour trip into a six-hour ordeal. He used time on the train to read the pages of *the Morning Chronicle* newspaper that had been left for him by Patrick.

He read with curiosity about the trial of Patrick Geehan and Johanna Hamilton. *The Morning Chronicle* had included all the witnesses' testimonies, the counselors' sumsarahs and the sentence. He also read Patrick Fitzgerald's testimony. He saw nothing in there about Patrick Fitzgerald hiding a body or anything about his relationship with Johanna Hamilton.

Then Father John saw another article that had been clipped from the *Harbour Grace Standard* dated December 8, 1871. It was a report of the Coroner's Inquest into the death of Garrett Sears which was held the day after Geehan and Johanna's arrest.

Patrick had underlined the testimony of Thomas Morrissey, the man who had sworn in court that he had seen a fetch or ghost, which appeared to be that of Garrett Sears. Morrissey stated that he spoke to Garrett on the same morning, long after Garrett had been buried. The reporter described the courtroom's response to Morrissey's testimony. Most of those in attendance treated Morrissey's words as frivolous and untrue.

Father John pondered if this reported apparition could really have been that of Garrett Sears. Had Sears escaped from his grave that morning? Was that the subject of Patrick Fitzgerald's confession to Father John? His confession, recalled Father John, recounted that Patrick Fitzgerald hid a body for an accused woman. Patrick confessed to giving the man another blow to the head as he wanted to make certain that the man was dead. The priest also recalled that Patrick had said something about causing the accused woman to lose her child. What, then, became of the baby?

The priest wondered if the sentence had been carried out as issued. His interest in the case had now been sparked. He saw it as his mission to find out exactly what had transpired to make Patrick feel so guilty. Did he feel guilty about not helping Garrett Sears? For hitting him with a rock? For not speaking up for Johanna at the trial? Maybe causing Johanna to lose her child and leaving that youngster an orphan were the things that bothered him most.

Father Falconia was at the Harbour Grace Railway Station to

greet Father John. They watched as Mr. Parsons, the undertaker, had his men off-load the pine box containing Patrick Fitzgerald. Father John's stay at the Roman Catholic presbytery, known locally as the Palace, was very pleasant. Over supper, he met Bishop Ronald MacDonald, the third Bishop of the Diocese of Harbour Grace, and other parish priests. Bishop MacDonald knew Bishop Howley very well and told Father John that they socialized as often as they could. He said Bishop Howley had spoken to him about Father John. Although he knew he hadn't accomplished very much for Bishop Howley to single him out, Father John was truly complimented.

It was Father John's first time at St. Joseph's Church in Riverhead, a community he had never visited. He wondered how well attended Patrick Fitzgerald's funeral would be, given his status as a murderer and the fact that he had been locked away in prison for such a long time. Patrick had said he left the Southside and moved to St. John's shortly after the trial in 1873. He never returned.

The turnout for the funeral the next morning was outstanding. People stood in the aisles, at the rear of the church and outside on the steps. There was no doubt that the Fitzgerald family was well liked. The community of Riverhead showed great character. Patrick Fitzgerald would have been proud.

Father John had been asked by Father Falconia to do the homily. It was not permitted to eulogize persons in a Roman Catholic Mass. However, some license was given for the preacher to connect the gospel and the readings to the deceased. John hadn't been ordained very long, but this was the most difficult and emotional funeral service he had ever conducted. Something had moved within him.

The Gospel Reading which followed the regular church calendar was about mercy for sinners. John thought Father

Falconia couldn't have picked a more meaningful scripture for Patrick.

Father Falconia's voice was reassuring as he said, "The Gospel according to Matthew: As Jesus passed by, he saw a man named Matthew sitting at the customs post. He said to him, 'Follow me.' And he got up and followed him. While he was at the table in his house, many tax collectors and sinners came and sat with Jesus and his disciples. The Pharisees saw this and said to his disciples, 'Why does your teacher eat with tax collectors and sinners?' He heard this and said, 'Those who are well do not need a physician, but the sick 'do. Go and learn the meaning of the words, *I desire mercy, not sacrifice.* I did not come to call the righteous but sinners.'"

Father John went on to speak in a theological way about the gospel. He saved the following few words until last: "Like all of us here today, Patrick Fitzgerald was a sinner. We all know that. Jesus knew that. But Patrick, as you all know spent twenty-three years praying and asking for forgiveness for what he did on this earth. Jesus came for him a couple of nights ago. He was looking for a sinner, not a righteous person, a sinner who had desired mercy. Patrick Fitzgerald was the man God picked."

Father John suddenly surprised himself by weeping. Tears rolled down his cheeks. It was as if he had lost a loved one he had known a lifetime. After regaining his composure, he and Father Falconia continued on with the service.

Patrick Fitzgerald was laid to rest in the Roman Catholic Cemetery in Bennett's Lane, Harbour Grace. As Father John was leaving the graveyard, an older woman approached him.

"Hello, Father," she said. "My name is Catherine and I wanted to thank you for doing this today. As you said of Patrick Fitzgerald, we are all sinners. I've been made aware of your kindness to Patrick. No doubt, he must have informed you of his relationship with Johanna and her struggles in life. Please pray for her."

"You were in communication with Patrick Fitzgerald?" Father John asked, his interest sparked.

"No," she said. "I wasn't in touch with him, but we have a mutual acquaintance that knows of your good work and told me about it. I'm sorry, but I am not at liberty to reveal who that person is."

The woman immediately turned and walked away. Father John waited until Father Falconia caught up with him and asked him if he knew the woman who had just spoken to him.

"That was Catherine Drake," Father Falconia answered. "A long time ago, Patrick Fitzgerald was a friend and neighbour of her sister, Johanna Hamilton." Then Father Falconia whispered, "Many years ago, long before my time, Johanna Hamilton, along with another man from here, were charged and convicted of murder."

"Were the sentences carried out? Are they buried in this cemetery?"

"I'm not certain, John. I think eventually there was an execution. It's not spoken about here, especially when there are relatives still living in Riverhead and on the Southside. I'm afraid you'll have to check with somebody else. I have learned to concern myself with the present."

Father John would return to St. John's the following day. He was now anxious to find out if *The Morning Chronicle* kept back issues. He hadn't heard of the paper in recent years. However, it occurred to him that Sister Madonna had been doing service at the penitentiary for nearly twenty-five years. Maybe she could answer some of his questions.

CHAPTER TWENTY-ONE

Newfoundland Supreme Court
May 30, 1872

Court began the next day with much less ceremony. Johanna looked tired but was optimistic since her counsel, Mr. Emerson, had made such a good opening statement yesterday. Sister Madonna was seated behind her. This would be the nun's designated place for the rest of the trial. Johanna could look back at her as often as she wanted. Catherine had also returned and sat behind her to reassure her of her support.

Patrick Geehan had been told to remain quiet and not to attempt to communicate with Johanna. His lawyer, Richard Raftus, didn't want to give the Crown an opportunity to remind the jury that Patrick had been intimate with Johanna. This would make him appear as a monster who took control over an innocent young girl. Raftus wanted to portray the opposite. He wanted Johanna Hamilton to be perceived as nothing more than a servant girl who had romantic notions about Patrick Geehan.

The Crown's first witness was the elder Dr. Allan. Attorney General Carter approached the witness box and placed his foot on the stand.

Holding a sheaf of papers in his hand he said, "I hold here in my hand the report on a postmortem you carried out as District Surgeon on the body of Mrs. Jane Geehan on November 23, 1871. You presented this document at the Coroner's Inquest into Jane Geehan's death. You were clear in this report and I quote now your words: 'I conclude that Mrs. Jane Geehan died from natural causes.' Having heard and read further written statements from this trial, in particular that of Patrick Geehan, would you like to expound upon your original findings, or change your conclusions regarding the death of Mrs. Geehan?"

Both Raftus and Emerson jumped to their feet almost simultaneously. They had expected this tactic.

"I object, Your Honour, we are not trying Patrick Geehan and Johanna Hamilton on the death of Jane Geehan," Raftus said loudly. "I move we exclude Dr. Allan's postmortem on Jane Geehan at this trial, and not allow any further testimony about Jane Geehan."

"I concur, Your Honour," said Emerson.

Both counsels remained standing in protest.

Carter rebutted. "Your Honour, the Crown would like to establish that there was a conspiracy between Patrick Geehan and Johanna Hamilton in the death of Garrett Sears. If the Crown can show probable motive for Sears' death, that being criminal intimacy between the accused, and if Dr. Allan has a different perspective which could cast doubt on the real causes of Jane Geehan's death, I think he should be permitted to add or change conclusions set forth in the Coroner's Inquest into the death of Mrs. Jane Geehan. It is not the Crown's intention to try Patrick Geehan or Johanna Hamilton for the murder of Mrs.

Geehan. However, the Court can't ignore that there may have been other reasons surrounding her death which may have implications for Garrett Sears' passing. The fact that she may have been dead for a couple of days before she was found and that she hadn't been to Brigus is something about which the Court needs to be concerned."

"I will allow the testimony for today," said the judge. "However, I will have to confer with his Lordship Judge Hayward on this matter. I cannot make an absolute judgment right now. I will have a ruling tomorrow to see if such testimony remains admissible. If it is, we will allow further evidence regarding the death of Mrs. Jane Geehan. If my learned colleague discovers something different, we will strike Dr. Allan's testimony specific to Mrs. Geehan's death. My ruling tomorrow will be the first order of business."

Raftus and Emerson looked at each other. Had His Honour sided with them or was he going to allow Dr. Allan's testimony relevant to Jane Geehan's death? They didn't have to wait long for an answer.

"For today, Mr. Carter, you may proceed with your line of questioning," said the judge.

"Now then, Doctor Allan, please describe your findings having revisited Mrs. Jane Geehan's postmortem," said Carter.

"My son, Dr. W. Allan, and I based the postmortem on Mrs. Geehan's history of heart disease. Having been informed that she had travelled to Brigus, we thought that her death was accelerated by fatigue and exposure. Knowing now that she didn't go to Brigus puts her death in a whole different light. Her heart and lungs were in such poor condition that other causes might well have come into play. Sudden excitement, a blow, or suffocation by a pillow might also have caused her death," the doctor said.

Emerson jumped to his feet, "Your Honour, the Crown is definitely implicating my client in allowing that statement. I want that testimony struck from the record."

"No, Your Honour," appealed Carter. "We are only relaying new facts surrounding Mrs. Geehan's death. The time of her death and the manner of her death are being introduced as subjects of concern which may have implications towards the motive of the accused, that being criminal intimacy."

"That's correct. Continue, Mr. Carter," said Judge Robinson.

Lawyers Raftus and Emerson were clearly upset with Judge Robinson. They felt that the judge, by allowing the cause of Jane Geehan's death to be entered at this time, was prejudicial against their clients. While it was true that their clients were not being charged with Mrs. Geehan's death, the implication was that she could have been murdered, and her death could have been part of the prisoners' conspiracy to get rid of both Garrett Sears and his sister.

In the days leading up to the trial, Emerson had warned Johanna that Frederick Carter was going to bring up Mrs. Geehan's death. He'd advised her that the judge could permit Dr. Allan to introduce other probable causes of her demise. However, the judge, by law, could not allow a link to be made between Jane's death and the charge of murder against her or Patrick.

Johanna was beginning to panic again. Emerson attempted to reassure her. "The jury has to keep an open mind about this, Johanna," he whispered in her ear. "They can't tie Mrs. Geehan's death to you or Patrick Geehan. Jane Geehan's Coroner's Inquest is long over. As far as the jury is concerned that inquest is done with and she died of natural causes."

Johanna knew the difference. Such a connection might not be legally acceptable to the Court, but she knew that Frederick Carter had begun to unravel the web that Patrick Geehan had woven. At any rate, Judge Robinson had allowed the testimony for today. And it was damning! He might very well uphold and reinforce his own decision tomorrow.

Carter continued, "Dr. Allan, you did a postmortem on the remains of Garrett Sears. Please read the postmortem report for the Court."

Allan cleared his throat and began: "We examined the body of Garrett Sears on its being exhumed from the pit and after having been brought into the Geehan house. We found a depression on the left side of his head caused by an extensive fracture; the fingers of the right hand were removed from the second joint. There was a fractured wound behind the right eye into which I could put my finger about two inches. A gaff or fork might have caused it. There were contused wounds on the left side of his head, also on the right side. On putting my fingers into the wounds on the right side, I discovered a fracture of the skull. On examining the wounds on the left side I found that three of them were fractures of the skull. About three inches below the right shoulder there were two small holes in the arm, which I suspect are gunshot wounds." [iv]

Dr. Allan stopped to take a sip of water from a glass passed to him by a court attendant. Patrick Geehan kept looking straight ahead, showing no emotion whatsoever.

Allan cleared his throat again and continued. "The next day we carried out a further postmortem on Garrett Sears at our surgery. There were thirteen wounds in all. As described before, there were extensive fractures of the skull and the bones on the right side of the head were driven into the brain. The fractures on the left side were communicating with those on the right side of the head and the lower part of the skull. All fractures were round, being completely broken. The fractures on the left side of the head were caused by a heavy blunt instrument. The stock of a gun was likely to produce them." [v]

When Dr. Allan finished, he removed his glasses. Carter then walked over to the evidence table and picked up a long rifle with a yellow stock.

"Would a gun like this one belonging to Patrick Geehan cause such damage to a man's head as you described?" he asked the doctor.

"No question. A gun like that could inflict such damage," answered Allan.

"I object, Your Honour. This implies that my client's gun was the actual one which was used," appealed Raftus. "I ask that that question and answer be stricken from the record."

"To the contrary, Your Honour, my question was to the likelihood of such a gun being used," Carter said.

"Carry on, counselor," said the judge. "The answer of the witness will be kept in the record."

Carter reached for a rusty pitchfork. He pointed to the handle. "This end is rounded," he said to Dr. Allan. "Did you insert the end of this tool into any of the rounded holes in the skull of the deceased?"

"I did, and it fit the holes perfectly," Dr. Allan answered as the Court erupted with discussion.

"Order! Order!" shouted the judge. "There will not be another outburst." Judge Robinson paused, "Do either of the counsels have any questions for Dr. Allan?"

Raftus rose. "I have one question. Could any of the described wounds have been inflicted after Garrett Sears' death? For example, might some of the fractures to Mr. Sears' head have been the result of being buried?"

"Of course, but why would somebody try to bury the man with the stock of a gun?" replied Dr. Allan. The Court erupted in laughter. The judge hit the gavel.

"Order please! Order please!" he shouted.

Dr. Allan went on, "Why would somebody cut off the fingers and the ear of a dead man? Unless such action was driven by perversion."

Patrick Geehan began to shuffle his feet back and forth. His fists were clenched tightly. Raftus took notice and tried to settle him down. Geehan had made it known in his statement that the injuries to Garrett Sears resulted from the pigs being at his body. He had now reached a breaking point.

Patrick Geehan suddenly jumped up and shouted at the doctor. "We didn't do anything to disfigure Garrett's body. The animals did the damage before we had a chance to bury him."

Johanna felt sick when he used the word "we." Here she was being implicated with him again.

"Please refrain the prisoner from speaking in this room, counselor," demanded Judge Robinson. Geehan sat back in his chair.

Emerson declined further questioning, opting to get the trial to move away from the gruesome details. He saw Johanna was being included in the crime, especially after Patrick Geehan's outburst.

Carter then called his next witness, Patrick Fitzgerald. After he was sworn in, the court business continued.

"Describe to the Court what you saw at the Geehan household on November 20, 1871," demanded Carter.

"I was with my brother John Fitzgerald and his wife at the potatoes up in our garden. We live west of Geehan and there is a grove of trees between our property and theirs. I heard the report of a gun around noon or so and thought nothing of it. I then saw Mr. Shugarue run as far as his wall which is behind Geehans. He didn't go any further than his fence."

"Do you know Johanna Hamilton?" asked Carter.

"Yes, I've been at Geehan's house on the Labrador. I've seen her there." Patrick Fitzgerald took a quick glance down at Johanna.

She was very nervous, knowing their history and the way she had ended their relationship.

"Where did Johanna sleep on the Labrador? Where in the hut, I mean? Did you take notice of the arrangements?" asked Carter.

"People on the coast haven't got much privacy. There was really only one room in the Geehan pace. Johanna slept in a bunk in the same room as Patrick Geehan. Sears had a linhay out back. I never saw a curtain or anything like that separating the room," said Patrick.

This time Patrick Fitzgerald couldn't look at Johanna. She remembered him and John Hearn coming over and waiting for Patrick Geehan and Garrett Sears to help with their boat. They waited with her behind the curtain while the men got ready. She wondered how he could not have remembered that. Indeed, he hadn't forgotten. He was lying.

Carter went over to his desk to review his notes as Johanna whispered urgently to Emerson, "Patrick Fitzgerald saw the curtain at our place in Nowlan's Harbour. He is lying out of spite," she said. "Patrick Fitzgerald had intentions for me, and at one point we were briefly intimate." She hated to admit that to a total stranger, but she felt she had no choice.

Emerson was about to get up when she pulled him back down.

"There's something else I should have told you before today," she said. "Garrett was not quite dead when Patrick Geehan buried him that night."

"What?" Emerson was shocked. "You're telling me this now. Holy Jesus, woman. Hurry up and tell me if there's anything else I should know."

Thankfully for Emerson, Carter continued to study his notes.

Johanna continued, "After Geehan had buried him and fell off to sleep, I heard a noise at the back door. I discovered Garrett gone from the shallow pit and had Patrick Fitzgerald help me find him. Garrett was dead in a drain by then. Patrick Fitzgerald carried him back for me and he re-buried him for me."

"I read at the Coroner's Inquest for Garrett Sears that a man claimed to have seen Garrett Sears fetch or ghost. You are telling me that he really did see Garrett Sears?" Emerson asked. He was now completely thrown off. What was he to do? He had to be calm despite the shock of hearing what his client had to say.

"Do you have any questions, Mr. Emerson?" asked Judge Robinson.

Emerson could see that Carter had decided to end his round of questioning, and he had to be careful with his new information. It could portray Johanna wrongly in the jury's eyes. He had to stall for time to get his thoughts together. There might be a question of why Johanna didn't try to save Garrett's life at that time. The jury might think she had one more chance to help Garrett Sears but opted not to save him.

Judge Robinson was getting frustrated, "Mr. Emerson, for the last time, do you have any questions for this witness?'

"Yes, Your Honour, I do." Emerson turned to Patrick Fitzgerald. "How long have you known Miss Hamilton?"

"Four or more years. As long as she was with the Geehans."

"Do you know her to be a good woman? A woman of good character?" pressed Emerson.

"I don't know anything about her character but I have nothing against her." Johanna knew that wasn't true. Patrick Fitzgerald was still hurting because she had denied him

At this time, Emerson thought it best not to question Patrick Geehan about the information he had just been given by Johanna. He did not want to malign Johanna's character if Patrick Fitzgerald stood his ground. Also, he worried about the jury believing that such an event had actually happened, particularly when Thomas Morrissey's testimony was thrown out at the Coroner's Inquest at Harbour Grace.

"May I reserve further questioning for this witness for a later time, Your Honour?" asked Emerson.

"We don't usually honour this kind of request," replied the judge. "I have a busy docket this week so let's get on with it now, shall we?"

Emerson made a choice. "I have no further questions, sir," he said as he sat down by Johanna. "I had to make that call then," he whispered to her. "It was too risky. There were too many variables that could backfire on us. I'll explain when I visit you tonight."

The Court called Daniel Shugarue, an aged man and well respected in the community. When called upon by the Crown, he slowly made his way to the witness box with the use of a cane. This man was known to be of outstanding character.

"I heard three shots coming from the Geehan farm around noon on Monday," said Shugarue. "Later that day Patrick Geehan came to my barn. He had scratches on his face and arms and was bloodstained as well. I asked him how he got all scratched up and he said he hurt himself getting up in the hayloft. We talked about our own affairs but he seemed shook up. The next day, he came over to help me kill a pig. He made special mention that his missus and Garrett were headed to

Brigus. He said he would have to leave tomorrow or the next day to go and get her. That was Tuesday. On Wednesday, I never saw them for the whole day."

Raftus stood up. The Shugarues had been neighbours of the Sears for many years, long before Patrick Geehan married into the family. But Geehan had noticed lately that Daniel Shugarue wasn't as sharp as he used to be. He had told Raftus about Daniel's poor memory.

Raftus asked, "Was it on Monday or Tuesday that you saw the scratches on Patrick Geehan, Mr. Shugarue?"

"I think it was Monday. But it might not have been till I saw him later with his sleeves rolled up, as he killed my pig on Tuesday."

"After he killed your pig, was there much blood around?"

"Of course," said Shugarue. "Patrick Geehan is among the best on the Southside at killing pigs and there can't help but be blood after killing one."

"Well, might the blood you saw on Patrick Geehan be from the pig? After all, you don't really know what day it was you saw it, do you?"

Shugarue couldn't answer. Patrick Geehan couldn't contain his glee. He began to smirk.

"Stop smiling, Patrick, the jury might see you," whispered Raftus as he stood directly in front of him so that the jury couldn't see him.

Emerson picked up on Daniel Shugarue's poor recall and decided not to ask any questions. He didn't know where they might lead. Judge Robinson adjourned court for the day after Daniel Shugarue's testimony. Johanna and Patrick Geehan were led out through separate doors.

Sister Madonna rode back to the prison with Johanna as she had been doing since the opening of the trial. "How do you feel about today's proceedings?" she asked as they jogged along in the horse drawn wagon.

"I think it's slipping away on me, Sister," Johanna answered, her face drawn and pale. "There's no doubt that the jury will convict Patrick Geehan. The only question now is if the remaining witnesses can uphold my character. I thought for certain that Patrick Fitzgerald would have been truthful."

Johanna then explained her relationship with Patrick Fitzgerald and how he had helped her with Garrett's re-burial.

"Patrick Fitzgerald was aware that my worst fear that night was being blamed for this murder. Yet, today in court, he went out of his way not to help me. He knew about Patrick Geehan's cruelty; he knew that Patrick Geehan is Garrett's killer." She began to cry. "Is he that angry at me for not wanting him? Maybe he feels he would be implicated in some way if he came forward? You know, he couldn't even look at me while he testified. If I die for this, Patrick Fitzgerald may as well have been the man who put the noose around my neck."

Johanna suddenly took very sick in the wagon. Sister Madonna wiped her face with her handkerchief and wondered how much more the poor girl could take.

CHAPTER TWNTY-TWO

St. John's Railway Terminus
September 22, 1896

Father John endured a long trip back to the city of St. John's by train. His visit to Riverhead had left him exhausted. He knew that Patrick Fitzgerald's passing shouldn't have bothered him like it did. He had only known the man for a few months. But now, for some mysterious reason, he had an insatiable desire to know more about the Geehan and Hamilton affair. He was hopeful that Sister Madonna Lynch would be able to give him some details or at least direct him to a place where he could access the information.

The whistle of the train indicated it was nearing St. John's. The city finally came into view and he hoped that one of the priests from St. Patrick's would be there to greet him. It was six o'clock when the three-car passenger train pulled into the station. Much to his surprise he saw a very somber looking Sarah Keough standing on the platform and waving to him. He exited the train carrying his case and gently kissed her on her cheek.

"The news can't be good for you to be meeting me here. Who is sick now?" he asked.

"I'm sorry, John. It's Sister Madonna. She fainted at the Penitentiary during her regular visit this morning. She fell into a coma as the prison doctor was rushing her to the General Hospital. All efforts to revive her failed and she passed away around eleven o'clock without regaining consciousness."

John felt devastated. How much more bad news could he handle?

"She looked ill when I saw her last," he said finally. "But I can hardly believe she's dead. She'll be very much missed, especially at the prison and certainly by me. She looked stern but she had a true heart of gold."

"You grew very close to Sister Madonna in the short time you knew her," said Sarah as she led him towards a fancy horse and carriage accompanied by a driver. Father John was surprised to see the upscale rig.

"Who owns this rig?" asked Father John as he held open the door for her to climb aboard.

"Where to, Miss?" asked the driver before she had a chance to answer.

"Head to St. Patrick's Parish presbytery, please," Sarah replied. She settled into her seat and then turned to John and said, "This belongs to Dr. Shea. He's Chief Medical Superintendent in charge of the hospital. He's been around the hospital as a surgeon but he's new to the position of superintendent since Dr. Crowdy stepped down. He has just been appointed to overlook the new construction. I know he was familiar with Sister Madonna's work and he was also aware that you had been associated with her. I asked him if I could bring you the news about her death in person and he kindly offered the use of this rig."

"That was very nice of him. I really appreciate your coming to meet me." John smiled at Sarah. He was grateful for her consideration. As the driver maneuvered the city streets on the way to St. Patrick's, John quietly thought about how supportive and caring Sarah was to him. He needed some time with her before going back to St. Patrick's. This wasn't the time for him to be alone in his room at the presbytery.

"Is there a place where we can go to chat for a while? I just need to be with somebody," he asked, the words spilling out almost uncontrollably.

"Of course. We can go to my place. Mother won't be there." Sarah was aware that a priest shouldn't be seen alone with a young woman. "Mom left to be with her sister in Placentia for a few weeks. We can have some tea and talk. You need some time to unwind."

John unhooked his collar and stuffed it down into his top pocket. "I've had a rough few days," he said.

Sarah slid open the front window of the carriage and called, "We're going to 189 Campbell, please driver." When they pulled up at the door, Sarah jumped out before the driver got down from his seat. She reached up and passed him up some money. "Thanks for the ride. You can bring this carriage back to Dr. Shea and tell him we are very thankful he let us use it."

She quickly opened the door of the house and John slipped into the porch as quickly as he could. He dropped his bag in the porch and went to the parlour where he collapsed in one of the overstuffed easy chairs.

"Relax there while I get a glass of sherry for us," said Sarah, recognizing his fatigue. The priest put his feet up on the ottoman as she left the room. On her return, she found that he was fast asleep.

Sarah laid the glasses of sherry on the mantle and proceeded to light the fire. Her mom's eiderdown was on the couch. She gently covered John with it and sat back to sip her glass of sherry, her eyes fixed on the man she loved.

The grandfather clock, which only occasionally chimed, rang loudly at nine o'clock, awakening John and Sarah, who had also dozed off. Both were momentarily disoriented. John was now overheated and rolled back the eiderdown. The room was dim as only one electric light was burning. The fire had faded but flames occasionally flickered.

"I must have been exhausted. I am sorry," said John as he stood up. "It's after nine and the priests are expecting me. I'd better get moving." He wanted to tell Sarah she should have called him, but wisely refrained. "I'm sorry. I'm afraid that I've been very poor company."

"That's fine," said Sarah. "I knew you wanted to talk but I could tell that you needed sleep more than discussion."

"Sarah, my involvement with Patrick Fitzgerald and Sister Madonna Lynch has me disturbed. Sister must have known Patrick's background. Her time at the prison pre-dated Patrick Fitzgerald's incarceration by eight years or more." John wrinkled his forehead in thought as he spoke. "I can't help but wonder if Sister knew Johanna Hamilton and Patrick Geehan. Patrick shared his confession and while I can't divulge his sins I can say that Johanna had a child sometime during her stay at the Penitentiary. Patrick had great guilt about the child and Johanna's loss of the child."

"So why is all of that disturbing to you? Your role as priest was to console and help him find forgiveness. You've done your work. What's disturbing you?"

"I was about to have this conversation with Sister. She directed me to Patrick Fitzgerald from my first day at the Penitentiary. After he confessed to me, he told me that he was finally able to find peace."

"I'm still confused as to why you are disturbed about that. Can't you accept that it was your work and the mystery of the Holy Spirit which gave him relief?" asked Sarah.

"I would have thought that. However, it took more than twenty years to find peace. There had been other priests who I'm sure gave him similar counseling. Why did he find solace in me?" John paused before continuing, "Sister took it upon herself to make sure that Patrick Fitzgerald and I stayed close. She ensured that his wish to have me at his funeral came to pass. At the funeral Mass in Riverhead, I had this feeling of being bonded with Patrick Fitzgerald. I was stricken with grief for a man I had hardly known. I really am at a loss to explain it."

"Do you think Sister Madonna knew something about Patrick that would allow you to have a connection with him?" asked Sarah.

"Any connection between Patrick Fitzgerald and me would be impossible," John said, as he continued to try and explain the enigma. "We met in prison. He was a total stranger to me. Yet it only took minutes for our conversation to turn personal. He spoke to me as if he had known me all my life. There was a comfort between us, an ease reserved for people who have a relationship."

"You mean you and he had a rapport such as ours." She hoped that John would recognize that they had more than a rapport. She wanted him to come to the realization that they loved each other.

John had to be careful of what he said for he knew where she was leading. A man of the cloth is still a man after all. "Sarah, there is nobody on this earth I cherish more than you," he said. "In another life, given different circumstances, we would be married." He got up from his chair and took her hands with every intention of saying goodbye.

She looked up at him, her eyes wide and searching. "This isn't a rehearsal, John. We aren't players on a stage waiting for Act Three to be over so we can begin another play. We are on this earth only once."

Without warning, he pulled her up from her chair as if he were angered by her words. There was no more discussion. Years of resisting Sarah's love were bound up within him. Nature has its way in reclaiming what man tries to control. Wave after wave of passion washed over the two lovers. They were lost in an ocean of unabated bliss, hoping against hope that reality would never allow this moment to end. Then the storm quickly passed. It was over.

Afterwards, as they lay in each other's arms, John knew that finding calmer waters was not going to be easy. Sarah hoped he would abandon his elusive desire to find something beyond what he already had. This time, Sarah was the one who drifted off to sleep. It was now John's turn to cover her and lend her some comfort.

As brilliant sunlight was sneaking its way up over the Narrows, Father John made his way towards St. Patrick's. He was now compelled to speak to his spiritual confessor, Bishop Michael Howley, as soon as possible. He had to make a choice. Would it be the way of the cross or would he take off his collar for the woman he loved?

CHAPTER TWENTY-THREE

Her Majesty's Penitentiary, St. John's
May 31, 1872

At about four in the morning, a huge clap of thunder woke Johanna. Thunder and lightning storms were unusual in Newfoundland. With only two lights burning in the entire cell block, it was eerie how lightning flashed in through the tall windows creating total daylight for a split second then plunging the place into complete blackness again. She thought about her execution. Would her death be as quick as a lightning flash? Would the darkness be as immediate? Or would it be a prolonged painful, choking death? Johanna wanted to scream. She couldn't though. It would only result in more abuse, if not from the guards, then from the other prisoners.

In the darkness, she found her only comfort, her prayers. Johanna had said the rosary so many times that she could tell by the shape of each bead the particular Hail Mary she was saying. Rote praying had become a form of meditation for her. She whispered the Lord's Prayer over and over, "Thy will be done on earth as it is in heaven." God had become her only refuge. She hoped and prayed that He understood.

The guards had placed a package from Catherine at the bottom of her cell. It was three days late and had been torn apart. The guards told her it was opened for security reasons. Johanna knew differently. It contained a sweater, socks, biscuits and some candy wrapped in brown paper. Catherine had written a very uplifting letter, saying that Johanna was welcome to her home in Riverhead when she was released from prison. Johanna was bolstered by her sister's confidence of a positive outcome in the trial.

Today was to be a pivotal day in the trial of Johanna Hamilton and Patrick Geehan. Both defense lawyers were on edge. A decision was to be made whether to admit evidence linking the death of Mrs. Jane Geehan with that of Garrett Sears. The Chief Justice began by reviewing yesterday's objection raised by the defense. Judge Robinson had given further thought to the motion, and based on legal case research, he entered his decision into the court records:

"I have carefully considered the question, and am of the opinion the evidence is relevant and should be received. The case of the Crown is that it was the objective of these parties to get rid of Mrs. Geehan in order to complete carrying out their criminal intimacy; and having done that, then to get rid of Sears to prevent him from instituting enquiries and bringing them to justice, which was, they contend, the motive which influenced the killing of Sears. If this motive can be shown for the commission of the crime charged in the indictment, the evidence against the prisoners becomes clearer, more pointed and more conclusive. It is competent for the Crown to show that such was the motive. *Regina vs. Clews*[vi]"

Carter, Raftus and Emerson were called to the bench once the judge had rendered his decision.

"Gentlemen, there you have it," he said to them. "The Court will not stand for any more delays and unnecessary interruptions. Make sure you have good reason for future objections. I hope my ruling has been clear. Any questions?"

All three lawyers knew when to say nothing.

"Clerk, call the next witness," ordered the judge.

Judge Robinson had now opened the floodgates. This was exactly what the defense didn't want. Anybody who had seen anything remotely connecting Johanna and Patrick with Jane Geehan's death was summoned to speak. Emerson and Raftus had good reason to fear these next few witnesses. Such testimonies might serve to knock down what was already a shaky defense. The judge's decision could seal the fate of Johanna Hamilton and Patrick Geehan.

John and Catherine Hearn were bitter about the deaths of Jane and her brother Garrett. They were relatives and longtime friends of the Sears family. They were among the earliest to come forward with statements to the police.

John Hearn was called on behalf of the Crown. Firstly, he recounted his friendship with the Geehans on the Labrador and his acquaintance with Johanna Hamilton. It was evident that Attorney General Carter had done his research. The Hearns had a long and close affiliation with the Sears family. Like an accomplished hunter seeing an opportunity to take his prey, Carter spied an opportunity to show Geehan and Hamilton's motive in this witness. Carter now had the case in his crosshairs, so he took accurate aim.

First, Carter asked, "Can you, Mr. Hearn, recall any conversation with Johanna Hamilton on the Labrador which would indicate to you she may have had some desire or motive for Mrs. Jane Geehan's death?"

Johanna looked at Emerson, waiting for some intervention at

this point. However, Judge Robinson's ruling forced Emerson to remain silent.

"Yes," answered Hearn. "We lived about one hundred and forty yards from Geehan in Nowlan's Harbour. I don't why the girl came over to the house, but I do recall her shocking statements when we inquired about the news from home."

"I went to see Mrs. Hearn, just once last summer. Is that what he is talking about?" Johanna whispered to Emerson.

Hearn stated, "Johanna Hamilton said she had a letter from home and everything was fine, except that her mistress was sick all summer. She then said something we will never forget. Johanna Hamilton said that it was a pity such a smart young man as Patrick Geehan was tied to such a bloody old bitch."

Johanna lost all control and jumped up shouting out, "I didn't say that. I said to Mrs. Hearn that Jane was sick. That's all. John Hearn was nowhere near us to hear what we were saying! He's lying!"

"Order! Order!" said the judge. "Sheriff, if the prisoner interrupts these proceedings again, remove her! Counsel, control your defendant."

"Sit down, Johanna. Please," Emerson said as he pulled Johanna back from the table and dragged her down into her chair.

Carter moved in for the kill. "How did you react to such terrible words?"

"I told Johanna that her mistress was a smart young woman and would live to bury her and Patrick Geehan." Hearn was getting visibly upset.

"Did the defendant, Johanna Hamilton, say anything in response to that?"

"Johanna said that Mrs. Geehan wouldn't live till Christmas day."

The Court began to rumble again, this time much louder.

"Order! Order! I'll clear the room right now if there's one more word said!" Judge Robinson shouted.

Only the sound of Johanna's weeping could be heard after the judge's reprimand.

Carter went on, "Do you recall her next words?"

"How could I forget them? They still send cold shivers up and down my spine. She said 'It is Uncle Pat and Aunt Jane now, but soon it will be Uncle Pat and Aunt Johanna.'"

"What about Patrick Geehan? Was he a man who demonstrated a motive to see Mrs. Geehan dead?" Carter asked.

"I know nothing of Patrick Geehan. He kept to himself and seemed to work well with his brother-in-law. I never once saw him argue with Jane."

"Did you ever see Patrick Geehan and Garrett Sears fight or argue?"

Carter knew he was on thin ice with this question for he truly didn't know how Hearn would answer. The more motives that Carter could build up against Patrick Geehan the stronger was his case.

Patrick Geehan stared at John Hearn. Hearn looked back at Geehan.

"No," answered Hearn, "I think they got along well."

Johanna shook her head in disbelief. The Hearns must have heard Garrett Sears and Patrick Geehan squabble, especially during their last summer in Labrador, when Patrick Geehan drank every day, and kept ordering Garrett around and putting him down.

To make matters worse for Johanna, Emerson's cross-examination was weak. He asked Mr. Hearn, "Did others hear the conversation between you and Johanna?"

"Yes," replied John Hearn. "My wife was seated on the front

step and she was the one who began asking Johanna about home. She and our servant girl heard every word that Johanna said."

Emerson hadn't prepared for that answer. Johanna remembered that the servant girl had been in the kitchen. She couldn't possibly have heard anything. Johanna quickly scribbled down the location of Hearn's young servant girl. She passed it to Emerson when he walked back to his seat to get his notes. Emerson read her note and thought, at this point, it was an irrelevant detail. But he decided to ask the question to appease Johanna.

"Mr. Hearn, where was your servant girl when Johanna is alleged to have made those statements?" he asked.

"She was in the kitchen. My house has board partitions in the exterior walls that are nailed together, but there's no trouble to hearing what is being said outside," replied John Hearn.

Emerson returned to his seat. He looked dejected.

Raftus passed on asking any further questions since John Hearn had clearly showed Johanna's infatuation with Patrick Geehan. Hearn had also dismissed any tension between Garrett Sears and Patrick Geehan. This would most certainly help lessen Geehan's motive.

Then came the most damning testimony of all. Four years earlier, at Nowlan's Harbour, Patrick Geehan had warned Johanna about Mrs. Catherine Hearn. She should have listened. When Johanna heard her called to the stand, she knew what was about to unfold.

After Mrs. Hearn was sworn in, Carter got right to the point. "Mrs. Hearn, you were in conversation with Johanna Hamilton in Nowlan's Harbour last summer. Is that true?"

"That it is, sir. Although I only saw her once or twice during the entire summer."

"Can you remember anything Johanna may have said to show that she disliked Mrs. Jane Geehan?" asked Carter.

"Yes. I was there on the day she spoke to my husband and me and our servant girl. I heard her saying that Mrs. Geehan wouldn't live till Christmas. When I was young I lived with Jane Geehan. She was my cousin and my husband and I called her and her husband Uncle Pat and Aunt Jane. That's why Johanna said that later it would be Uncle Pat and Aunt Johanna."

"Can you recall anything else Johanna said?'

"Yes, indeed. I really don't know what the word means, but Johanna called Mrs. Geehan a mean old hake," said Catherine Hearn.

"In your police statement, you noted some things about Johanna at Mrs. Geehan's wake. You said you asked Johanna if Garrett Sears would be notified about his sister's death. For the Court, what did she have to say?" asked Carter.

"Johanna insisted that Garrett wouldn't be coming back because Patrick Geehan didn't want him back. She said that Patrick Geehan blamed Garrett for Mrs. Geehan's death. Johanna knew all along that Garrett was buried outside the house in an old pit. That was an out and out lie! Johanna knew the difference."

With the end of the trial drawing near, Emerson was overwhelmed with the evidence against Johanna. His only rebuttal was that all of the evidence was circumstantial. His summary leaned heavily on the fact that not one piece of evidence demonstrated Johanna's direct involvement with the killing.

Emerson emphasized that even though the police had found Johanna and Geehan had slept together; it didn't prove that she had killed Garrett Sears.

Patrick Geehan, on the other hand, had no defense. He had

admitted to his crime. Raftus' summation defined Patrick Geehan as a man who killed Garrett Sears out of mercy after having mortally wounded him.

Nevertheless, the Attorney General had clearly and effectively established the motive of criminal intimacy between Hamilton and Geehan with testimonies from several witnesses. Patrick Geehan's statement implicating Johanna, and the fact that Johanna had lied in her earlier statement, appeared to clinch a guilty verdict for the Crown.

The trial was over. Johanna had lied to protect Patrick Geehan, and out of fear, she had helped conceal the bodies. Patrick Geehan had threatened her with the fear that she would be implicated in Garrett and Jane's death if she didn't assist him. Johanna had transgressed the law but she hadn't killed anyone. Now, however, it was quite apparent that the jury wouldn't see it that way.

CHAPTER TWENTY-FOUR

Her Majesty's Penitentiary, St. John's
June 1, 1872

When court ended on Friday, May 31, 1872, there was no question that both Patrick Geehan and Johanna Hamilton would be convicted in accordance with the laws of the Dominion of Newfoundland.

A newly ordained priest by the name of Father Michael Howley had taken up duties at the Cathedral of St. John the Baptist in St. John's. Bishop Thomas Power assigned Father Howley the challenging task of counselling prisoners at Her Majesty's Penitentiary. He was to work closely with Sister Madonna Lynch.

Sister Madonna by now had become a confidant of Johanna Hamilton. Since Johanna's incarceration in December of 1871, Sister had visited Johanna every single day, taking care of her needs to the extent she was permitted to do so by the prison. The two had developed an emotional attachment, not unlike that of siblings. Whenever Sister left Johanna's for the day, there would always be a reassuring hug. Johanna had grown more spiritual than ever. She received Holy Communion whenever Father Howley visited.

Coming from court on May 31, 1872, was the worst day of Johanna's imprisonment. Distressed and in tears, she had made herself physically sick. She had no desire for food that evening. She no longer had the will to live. Johanna lay on her bunk, turned in towards the wall, and covered herself with a blanket. Refusing to talk to anyone, even Sister Madonna, she resigned herself to the fact that she would be found guilty. Johanna remained that way Friday night and all day Saturday. She refused to eat. Sister Madonna offered to get her a doctor. Her answer was no to that offer.

News was now circulating among the nuns that Johanna might have good reason to be sick. Nobody had asked, but it was said she might be expecting a baby.

On Sunday afternoon, prior to her last appearance in court, Father Howley walked by her cell and saw Johanna in a fetal position. He hadn't met her but the Sisters had told him about her. He and the nuns had met with Patrick Geehan earlier that weekend. At times, Geehan seemed to be at peace with himself and resigned to facing his sentence. Then his mood would switch and he would become arrogant and brazen. He told Father Howley he wanted to go to confession and receive Holy Communion. He also seemed very concerned about Johanna and requested a meeting with her.

On the evening of June 2, the day before the verdict was to be issued, Father Howley went to Johanna's cell. She was lying on her bunk, her face towards the wall. He knew she'd heard him approach but she ignored him.

Undeterred, he cleared his throat and said, "I've been to Ireland and loved it there. The thing I would have to ask is why would anyone want to leave such a wonderful place? I served in a couple of parishes near Cork, where I believe you were born?"

There was no response. Howley was an extremely astute individual who had attained a Doctorate in Theology. Always one to strategize, he was a determined problem solver. He baited her to reply when he tried again. "I've seen Saint Latiaran's well. I'm sure you know all about that?"

Saint Latiaran was a well-known saint in the community of Cullen near Cork. There is a famous story about how angels appeared to her and her two sisters in the fifth century, giving her the power to carry hot coals in her apron without getting burned. Being an extremely beautiful woman, she became prey to many men. A blacksmith, who was consumed with the girl's magical ability, duped her to commit sin by complimenting her legs. He asked if he could see how she was able to carry the coals. She lifted her skirt and exposed her legs, which the Irish believed to be cause for eternal damnation. Celtic myth says Latiaran then sank down through the earth, and that there in that spot there remains a well filled with holy water. Ever since then, the people of Culllen have made much use of the holy water. Father Howley knowingly picked this topic hoping it would arouse her interest.

Johanna turned to look at him. "When were you in Cork?" she asked quietly.

"Last summer. I studied at St. Patrick's College in Maynooth and went from there to your old hometown."

"I visited Saint Latiaran's Well many times as a child," said Johanna as she stood up and walked towards the priest. "God shouldn't have abandoned me. Patrick Geehan was as evil as the Irish blacksmith in that story."

"God didn't abandon you, my child. I know you think the trial hasn't gone well, but we still have to wait for the verdict." Father

Howley tried to be as positive as he could be under the circumstances. "Johanna, you know in your heart you are innocent and Sister Madonna has told me you are a woman of faith. Let's see what tomorrow will bring. Take it day by day."

Father Howley asked a guard if he could keep Johanna company in her cell. He sat beside her as she lay on the bunk and held her hand and prayed with her until she fell asleep.

It was a long muggy night at Her Majesty's Penitentiary. On the morning of June 3, 1872, Johanna Hamilton and Patrick Geehan were escorted to the Supreme Court by paddy wagons. Crowds of spectators lined Duckworth Street and Water Street. For several days, the local newspapers had published Letters to the Editor calling for a guilty verdict to be accompanied by the death sentence for both prisoners.

Nothing less than a mob atmosphere was being played out on the streets of St. John's. The Terra Nova Constabulary was out in full force, having called on extra police to man the barricades as the wagons drew closer to the courthouse. The first wagon came to a stop and Johanna Hamilton was quickly hustled out and escorted up the steps as some of the more boisterous public tried to reach her. There were shouts of *Guilty* and *Hang her*. Johanna held her hands up to her ears as best she could given her restraints.

The crowd then turned to the paddy wagon holding Patrick Geehan. The Constabulary barely managed to prevent it from being overturned as they opened the door and dragged him through throngs of people who had become fierce and aggressive. The scene was far more volatile than what the police had experienced in May when the trial opened. There was no question that the publicity about the murder trial had heightened public emotions.

Inside the courtroom, anticipation had begun to build. The Chief Justice realized it would be wise to get the trial concluded without delay.

The case for the Crown having been closed, and there being no further witnesses called for the defense, Mr. Emerson addressed the jury on behalf of the prisoner Johanna Hamilton, speaking fully an hour, and urging with much ability and legal acumen that the evidence against her did not prove her complicity in the murder of Sears.

Mr. Raftus, for the prisoner Geehan, addressed all that could be said in his defense.

Mr. Carter, Q.C. then addressed the jury on the part of the Crown. The learned gentleman, on a comprehensive review of the evidence, urged that the charge of murder against both prisoners was fully sustained, and called upon the jury, however painful to their feelings, as it was painful to all engaged in the trial, to give a verdict in accordance with their conscientious convictions, on the evidence placed before them.

Judge Robinson, then, after paying a well merited compliment to Inspector Foley, for the zeal and ability he had evinced throughout the investigation, charged the jury, making an able and lucid analysis of the evidence against each of the prisoners separately, and giving full weight to all that had been urged by their counsel in their defense.

The jury then retired, and after an absence of three hours, came into the court with a verdict of Guilty against both prisoners but strongly recommending Johanna Hamilton to mercy….

The Chief Justice then proceeded to pass the following sentence:

" 'That you, Patrick Geehan and Johanna Hamilton, be taken to the place whence you came, and that you be there hanged by the neck until you are dead, and that your bodies be buried within the precincts of the prison; and may God in his infinite wisdom have mercy on your souls.'" [vii]

For a few seconds after the verdict was pronounced, there was complete silence in the courtroom. Then a commotion ensued as reporters scrambled to get outside and relay the news. Spectators in the courtroom mumbled and cries were heard. Catherine Drake fainted and had to be carried out of the room.

"Order, please! Order, please!" Judge Robinson had prepared himself for a rowdy reaction so he wasn't surprised at what was happening. After waiting for a few minutes, he swung the gavel several times until he got absolute silence.

"Do you wish to address the Court, Mr. Geehan?" he asked.

Patrick Geehan hung his head and said nothing.

The judge turned to Johanna. "Miss Hamilton, do you wish to address the Court?" he asked.

Johanna stood up. Again, it was as if the entire gallery was holding its breath.

"Sweet Jesus, Your Worship, please don't put a rope around my neck," Johanna cried out in a loud voice. "I don't want to die like that! I'll spend the rest of my life in prison instead. Please don't have me die like that." She then fell to her knees and clasped her hands together as though in prayer.

Johanna and Patrick Geehan were escorted out of the court in shackles amidst applause from the crowd. There were shouts of joy that such monsters had been condemned to death. Fists were jabbed high into the air. If it weren't for the presence of the police the worry of a lynch mob would have been very real. Policemen were positioned on both sides of the street as the two prisoners were separated and put into different prison wagons. This would be their last trip to the Supreme Court.

CHAPTER TWENTY-FIVE

St. John's
September 23, 1896

Father John Coombs dropped off his suitcase at the presbytery.

"You are only getting home now?" asked Mrs. Donahue.

"An old friend met me at the train. I spent the night there. I guess you have heard the news about Sister Madonna?"

"Yes, the Superintendent from the prison came by last night. He thought you were on the train and came by to see you. They had a service at the prison this morning before the wake at the Mother House. They'll be looking for you today."

"I have to drop by to see Mom and Dad, and then I will be going to the Diocese office."

Father John was eager to talk to Bishop Howley. But he hadn't seen or spoken to his parents for three days so he'd decided to go in and see them on his way to the Cathedral.

Theresa Coombs was washing dishes and looking out the window over the sink as they talked about Sister Madonna's death. John noticed that his mother never stopped working. She didn't know how to rest, even though she was now retired.

"How was the trip to Harbour Grace, John?" asked his father, who had just finished reading the newspaper. He was in the old creaking rocking chair and puffing on his pipe.

"You knew I went to Harbour Grace?" John hadn't communicated with his parents since Patrick Fitzgerald's death so someone else must have told them about his trip. "You must have dropped by the Church."

"Yes," answered his mother. "We were at Mass and wondered if you were interested in taking a walk down Water Street. When we went to the presbytery Mrs. Donahue said you weren't there, she said you had to attend a funeral in Harbour Grace."

"That's right. One of the long-time inmates I had gotten to know quite well passed away and I went to his funeral. His name was Patrick Fitzgerald. You may remember a criminal case in which he testified many years ago in Harbour Grace. Patrick Fitzgerald was a neighbor of a man accused of murder. Poor Patrick took a liking to a young Irish girl who was accused of being the man's accomplice. She worked as a servant girl in the family household where the tragedy took place. The young woman was eventually convicted of murder."

"Can't say that I do remember the case," responded Theresa.

"Now that he's passed away, I guess it's no harm in mentioning this to you. He never got beyond his guilt about her demise. Having taken a false oath in court, he blamed himself and felt great remorse for getting the young woman put in prison. She eventually lost her child because of her imprisonment."

Theresa continued to wash the dishes, listening intently to every word uttered by John.

"The young woman's name was Johanna Hamilton," he said, and Theresa suddenly dropped her favorite crystal dish in the sink, smashing it to smithereens.

Mark and John rushed to see if she was all right.

"Damn it," she cursed. Now she was embarrassed. This was the first time she'd sworn in Father John's presence. "I've broken my beautiful dish."

Theresa grabbed a cloth to stop the blood and then she sat on a kitchen chair and cried as if she had lost a friend. John couldn't understand why his mother was reacting like that about a broken dish.

"Don't worry about it, Theresa, as long as you didn't hurt yourself. We can replace that old dish." Mark had taken her hand and was checking her injury.

"You can't fix something you cherished once it is broken, Mark." Theresa looked sad. John could see the sorrow in her eyes.

After the drama had finally subsided and the cleanup was over, John gave his mother a hug and kissed her on the cheek.

"Well, I have to be going," he said to his parents as he put on his coat. "I'm on my way to the Diocese. I have to see the Bishop."

After Father John left, his parents stood and looked at each other in absolute disbelief. Theresa began to tremble. Mark held her and said, "If the time comes, we'll find the courage."

"I can tell that John is not himself. He seems preoccupied about something." Theresa knew John well enough to perceive his anxiety.

"Priests have it tough these days. Maybe he is concerned about his visit to see the Bishop."

Father Harold Cooney was just stepping out of his office when Father John arrived. Father Cooney's office was next to Bishop

Howley's and John noticed that the Bishop's door was open.

"This is an unexpected visit, John." Father Cooney smiled at him. "How are you doing at St. Patrick's? We have been hearing good things about you."

"I am doing fine, thank you, Father," replied Father John. "Now I am wondering…is there any way I can see His Excellency today?"

"He's completely booked for today and all day tomorrow. How about Friday morning?" offered Cooney.

"No. I'm afraid it can't wait. I wouldn't mind coming back tonight. I really need to see him."

"John Coombs, is that you?" came a voice from within the Bishop's office. A minute later Bishop Howley walked out. He had heard the consternation in Father John's voice.

"Yes it is me, Your Excellency. And I was hoping I could see you."

"Come in. I always have a little time for you. Father Cooney, have my next appointment take a seat and wait in the parlour."

Father John walked into the office. The Bishop could read the young priest's expression. "Sit down, my son. You seem troubled. Is there anything I can do?"

"Yes, Your Excellency. I need to go to confession. I've sinned."

The Bishop got up from his chair and shut the door. He turned the key to lock it, so that he and Father John could have some privacy. Opening his drawer, he took out a match and lit a blessed candle which stood in an ornate silver candleholder on his desk. He carried the candle to a small table next to the couch. A white stole hung behind his office door. He took it down and draped it over his shoulders. He then donned a red beanie and sat on the couch. A kneeler, placed in his office especially for his own prayer time, was next to the couch.

"Kneel, my son. There is nothing you can share with me that

God doesn't already know," said the Bishop. He began the introductory prayer in Latin. When he finished he put his hand on Father John's shoulder. 'Begin your confession."

"Father in heaven. I have transgressed the laws of God by breaking my vow of celibacy. I've been with a woman whom I deeply care about and love," said Father John.

"Has this been an ongoing relationship, John?"

"Not really," replied Father John. "I've known the woman for many years. This is the only time we have been intimate with each other."

"John, you have to make a decision. It's one thing to bring your sins to God, but it's another to leave them behind and make amends. Yes, you have broken your vow, but God is all forgiving."

"How do I make amends?" he asked. "I can't put together a broken dish. I have made love to this woman. How can I change that?"

"Amends in this case means that you have to stop your behavior. The devil tempts us all, each and every one of us, every day. We are all sinners. Our reconciliation is built on resisting further sin. When temptation is always present, it makes it more difficult to resist."

John bowed his head. "Therein lays the sin. I'm not sure if I want to stop. I know that I love her very much, yet I realize that I have made a vow to God."

"Then it's your choice. John, I don't want to lose you as a priest in our church. This isn't going to an easy decision for you."

"No matter how much I try to put her behind me, we keep ending up together. Oftentimes, it seems as if fate brings us together in times of need. I wonder if I didn't make the wrong choice when I entered the church. I'm so confused, Bishop. This woman was my support when I've recently lost two people I had grown close to. Relying on God alone hasn't been enough for me."

"That's the challenge, John," said Bishop Howley. "Sometimes we don't realize that God has been there for us all the time. You are a still a very young man with a full life in front of you. You don't have to be unhappy, regardless of what path you choose. If you want to be with this woman, then we'll find a way for that to happen."

Bishop Howley knew you can't force people to be something they don't want to be. He had been around long enough to know that there were too many religious and lay people who were unhappy.

"I can recommend to Rome that you be a candidate for laicization. You can decide if you want to be with the woman you love. However, you would no longer be a practicing priest in our Church."

"I understand." Father John shifted his position on the kneeler. He was clearly uncomfortable with the Bishop's words.

"John, you must also be aware that I cannot give absolution until you've made a decision, to stay with the priesthood or to be with the woman you love." The Bishop had to be bluntly honest and alert the young priest of the possible consequences. "Mind you, your indiscretion could be looked upon very seriously. If we are not careful about this entire process, you might face excommunication."

Having listened to the Bishop, Father John still hadn't decided on a course of action. "If I go through with all of what you have said and go back to being a lay person, there are still no guarantees that I will feel fulfilled," he said. "If I am unhappy then it would destroy the woman I love and me. This woman has been waiting for me a long time. I think our being together last night may have led her to believe that I have chosen her.

I've never felt so torn and bereft as I do today. Can I really face losing another person from my life?"

The Bishop began to speak again, feeling that he had to lay everything on the line this time. "If you are going to stay in your role as a priest, I have to be clear with you that you have to move from this area. We need an assistant priest at the Church of the Assumption in St. Kyran's, Placentia Bay, in one week. If you decide to stay with the priesthood, you can leave on the coastal boat in two days."

While still kneeling, Father John bowed his head. "I know my sins haven't been absolved. But may I have your blessing?"

Bishop Howley put both his hands on Father John's head and gave him his blessing.

"I need a day to reflect and pray, Your Excellency," said John. "I'll return tomorrow at four if that's a good time for you."

"Of course. Take some time today to pray, and let me know what you decide tomorrow. If you choose to stay with us, I'll make all the arrangements for your trip to Placentia Bay. Either way, tomorrow, once you've decided, I'll confer absolution."

They both stood and Father John reached out to shake Bishop Howley's hand. But the Bishop pushed his hand aside and embraced him as he would a son.

"Go in the peace of Christ, my son," he said. "You'll be in my prayers. I'll accept your decision whatever it may be. God bless you."

CHAPTER TWENTY-SIX

Her Majesty's Penitentiary, St. John's
June 13, 1872

Both Johanna Hamilton and Patrick Geehan were now on death row. Neither of their cells was near enough for them to have contact with each other. Prisoners awaiting the death sentence, ironically, were given special treatment at Her Majesty's Penitentiary.

Rumours were rampant that the execution date would be announced today. British law had made it clear seventeen years ago that there were to be no more public executions. This would be the first private execution in the Dominion of Newfoundland. Several reporters were to be permitted access to the prisoners if Johanna Hamilton or Patrick Geehan agreed to interviews. As well, a number of reporters, one from as far away as New York, had been given permission to cover the execution.

At about nine o'clock on the morning of June 13, 1872, the Court Sheriff arrived with Father Howley and Sister Madonna. The priest asked the Superintendent to allow their presence while Johanna received the news. Father Howley and Sister Madonna filed into her cell with the Sheriff. The nun and the priest each took one of Johanna's hands. They stood by her side as the Sheriff read the proclamation:

"Johanna Hamilton, I come here at the behest of his Lordship, Sir Bryan Robinson and the Supreme Court of Newfoundland. I hereby proclaim your day of execution, as sentenced in the Supreme Court on June 3, 1872, to be carried out on July 1, 1872, at 6:30 a.m. on the precinct of Her Majesty's Penitentiary where your remains are to be interred. God rest your soul."

Johanna listened in shocked silence and then watched numbly as the Sheriff left the cell. Father Howley and Sister Madonna gently eased her down onto her wooden bunk and she buried her face in her hands. Father Howley had been preparing for this moment.

After giving her a few minutes and without asking for permission, he said, "Let us pray together, the Lord's Prayer." Father Howley's background had taught him that even during times of crisis the act of prayer has a way of soothing people.

After the prayer, he reached into his pocket and asked Johanna and Sister Madonna to kneel as he opened a small gold pyx which contained the Blessed Sacrament. Carefully removing the host, he held it up. Making a sign of the cross with it, he said to Johanna, "Corpus Christi." She replied, "Amen" as she opened her mouth to receive the Body of Christ. He then did the same for Sister Madonna.

After receiving communion, they said the rosary. Father Howley had Johanna pray all five decades aloud. He and Sister Madonna did the responses. Father Howley knew that her faith was all that remained for Johanna. Most people know not the day, nor the hour of their death. But Johanna had been made aware of when she would pass into the next world.

There were no words which could lighten her heart. Father Howley left her cell quietly leaving her with Sister Madonna. When Sister left the cell that night, Johanna seemed resigned to the fact that her death was looming.

As time passed in the prison, Johanna became more of a recluse. On one occasion she said to Sister Madonna, “I would rather die by my own hand.”

“You shouldn’t say such a thing, my child,” implored Sister.

Johanna’s nausea got worse. When guards walked by her cell, there were times when she would be on her hands and knees throwing up. Speculation was growing about her condition. The woman was beyond pitiful. Something had to be done to assist her. Sister Madonna and the other nuns had their suspicions about why Johanna was so sick. Although she had to approach it delicately Sister Madonna felt compelled to talk to her.

Because Johanna was about to be executed, she was given the privilege of having tea whenever she desired. One day, Sister made tea and brought it to her cell. It was during that visit that Sister Madonna began to question her.

“Johanna, you’ve confided in me that you had been intimate on a number of occasions. Do you think your illness has anything to do with that?”

“No, I am just sick. I think it’s the worry and strain,” said Johanna.

“True, you’ve been through a great deal, but I have to ask you something. Have you been alright these last few months? I mean, as a woman?”

“No, not really.” Suddenly, she began to panic and became unable to breath. “Mother of Mercy. You’re not telling me I am having a child?” Sister couldn’t believe that Johanna hadn’t come to that conclusion herself. Was it possible that a woman, at the age of nineteen, wouldn’t know she was expecting?

Johanna's reaction was unexpected. "Get out of here! Leave me alone! You don't know what you are talking about, you bitch," she yelled, flailing her arms around as if she was about to attack the nun. Uncharacteristically, she began to curse and utter obscenities unfamiliar to Sister Madonna. It was as though Johanna had become possessed. The nun began to fear for her safety. She held Johanna's wrists until the prison warden arrived. Just as the guard turned the key to come to Sister's aid, Johanna suddenly stopped and sank to her bunk. Sister Madonna put her arms around her and rocked her back and forth as she wept.

"Shush! My child. It's all right. I'm here with you," she said.

Johanna cried on Sister Madonna's shoulder like a baby, grasping her blanket more for comfort than for warmth. She finally fell asleep. When Sister Madonna left her cell, she thought that Johanna had been convinced to see Doctor Simms, the prison doctor. In days to come, however, Johanna presented very differently. No matter how hard Sister Madonna tried, Johanna continued to refuse help. She knew she had every right to keep her condition to herself. She began to slip into a self-destructive mental state, often seen when prisoners faced certain death. With each passing day Johanna worsened. She stopped eating almost completely and slept most of the day.

One night, late in June, a guard was making his rounds when he heard moaning coming from Johanna's cell. She had fallen on the floor and was unresponsive when the guard spoke to her. The guard ran to the prison bell and rang it as loudly as he could. He feared that she had passed away. Johanna was put on a stretcher and carried to the doctor's room. Dr. Simms was called in at four in the morning. After close examination, he reported to the Superintendent that it would be necessary for Johanna to be further examined for official reasons. She was returned to her cell and remained there for the next two days, refusing to communicate or take food.

Dr. Simms returned on June 24, six days before her scheduled execution. A jury of six matrons and Dr. Simms had been empaneled by the Supreme Court to determine whether Johanna Hamilton was, in fact, "quick with child."

Sister Madonna and Father Howley were very concerned about the timing. They knew Johanna would not be executed if she was pregnant. With only six days remaining before the execution was carried out time was of the essence. But despite Father Howley's continuous appeals to Judge Robinson for a speedier response the execution appeared to be on schedule.

For her part, Johanna had decided it was time to accept her fate. She seemed oblivious to everything. Her mental state had deteriorated to such a point that she was without logic and devoid of feeling. The nuns knew she was intent on giving up her own life and the life of her unborn child. Each day she ate only enough to ward off her nausea. With her rosary beads in her hand, she walked around her eight by ten foot cell from morning till night, praying under her breath. She ignored everything and everybody.

In the meantime, Father Howley was committed to work with the other prisoner on death row, Patrick Geehan. While on his way to visit him, he came up with an ingenious idea he thought might work to assist Johanna. When he arrived at Patrick's cell he was surprised to see that the prisoner was sitting and talking to a reporter. He wondered if he was one of the reporters who had been selected to view the execution.

"He's been in there with him for nearly an hour," nodded the guard seated outside the cell. "I can't believe that Geehan. He's as hard as nails. Only hours from death and listen to him talk."

"Well, how much is your newspaper willing to pay?" Father

Howley heard Patrick Geehan ask the reporter.

"I'd say they'd pay forty pounds for a picture of you. I'll have to check with my editor and let you know tomorrow," the reporter was saying as he gathered his notes and put them in a case. He hurried out of the cell and rushed past the priest and the guard without acknowledging either of them.

Howley couldn't understand why Patrick Geehan, who was about to die, was bargaining for money, something of no earthly value to him. He saw that Geehan was now sitting back puffing on his pipe, making rings of smoke with his pursed lips. The reporter he'd been talking to described him as "audacious" in the article he wrote the following day.

"Patrick, would you like to have a prayer with me tonight?" asked Father Howley.

"Not much need of a prayer now, Father," Patrick replied as he peered through the bars of the cell. "If the court couldn't help me, there's nothing you can do."

"I wouldn't say that. A man of your strength and character must realize that there is one greater than us." Then Father Howley took a chance and played a card he thought might work to help him carry out his idea.

"I've read that you were a hard-working man. Years on the coast of Labrador and then coming back to spend the rest of the time farming, getting wood, and living life as best you could."

"Yes, Father. What did it get me though? I'll be swinging at the end of a rope soon enough."

"Well, Johanna Hamilton must have seen something in you to love you like she does."

Geehan came to his feet. "What do you know of Johanna?"

"She's in a bad way," Father Howley said, unsure whether Geehan was angry or concerned.

"How so? Is she not well? There isn't a moment goes by when I don't think about her. They haven't let us talk to each other. Besides I don't think she would want anything to do with me now." Within seconds, he had morphed from being a boisterous braggart into a man of quieter disposition. "I wish I had known that you were in contact with her. I would have tried to see if she would speak to me."

"Patrick, I have been by your cell with the nuns on several occasions and you have refused to talk to me so I had no way of knowing you wished to speak to Johanna," Father Howley paused before continuing. "Johanna is now very ill. While it can't be said with certainty we think she is expecting a child."

Father Howley wanted to get his plan to work. He figured he had nothing to lose at this point. Besides, Geehan had every right to know about Johanna's pregnancy, if he indeed was the father.

"Jesus, Mary and St. Joseph," Patrick pushed the palms of his hands against the sides of his head as if he was experiencing a terrible headache. "Has she been asking for me?"

"As I said, she is in a bad way and refusing to speak to anyone. If I can arrange a meeting would you try to speak to her?" Howley knew he was treading on very thin ice. The two prisoners were about to die and this was his last chance to change that. Patrick Geehan could be the very one to save Johanna from the noose.

Later that night, after getting permission from the Superintendent, Father Howley and Sister Madonna walked Patrick Geehan, in manacles, up to Johanna Hamilton's cell. Howley was intent on getting his plan to work.

"Johanna, we have someone here to see you," he said. Johanna lay facing the wall and refused to look.

"Johanna, it's me." Patrick Geehan said as he put his face close to the bars of her cell. "I came to talk to you. I came to say that I am sorry. Please forgive me for what I have done to you."

Johanna finally twisted around and sat up on her bunk. "Patrick, I have nothing to say to you."

"Johanna, please listen to me. I came to tell you that I am willing to confess to everyone, before God, that I lied about your involvement." Patrick Geehan began to cry. "Please forgive me, Johanna. Please! Think no more of me, but only of yourself and our unborn child. I pray for you to be calm, not only for your own sake but for that of the unconscious and innocent being within you."[viii]

Father Howley and Sister Madonna were astonished at Patrick's words. And then Johanna came over and stood in front of the bars and looked at him.

"I forgive you, Patrick," she said. "Go now to meet your God. We are to suffer for our sins and there's no stopping it now."

"I love you Johanna. Do you still love me?" Patrick asked.

Father Howley hoped that Johanna could find the right answer. He wanted Geehan to remain in a frame of mind which would allow him to confess as he had promised.

"God help me, but yes, I still love you, Patrick." Johanna put her hands out through the bars and Patrick bent down to kiss her fingers.

After his visit with Johanna, Patrick confessed his sins to Father Howley and made his peace with God. However, the wheels of justice continued to turn slowly, and the empaneled jury's recommendation on Johanna still hadn't been released. Time had run out and it seemed Johanna Hamilton and Patrick would both die as scheduled.

"At five o'clock Patrick Geehan was aroused from his fitful sleep, and recommended to prepare himself for the last offices of the

church of which he declared himself to be a member. He then ate some muttonchops, toast, and coffee with great relish, after which he said he felt "plucky."

But the more worthy object of human sympathy in this case was the frail but lovely creature, Johanna Hamilton, who sat wearied yet sleepless upon the miserable pallet within her last abode on earth. Her tears had steadily fallen during the night; but when the priest announced himself to her, she cried aloud for many moments before speaking to him. At length he succeeded in calming down her grief, but only to hear from her the distracted and plaintiff appeal- "Oh Father! For the love of sweet Jesus, save me!" The priest then gradually led her thoughts away from the earth. She slowly grew resigned to her fate.

At six o'clock, a company of policemen marched into the yard, and upon hearing them the doomed woman shuddered involuntarily. And had new recourse to tears. On leaving her cell at the request of the Sheriff, she drew back and sobbed hysterically. Being quietly pressed to move on, she advanced a step, and again shrank from the terrible journey. At length it was found necessary to employ violence in removing her from her cell; but at the request of the clergyman he was allowed to re-persuade her to obey the sentence of the law. The priest finally succeeded in taking her into the passage where her dress was looped, her arms pinioned, and the fatal noose adjusted. In the meantime, Geehan, dressed in a suit of black, had been fitted out for his leap into death, and he stood before his beautiful accomplice.

"Poor Johanna," said Geehan aloud; but the condemned woman did not even raise her eyes towards him. She held down her head meekly, and seemed fully to realize her shame. But her tears had all dried up, and her sobs were hushed; nothing save an occasional sigh was left of the grief and distraction of her last night on earth.

"Are you ready?" asked the Sheriff, and Geehan answered

promptly, "Yes, sir."

Geehan then received the white cap, as did also the unfortunate Johanna. Geehan, accompanied by a clergyman and two deputy sheriffs, led the way to the cortile of the penitentiary.

Approaching the platform upon which the fatal trap-bars were the doomed woman again shrunk back and cried bitterly. But again encouraged by the counsel of her spiritual advisor, she went courageously up to the platform. There she knelt and prayed ardently. Geehan also prayed. Their prayers being finished, they arose and the black caps were drawn over their eyes by the deputy sheriffs, and the noose of each was adjusted to ropes, which dangled from two protruding beams…Great sympathy was felt for the girl, and it was hoped by many that the governor would relent before the sentence had been fulfilled."[ix]

The black hooded hangman left the platform and took his position underneath, where he awaited the signal to pull the trap door. The prisoners, with a sheriff behind each one, were ready to step onto the trap doors as a dozen witnesses watched. Once the captain dropped his raised arm the trap door would be opened. A deafening silence prevailed within the prison walls. The anticipation of such a macabre event created great tension.

Suddenly, the huge doors were flung open and a voice bellowed loudly, "Stop this execution! Stop this execution!"

A sheriff of the Supreme Court, in full uniform, marched up the steps of the gallows and stood between the two doomed prisoners. He then read aloud this proclamation: "On behalf of Sir Stephen John Hill, Governor of the Dominion of Newfoundland, I hereby issue an order to stop the execution of Johanna Hamilton. The prisoner's sentence has been respited until November 20, 1872. Return the woman to her cell."

Hearing the order, the sheriff standing behind Johanna pulled her back from the brink of death. He removed her white hood and quickly escorted her down the steps of the gallows and out of the cortile area, away from the western side of the prison.

As she was rushed away, Johanna continued to stare back at a hooded Patrick Geehan. The captain raised his arm and waited until he heard the main door slam, making certain that Johanna had left the area before proceeding with the execution.

"The gallows, rising about ten feet above the platform, consisted of a crossbeam supported by two uprights, from which hung a manila two-inch rope, with the noose. The doomed man walked still firmly under the noose and nervously looked at his feet to the left and to the right. He then shook both hands with the priest and bid a final adieu. Here the masked executioner adjusted the noose with much apparent ease…the Minister of Religion meanwhile offered the prescribed prayers….

All the ghostly preliminaries completed, the executioner descended the scaffold to position beneath the platform, and here upon a given signal he drew a large iron bolt or trigger, when the platform fell with a fearful sound and the unhappy man made a descent of about his six feet. At first his body hung motionless as if instantly dead, then the knees were drawn up convulsively; soon after every limb quivered and from the action of the feet one of the shoes was shaken off. When this ceased, all was still forever. The neck was not broken by the fall, but insensibility must have been supervened almost immediately and there must have been little or no suffering, a result for which we must all feel thankful and which reflects credit on the care and judgment exercised to prevent any pang that it was possible to spare." [x]

CHAPTER TWENTY-SEVEN

Her Majesty's Penitentiary, St. John's
July1, 1872

As Patrick Geehan fell to his death, Father Howley and Sister Madonna were leading a shocked and shaking Johanna back to her cell. Johanna had been kept in the dark about the plan Father Howley had hatched after she met with Patrick Geehan prior to his execution. Now he and Sister wanted to confess.

Johanna was still trembling. Her eyes were wide. The trauma of being on the gallows had left her in shock.

"'I really don't know what respited means. I think the sheriff said that I have been respited until November 20th. Do I have to go through this again?" she whispered.

"The empaneled jury ruled that you are about six and a half months pregnant," said Sister Madonna. "They have also said you are to have your child here in prison before your sentence is enacted."

"So then, I am still to be hung?"

"That's what we need to talk to you about," said Father Howley as he took her hand in his. "After Patrick Geehan's visit to you, something happened that Sister and I think may help your cause. Patrick made a confession that completely exonerates you from any wrong doing in the death for which you had been convicted. His letter of confession establishes your innocence. With Patrick Geehan's permission, I sent a copy of the confession to the editor of the *Morning Chronicle*. I also sent copies of the confession by courier to the Chief Justice of the Supreme Court and to the Governor of Newfoundland and let them know it was going be published in this morning's paper. I think the respite you received is directly attributed to Patrick Geehan's letter of confession which will soon hit the streets. How could the Governor and the Chief Justice hang a woman when the public will soon be informed of her innocence?"

"Do you think they will overturn the conviction of murder?" Johanna asked tearfully.

"I think they'll have no choice but to do that once the confession is published. It may take some time but the Supreme Court will want to make sure they get things right," Father Howley spoke with great confidence.

Johanna struggled to her feet and embraced Father Howley and Sister Madonna.

"Johanna, based on your confession, which you gave me yesterday, it's likely the Crown will suggest jail time," Father Howley said. "There will still be the lesser offences of perjury and collusion. I'm not a lawyer, but I don't think the Court will accept your fear of Patrick Geehan as a reason for not coming to the police from the beginning. We'll have to publish your written confession to show how similar yours and Patrick's confessions are without either of you knowing what the other was saying." Father reached into his pocket and took out a letter.

"Read this, Johanna. It's my letter to *The Morning Chronicle*."

"To the Editor of The Morning Chronicle:
Cathedral, St. John's, Newfoundland, July 1, 1872

Sir, so many false and uncharitable rumors have gone around concerning the unfortunate Patrick Geehan, who this day suffered the awful penalty of the law, that I think it my bounden duty to make a few remarks upon this melancholy affair in which I have been called to take so prominent a part. No one appears to have anything but evil to say of poor Geehan. Perhaps when they read the subjoined statement, made on the threshold of eternity, they will mitigate their anger, and drop a tear or a prayer in memory of the man.

From the time I first visited Geehan shortly after his imprisonment, I found him to be the same respectful, submissive person. He felt the keenest anxiety for having dragged the poor girl Hamilton into trouble and for having, in a moment of anger, as appears below, endeavored to incriminate her.

Though she may be frail and weak, and guilty of defaults of a kind which are to be condoned before a tribunal higher than that of man, still it will appear she had no hand in the shedding of a fellow creature's blood. She is more to be pitied than blamed. The character she has gained for herself in the prison is one of gentleness, simplicity, and gratitude for the highest favours received, with a continued and heart-breaking repentance for her sins. She feels great sorrow that she did not at first state the whole truth, instead of risking her own life to save Geehan.

I obtained the following free and voluntary statement from Geehan, in the presence of Messrs. R. Raftus, Barrister, and J.P. Scott, Attorney

Michael F. Howley

THE CONFESSION OF PATRICK GEEHAN
Penitentiary, St. John's
Newfoundland, June 24, 1872

'I Patrick Geehan hereby solemnly declare that there never was any plot or conspiracy between me and Johanna Hamilton to get rid of either Mrs. Geehan or Garrett Sears. I never, up to the time of Garrett Sears' death, said one word to her on such a subject, nor did any conversation ever take place between us to that effect. I therefore freely submit my written confession as given at the knee of Father Michael Howley to my Savior the Lord God Almighty....

I clear Johanna Hamilton totally of any conspiracy. She had nothing to do whatsoever in it. The four witnesses that swore against her were false. She did not hand me the pitchfork as I stated in the prison. 'Twas in derision I stated that; to spite her because she said I killed the man. What I said about her wasn't true.

This is my free and voluntary statement and contains the truth.'
Signed Patrick Geehan
Michael F. Howley
Jonathan Martin"[xi]

Sister Madonna and Father Howley watched Johanna's expression change as she read Patrick's confession. The letter of confession relieved years of stress and anxiety for the young woman who had faced abuse at the hands of Patrick Geehan, his family, and an unforgiving public.

Three weeks later, the sheriff who had proclaimed Johanna's respite on July 1, arrived at her cell with much less drama. He referred to her as Miss Johanna Hamilton as he stood outside her cell in the company of a prison warden and proclaimed:

"Miss Johanna Hamilton, on behalf of his Lordship Byron Robinson, Chief Justice of the Supreme Court of Newfoundland, I am here to announce that your sentence, which was to be carried out on November 20, 1872, has been hereby revoked. After much deliberation, on July 25, 1872, the Court has commuted your sentence to life imprisonment. You are advised that the Dominion of Newfoundland, in conjunction with the country of Ireland, is negotiating the process of your deportation under the laws and conditions outlined by our countries' treaty for the immigration and emigration of convicted felons."

Hardly able to believe that she was going to be allowed to live, Johanna was now all consumed with her unborn child. Although news that her execution had been revoked was reassuring, the newly imposed life sentence stole her fleeting sense of hope. At best, she would escape this country by being deported back to Ireland. She was most certain, though, of one fact: she would be required to give up her child.

Now in her seventh month of pregnancy, she thought it most likely that Patrick Geehan was the father. However, she couldn't rule out her short intimate affair with Patrick Fitzgerald. But Johanna never intended to see Patrick Fitzgerald again. And it was her wish that he have nothing to do with any child of hers.

Despite everything that had happened, Johanna mourned Patrick Geehan, the man he could have been rather than the man he was. They could have been happy together. They could have made a good life together, she thought as she sang to her unborn child, nurturing the tiny human being growing inside her.

CHAPTER TWENTY-EIGHT

Her Majesty's Penitentiary, St. John's
September, 1872

In the early morning of September 10, Johanna Hamilton went into labour. A Sister of Mercy who was experienced as a midwife was called into the prison and Johanna was helped to the sick room where prisoners were treated. This was the same room where the empaneled jury had done their intrusive examination to determine that she was pregnant.

"She is bleeding profusely! It has to stop before the birth," Sister Edward said now as she went into quick action, having stripped off her veil and other parts of her habit that would get in the way. "We'll need cloths torn into tiny strips. Scald them. Let some cool and keep others as hot as you can," she told the nun who had been assigned to help her.

Sister Edward kept talking to Johanna and telling her what she was doing every step of the way. "I will begin packing you with hot then cold cloths. I'll let you know when I'll be switching.

Each time, I'll take a look to see if the hemorrhaging has stopped."

Johanna cried out with each contraction. "Don't push! Hold back as long as you can," said Sister Edward. She kept changing the cloths until finally the bleeding stopped.

"We have a partial breech," Sister announced at last and there was relief in her voice. "I think I can reach a leg and pull a little. Can you push now? Johanna, listen. You haven't got long to go now. I need you to push."

Johanna went through two hours of labour before Sister Edward got the baby in the right position and she gave birth to a healthy baby boy. After cutting the placenta, the nuns swaddled the crying child and gave him to Johanna to hold. Johanna looked at her son in wonder. He was beautiful and she never wanted to let him go.

But then she heard Sister Edward's voice, gentle but firm, as she said, "Johanna, we have to take a look at the baby now to make sure that everything is fine. With infinite tenderness, Sister Edward took the baby from Johanna and passed him to the other nun who carried him swiftly out of the room.

"Where are you taking him? Bring him back. He's crying. Please!" Johanna heard her baby's cries as he was carried out of the cell-block and away from the penitentiary. His cries echoed throughout the building. Johanna covered her ears and wept. Her baby was being stolen away from her. She had never experienced such torture. Then there was emptiness.

The sisters cleaned the room in a routine fashion. It seemed to be a normal act for them to steal someone's flesh and blood. The sisters were speaking to her and to each other, but Johanna didn't hear a word as the cries of her baby continued to echo in her head. A few weeks ago, she was standing on the crossbeams awaiting her death. Having her child ripped away from her was far more painful than facing death. She would have readily accepted the gallows, knowing now the pain of her loss.

Johanna was carried back to her cell shortly after giving birth. The only nursing care was that given to her by the Sisters of Mercy. Sister Madonna came to see her later that day. The nun's face was sad as she gazed at her.

"There's nothing that can be said. There are no words I can say to help you overcome the pain you are feeling. I'm so sorry for your loss," Sister Madonna spoke as though she was referring to a death that Johanna had experienced.

Sometimes grief presents itself in the form of anger. That was the emotion now uppermost in Johanna. "If he had died in my arms, Sister, I would have been distraught, distressed beyond belief. But it would have been over. I would know that his life had ended. Now I am left empty, wondering if he'll be loved and cared for."

Sister Madonna looked distressed. "You shouldn't think like that, Johanna. You have to thank God for allowing you to have brought a healthy child into the world. Look at you. You carried this child through a very turbulent time. It has to be a miracle that he survived. You have to thank God for that."

"How can I thank God for my place in life?" cried Johanna. "I am sentenced here for the rest of my life and I have just lost my precious son."

"Do you believe in miracles, Johanna?" asked Sister Madonna. Johanna looked at her in silence. "Less than two months ago you stood on the brink of death. We all thought you'd be gone by now. Then God sent to us a priest by the name of Michael Howley who was given a gift. This gift was a talent and an intellect which he put to use to save your life. Then God sent you another miracle. He gave you a healthy son who will bring someone great happiness. We aren't able to even begin to see the joy he will bring to the world. We'll probably never know."

Johanna seemed to find some solace in Sister Madonna's words. As she had accepted her pending death so she had no choice but to accept her loss. The idea of her son going on and doing wonderful acts of love for people was of some consolation. But she still felt as though her heart had been destroyed.

"Will I know where he is being sent or who will get him?" she asked.

Sister Madonna shook her head. "I'm so sorry, Johanna. It is the strict policy of the Sisters of Mercy that our orphanage never shares that information. You can be assured, though, that your son will be received into a loving and caring home."

"I ask but one favour," Johanna said as she reached inside her pillowcase and pulled out the rosary beads she'd found in Labrador. "Please see that these go with him. They will protect him as they did me." She blessed herself with the beads, kissed them, and handed the rosary to Sister Madonna.

"That I can do, Johanna," Sister promised.

Later that week Father Michael Howley was requested to do a baptism on September 16th for a young married couple who felt blessed in having received a newly born baby boy. The priest had helped the couple get the child.

Mr. and Mrs. Mark Coombs both knew Father Howley since Theresa Coombs was a cook at the Bishop's residence. The Coombs had been married for five years and, although they desperately wanted children, they had been unsuccessful in their efforts to have a child.

A week earlier Father Howley had asked Theresa and Mark to

come see him at St. Michael's Orphanage. Theresa hoped that the nuns weren't going to ask them to take in another child. Because of their work within the church and parish, she and Mark were occasionally asked to take children into their home until the sisters could get them settled somewhere permanently. They weren't in a position to refuse, since both their salaries, indirectly or directly, came from the church.

Father Howley was in the orphanage waiting room with Sister Madonna when the Coombs knocked on the door.

"Come in. It's good to see you both. And you probably know Sister Madonna?" he said.

"Yes, we do, Father. We've often seen her at mass in the Cathedral. It's good to see you again, Sister, and you too Father." Mark wasn't much for formalities. He and Theresa had already agreed that they would take a child for a short period if there were a need.

"We have a favour to ask," Father Howley said, knowing that the couple was anxious to find out why they had been summoned.

The Coombs thought they knew what was coming next, and they looked up in surprise as the door opened abruptly and a nun walked in carrying an infant.

Father Howley smiled at them. "We have a baby boy for you to adopt if you so choose. We know you have been waiting to have your own child so here is your opportunity."

Theresa immediately opened her arms and reached out to receive the child.

"You mean, we can keep this precious little boy and call him ours?" she asked in wonder. Tears of joy began to trickle down her face as she cuddled the sleeping infant. She looked at Mark. He was nodding his head in full approval.

"Normally, we never say where a child we are putting up for

adoption has originated," said Father Howley. "This case is extremely delicate so we have to treat the adoption a little differently. The baby is three days old and very healthy. His mother is a young prison inmate. You may have read about the case of a young woman wrongly accused of murder. Her name is Johanna Hamilton. Unfortunately, although innocent of murder, her circumstances mean she will spend the rest of her life incarcerated. It will be impossible for her to care for her child. Do you think you could raise this boy as if he is your own, knowing the difficult circumstances under which he was born?" Father Howley was being very sensitive about Johanna and her child. Again, in his wisdom, he had researched who he thought would be the right parents to raise the child.

"We'll be more than happy to raise this child. Thank you from the bottom of our hearts. He'll have a home full of love and kindness. We promise," Mark said as he and Theresa looked down at the most wonderful gift they had ever received.

The Coombs signed the necessary documents, with Father Howley and Sister Madonna as the witnesses. Sister Madonna then took out a case and opened it to reveal a beautiful rosary. The beads looked handcrafted.

"This set of rosary beads belongs to your baby. He is to receive it at his First Holy Communion," she said without further explanation as she passed over the case with the rosary inside. The Coombs left the orphanage with their boy. Nothing could have made them happier.

Johanna Hamilton served the next eight years at Her Majesty's Penitentiary in St. John's. By all accounts she had regular contact with her sister, Catherine Drake in Harbour Grace, but she always felt that her imprisonment wasn't warranted. After several letters of request for her release, the Governor issued the last proclamation for Johanna Hamilton, the one ordering her deportation.

On May 24, 1880, Johanna, at the age of twenty-seven, was escorted from the prison under guard. This time she wasn't in restraints. The prison wagon made its way to the waterfront. At customs, she signed her deportation order. Sister Madonna stood on the dock with her as the officials came down the plank to greet her.

Sister Madonna took out four ten-pound notes along with a letter and passed everything to Johanna. "This isn't much. Here, in this envelope, is the name of a person who will meet you in Dublin. She's a great and trustworthy friend of mine. Don't worry. She'll help you get situated."

"I intend to make something of myself, Sister," said Johanna. "My boy is eight years old now and he is in the arms of somebody else. I still have age on my side. Maybe there is some organization, some group, where I can put my efforts to good use." She embraced Sister Madonna one last time. "When you see Father Howley again, please give him my heartfelt thanks."

"You have our address. Please let us know how you are doing."

With a sense of freedom and hope for the future, and much regret for the past, Johanna boarded a steamer bound for her native home of Ireland. She had plenty of time to make something of herself in the Old World.

Eight weeks later, Sister Madonna met a new inmate who was now occupying Johanna's former cell. He had received a life sentence for killing a man during a fight. When she tapped on the cell door to see if he wanted to talk, Patrick Fitzgerald turned around to welcome her. He needed someone to whom he could relate his story.

CHAPTER TWENTY-NINE

St. John's
September 23, 1896

Father John Coombs left the Cathedral Palace and walked towards the Battery. Being late September, the evenings were beginning to close in earlier. Walking usually helped him think through times of anxiety and loneliness. At the Battery, he saw fishermen busy on the stage heads gutting and cleaning their freshly caught fish. Loudly cawing seagulls hovered over the fishermen. Eyeing the vestiges of cod being tossed into the water, they dove in to scavenge the remains.

The more John thought about his dilemma, the more he was leaning on the side of staying with the Church. It wasn't that he didn't want to face disgrace as a defrocked priest. He and Sarah Keough could leave the area, just as he would have to do if he stayed in the priesthood.

While on his way back to St. Patrick's Church, he made a visit to pay his respects to Sister Madonna. She was waking at the Mother House. The chapel was peaceful with several blessed candles adding to the sacred ambiance. The Sisters welcomed him. Many of the nuns offered their condolences to him for they knew what great respect and friendship Sister Madonna and Father Coombs had for each other. On being informed of his presence, the Mother Superior came to welcome him.

"She spoke highly of you, Father," she said, with a nod to the coffin holding the recently departed nun.

"Thank you for telling me that. We had a great relationship at work in the prison."

The Mother Superior reached into the side pocket of her habit and took out an envelope. "Because of your close working relationship maybe you can assist us with this," she said, passing it to Father John. "We received this letter from overseas today addressed to Sister Madonna. It didn't have a return address but it was postmarked in Ireland. Apparently, Sister was receiving regular correspondence from this woman who befriended her while she was incarcerated here in prison. The Convent hadn't been informed of this as it was Sister Madonna's personal business. However, from reading the woman's letter we would like to let her know of Sister's passing. For some reason this woman believes she owed Sister Madonna a debt of gratitude."

He took the letter out of the envelope. The letter read:

Dear Sister,

I write to you in good health and hope this letter finds you the same. Things are busy here at the orphanage. At day's end, we are very tired, but the work is very rewarding.

Your last letter said that Patrick Fitzgerald had passed away. God rest his soul. It brought back terrible memories, but I am glad that Patrick found somebody like that good priest, Father John, about whom you often write.

Well, Father John is fortunate to have you as a tutor in matters of spirituality. Without you, I would have been a vanquished soul lost in a den of iniquity.

I have requested our community to pray for Patrick's soul. May he rest in peace.

Your letters continue to bring me joy, hope and happiness.

Yours sincerely,

Johanna +

Father John realized that the writer of the letter had to be Johanna Hamilton. He'd had every intention of asking Sister Madonna about her. Sadly, the mystery might now have died with the nun. In true loyalty to Sister Madonna, he felt that he shouldn't reveal the letter writer's identity. That might not be what his good friend would want.

"I'm sorry I can't be of help to you, Mother Superior," he said as he passed back the letter.

Patrick Fitzgerald's mysterious last words then rushed back at him: "Keep with God. She'll find you one day."

Father John had a sleepless night. Tomorrow, he had to have two very difficult conversations before speaking to the Bishop.

Sarah was working so Father John had to find her at the hospital. Having made his decision, he wanted to have his conversation with her this morning.

Upon spotting her amidst the noise and confusion, he called out, "Can we have a moment, Sarah? Are you able to leave for a short time? We need to talk." John's somber appearance was a signal to Sarah that this wasn't going to be a pleasant meeting. The noisy hospital ward was crowded with ailing patients and medical workers. Without saying a word, she walked over to an attendant and tapped him in the shoulder. She pointed to the priest and then left with Father John.

Sarah pulled on her coat as they descended the steps of the hospital and began to walk down Forest Road towards Quidi Vidi Lake. "I haven't much time, John. You didn't drop by last night and I know something is up. What is it? Tell me."

John plunged in. "I've been to see the Bishop. I have to leave for Placentia Bay on the coastal boat tomorrow morning. I am to be assistant priest at the Church of the Assumption at St. Kyran's, Placentia Bay."

"So you are staying in the priesthood?" Sarah said and her voice was flat and calm. "I thought we had sealed our love during your stay the other night. But I suspected differently when you didn't get in touch afterwards." They walked on without speaking for a few minutes. "You know, John? I knew there was something illusory about that whole encounter. Even as we…"

"I know what you are were going to say," he broke in. "You were going to say that even as we made love, you didn't feel that I was committed. You were right. I wasn't. Sarah, I didn't lie to you. I do love you and will always love you very much. There'll never be another woman in my life, there could never be another woman like you in my life. My devotion, however, must be to Our Lord."

"Do you think your saying that makes this any easier for me? John, that means I have to accept losing you again." She sounded more angry than sorry. "Maybe your leaving will make the whole thing easier for me this time."

John reached out to hold her hand but she pulled it away.

"I should be saying that I am sorry for leading you on, for letting you think that I was ready to be with you," he said as he tried to continue his explanation. "I really am sorry for that. However, I have to be honest and tell you that you have completed me and for that, I will always be deeply grateful to you. Being with you was the most beautiful experience of my life, an experience I know I will never want to have with anybody else. I will always love you, Sarah."

"I'll never accept your reasoning! You are choosing to leave me in the name of God," Sarah said furiously.

John hung his head. "I know there is nothing I can say to help you understand that. I think time will allow you to move on. I pray every day for you to accept me as I am, a man dedicated to God."

Their walk ended back where it began.

"John, I have to get back to work. We could stand here all day, but I'll never accept your choosing the Church over me. How can I compete with God?" Sarah was unyielding in her position but she realized the battle was over. Knowing she was defeated, she concluded, "I'll never forget you and will always love you."

Sarah put her arms around him and he held her close. She gave him a fleeting kiss and then she rushed up the steps of the hospital and out of Father John Coombs' life. The door shut slowly behind her.

Father John's next stop was Prescott Street. This meeting wasn't going to be any easier than the one with Sarah.

"I knew yesterday there was something wrong. I could read your face." Theresa was upset on hearing John's news. "All the way to St. Kyran's in Placentia Bay? Sure there are so many places nearby where they could have sent you."

"Theresa, he can't tell Bishop Howley where he wants to go." Mark Coombs was as dismayed as his wife but he held his tongue.

"Mom and Dad, I'll write you every week. I promise. In no time at all I'll be back for a visit."

Theresa stalked into the front room. John hadn't seen his mother so angry in years. But he had an appointment at four. He had to leave.

"Don't worry, my son," said Mark. "We'll be there to see you off in the morning. Let us know which wharf you are leaving from and what the departure time will be."

"I will, Dad. Please try to make Mom see that I have to go."

As John got closer to the Cathedral he was sadly aware that two of the people in his life whom he loved dearly were now disappointed and angry with him. It was ironic. He was about to spend the rest of his days in service to total strangers, while those he loved refused to understand him.

Father John Coombs visited the Bishop and received absolution. The next day at eleven o'clock he was to set sail for Placentia Bay. Theresa and Mark Coombs would be at the wharf to wave goodbye.

CHAPTER THIRTY

St. John's
September 25, 1896

Father John arose early on September 25 and wanted to take a walk down Duckworth Street and over to Forest Road to clear his head before boarding his boat. He had plenty of time since he had packed the night before. The parish would arrange for his bags and other packages to be delivered to the boat at ten o'clock.

He decided to make one last trip to Her Majesty's Penitentiary to say goodbye to the wardens, the captains and the Superintendent. It was about eight-thirty when he rang the prison bell and was welcomed into the cell-block.

"Well, Father, you are leaving us. It's our loss indeed. Your new fella is working out very well, though, I have to say. You trained him well." Superintendent Parsons was always friendly. His personality was not characteristic of all Superintendents. "We had a little service here for Sister Madonna. She's a huge loss!"

"I couldn't make the service. I do apologize."

"Sister Madonna was a good woman. So many years here. I don't have to tell you that many have walked out of here who can thank her for putting them back on course."

Superintendent Parsons' comment caused Father John to think about Johanna Hamilton. "Do you have a record of releases, by name, as well as by year?" he asked.

"We do. Christine can find out exactly when it was that an individual was released." Christine was the prison clerk. She worked just off the Superintendent's office.

"I wonder would she know when a prisoner named Johanna Hamilton was released?'

"Christine," the Superintendent tapped on Christine's office window. "Can you come in, please?" he called. Christine entered the office. "Can you find out from the records when a woman by the name of Johanna Hamilton was released?"

"Of course, Sir. Give me a few minutes."

Christine soon returned with a file. "Johanna Hamilton was sentenced to hang on July 1, 1872," she said. "Because she was pregnant, her sentence was respited that day. The execution was to be carried out on November 20, 1872, after she gave birth. But the execution was then commuted to life imprisonment. She was exonerated from the conviction of being an accomplice. She was released on May 24, 1880, and deported the very same day back to her native Ireland."

"What became of the child?"

"The child was taken by the Dominion of Newfoundland and put under the care of the Sisters of Mercy on the day it was born. By law, we are not privileged to that information."

"We can assume the child was adopted back in 1872. He or she could well live somewhere in Newfoundland," surmised the young priest.

Father John now understood why Johanna Hamilton wanted

to keep in touch with Sister Madonna. She must have tried to discover where her child was. It was still a captivating story for Father John Coombs!

CHAPTER THIRTY-ONE

Dublin, Ireland
Sisters of Mercy Convent
October 20th, 1917
Twenty-one years later

Father Coombs was relieved when he stepped off the *SS Carlow* in Dublin. Arriving in Dublin after a rough trip along the British and Irish coastline, he found it anticlimactic after crossing the Atlantic Ocean on the *SS Olympic*. Eating and sleeping with fifteen hundred troops and five hundred crew had been intimidating for someone who had just departed St. Kyran's, a small rural community in Placentia Bay.

"Well, you finally made it, Father." It was Father O'Connor from the Diocese of Dublin who was there to welcome him. O'Connor was a middle-aged man who seemed very genuine.

Father John had been asked by the Sisters of Mercy to do some work in Dublin for a couple of weeks in that city before meeting the Newfoundland Regiment in England. Volunteering to be chaplain with the Newfoundland Regiment was his next challenge in life. He wanted to do his part in the world war that had started in 1914.

"It was quite the trip," he said to O'Connor. "I've never seen anything like the city of Liverpool. There were people everywhere. I hope that Dublin is a little slower."

"Things aren't as hurried here," answered Father O'Connor. "Where you are staying is very peaceful. You'll be at the Mother House on Baggot Street. It's wonderful quiet there. Archbishop Roche must have been impressed with you to make arrangements to do a retreat with the Sisters of Mercy before they head off to the Front in France."

"I don't know why he chose me when there were so many others," said Father John. "But I guess when he approved my leave as a chaplain with the Newfoundland Regiment he figured he could kill two birds with the one stone. He telegraphed me as soon as he got the request from Ireland. Your Archbishop had heard about my appointment to the Newfoundland Regiment and was looking for someone with a different perspective, I suppose. I haven't worked outside regular parish work for twenty years. My last experience was with the Sisters of Mercy who were caring for prisoners in a penitentiary back home."

"I happen to know that your Archbishop Roche and our Archbishop Brown were in Rome together not too long ago. It was more than likely they made the connection there. The Sisters of Mercy's Mother House is in my parish, so that's why he asked me to greet you."

The two priests drove along the streets of Dublin by taxi. This, in itself, was a treat for Father Coombs. The mode of transportation for him was generally by small boat.

Father O'Connor accompanied Father John to the Mother House and made the introductions after which they were treated to a wonderful supper. Father John was asked to join the nuns for an opening Mass the next morning. The next two days would be spent organizing the retreat. Scriptural readings, reflections, meditations and prayers were the general order of the day. Father John would repeat this retreat or mission four times throughout the next two weeks in various parts of Dublin and surrounding areas.

"Father," said the Mother Superior, "many of our Sisters are trained nurses and will be at field hospitals in France and England. The military have requested seventeen of our sisters and we have been preparing them for the past two weeks." The Mother Superior grimaced as she mentioned field hospitals. "We've lost several from our community these last three years. The Sisters you will be working with tomorrow are those that have been chosen."

This was a huge burden for Father John. He didn't know what the challenges were. Would there be anxiety? Sadness? Fear? Anger? He would soon discover a whole sea of emotions. He knew that only the Sisters themselves would be able to work through this, with the help of their faith.

The first morning of the retreat went well and Mother Superior said she found the experience stimulating and thought-provoking. The biggest surprise for Father John came during lunch hour.

One nun, Sister Mary Joan, a woman who looked to be in her sixties, made a point of sitting directly across from him. "So you are from Newfoundland. Which part?" she asked.

"St. John's. Have you been there?" he inquired.

"Yes, indeed. I spent several years there and in various other places in your beautiful country."

Father John knew that Bishop Michael Howley had helped establish the Sisters of Mercy in several communities in Newfoundland. And it wouldn't have been out of the ordinary for a Sister of Mercy to have left Newfoundland and returned to Ireland. Three nuns had left St. Catherine's Convent on Baggot Street in Dublin and crossed the Atlantic Ocean to form the first community of Sisters of Mercy in the New World in May 2, 1842. They arrived in St. John's on June 3, 1842, that date marking the establishment of the Congregation of the Sisters of Mercy of Newfoundland.

Father John Coombs didn't know it, but Sister Mary Joan had recognized his name. She had received letters from a dear friend of hers, Sister Madonna Lynch, who had written to her about him many years ago. Apparently he was a godsend, a replacement for Father Howley, whom Sister Mary Joan had known very well.

Only she hadn't been a nun at that time. Her name then was Johanna Hamilton and she had been incarcerated for murder but this wasn't something she was about to reveal to Father John Coombs. Twenty years ago, after not hearing from Sister Madonna for a considerable amount of time, she found out through the Order that Sister Madonna had died. This resulted in her losing track of Father John Coombs, the priest Sister Madonna had so much admired.

Sister Mary Joan also recalled communicating by letter with her sister, Catherine Drake, around the same time and about this same priest. According to Sister Madonna, Father Coombs had done great work in supporting Patrick Fitzgerald and had even attended his funeral. Catherine Drake, recently deceased, had also lost track of him for she never mentioned him in her letters after Patrick Fitzgerald's funeral.

"Did you like it in Newfoundland, Sister?" Father John broke into her thoughts.

"Well, yes. I did like it there," she said. "The people were very kind." She pondered that Newfoundlanders were a very close-knit group of people. In fact, Father John Coombs had a fleeting physical resemblance to Patrick Geehan, dark skinned with a chiseled chin and blue piercing eyes. He was a tall man as well.

"Do you know where on the Front you'll be sent, Sister?"

"All we know is that we will be stationed somewhere in France," said Sister Joan. "I hear that you are going to be with the Newfoundland Regiment. They have been involved in some very serious action during this terrible conflict and I understand they have taken some heavy losses."

"That is true. July 1, 1916, was terrible for our boys. 710 of them killed, wounded or missing at Beaumont Hamel. It's a date that will be forever remembered with great sorrow in Newfoundland. I can't say that I am looking forward to heading off to the trenches, but I feel this is my contribution to the war. It may surprise you that I am doing this at the age of forty-five." Father Coombs didn't mind sharing how old he was.

"Well, I am sixty-four, and I feel as you do. This is my time to help out. I'll be the oldest of our nursing unit. However, I am healthy and fit."

Father John and Sister Mary Joan had little or no conversation after that. The day before he left, he celebrated mass with the seventeen Sisters who were about to leave the next day. Father John did something during the Holy Communion which he had never done before. When he gave Sister Mary Joan the Blessed Host he smiled and placed his hand on her head. This was quite unorthodox but he felt a need to touch the woman who had so impressed him.

CHAPTER THIRTY-TWO

Masnieres, France
November 20, 1917
Twenty-one years later

"Why did you volunteer, Father?" asked Private Harry Best. "You could be back at St. Kyran's now getting ready for Christmas. But here you are stuck in a trench with shells flying over your head."

Private Best was from Merasheen Island, Placentia Bay. Father John knew the place well. He hadn't been there for several years but he knew the Best family. Harry, who was now nineteen years old, had been an infant when he was there,

"I could say that I am heroic. But knowing that I grew up in St. John's you would never accept that as a reason." They both had a much-needed chuckle at Father John's response. "When we get out of here, you've got to get that trench foot looked at." Harry had his boot off, and Father John could see that his right foot was severely infected.

Another shell came dangerously close to their position. They were expecting a call to move out of the trench and go forward towards the St. Quinton Canal. General Byng's Third Army was preparing to break through the Hindenburg Line and reach the German occupied town of Cambrai. It was a more ambitious plan than expected. The German defenses were merciless.

Darkness was closing in. It appeared that it might be another night in the trenches. Every now and then another comrade from the Regiment would come through and advise them to hold their position.

"Do you have family back home, Father?" asked Harry.

Distant machine gun fire was making Father John nervous. Harry was oblivious to the sounds of fighting.

"I did have family," said Father John. "At times like this, I get thinking of all the things I should have done. That's one thing in my life that I have lived to regret."

"You mean, having family?"

"No. Of course not!"

Harry had his boot back on and thought that he heard something above them on the top of the trench. "Shush!" Harry put his finger up to his mouth, gesturing to the priest to be silent and get further down in the trench. This battle hardened young man knew the intricacies of trench warfare more than the priest who had just arrived at the Front.

Harry raised his rifle and climbed up to peer over the edge. "Wait here," he said as he stood up and took aim. He fired repeatedly. Suddenly he slid back down. "There were two of them. I think I got 'em." There was no return fire. Harry got up again. Slowly he raised his head to take another look. He again slipped back down into the muddy trench. "I can tell you one thing, those guys won't be killing us tonight."

Father gave Harry a drink from his canteen. It was a cold evening. They were hungry and wet. Despite the chill, steam radiated from Harry's head when he removed his helmet. His hair was soaking wet. The young soldier's trembling wasn't from the cold. The deed of killing had taken its toll on him.

"So, you didn't mean you were sorry for having family?" Harry continued the conversation as if there had been no interruption.

"No, I was going to tell you that I feel I abandoned my parents. Taking a parish so far away from them at their age amounted to our complete separation. We may have been together only five or six times after I left for Placentia Bay."

"It's never too late! When you get out of here, Father. Go back to them."

"I'm afraid they both have passed. I couldn't even get to their funerals. My grieving took place at their graves, weeks after they were gone."

Another shell exploded a few meters up in the trench. Private Harry Best didn't flinch. "They'll soon order us back towards Marcoing to seek shelter," he told Father John. "We are going to need heavier artillery than this for us to advance. I can tell the enemy is advancing towards us now."

The order to pull back came within an hour. A runner came up to them, completely out of breath. "The Captain said to pull back. Don't go over the top. Stay where you are."

Within seconds there was a barrage of never ending machine gunfire coming at them from all directions. Harry, with his helmet still in his hand, took a direct hit to the head. Father John had seen many disturbing images, but he was traumatized to watch the side of Harry's head explode and disappear. He died instantly. The runner fell on top of the priest to shelter him with his body. When Father John tried to get up, he realized that the messenger was also dead.

With the trench foundering, he had only two choices. Disobey orders and climb out of the hole and head away from the gunfire or stay and wait for the enemy to come. He climbed out of the trench, secured his battle gear, and made a run for the forest at the end of field.

The soldiers of the Newfoundland Regiment began firing past him and towards the German advance. Father John was dodging bullets from both directions. His legs couldn't carry him at the speed he desired. Thankfully, dusk was serving as an effective camouflage. Only a few more yards and he'd be there.

Although he was still running, Father John felt the ground disappear beneath him. The sounds of gunfire stopped and he could no longer hear the shells dropping. There was absolute silence, yet there were explosions all around him, displacing rocks and uprooting trees. He could see the flashes of his comrades' guns.

The final one hundred yards took forever! When he arrived at the Regiments' position, he dived into the bunker. An officer crawled over to him and spoke. The priest could see his face and knew the officer's lips were moving but he couldn't understand what he was saying. Glancing down at his stomach, John could see that his uniform was full of blood. Oddly, there was no pain. Within seconds, dusk had turned to complete darkness for the priest.

Four days later, Father John began to move around in his hospital bed. "I can see a light," he said at first. He was looking directly up into the apex of the roof. A doctor in a white coat was standing over him. The pain in his abdomen was excruciating. An intravenous bottle was draining something into his body and hung directly over his bed. The doctor was shining a light into his eye, blinding him as he tried to determine where he was and what had happened.

"You're coming around? You've been hit badly, I'm afraid. We are giving you morphine to reduce the pain. Please don't try to move."

"Where am I?"

"You are in a field hospital in a place called Marcoing, France. We are doing what we can for you."

That didn't sound good to Father John. He began to violently throw up. A nurse was immediately by his side holding an enamel tray. It was clear to her that he was bleeding internally.

"We have your identification papers, Father, and your personal effects." The doctor was speaking in broken English but easily understandable. "Our intention is to keep you as comfortable as we can." The priest tried to respond, but drifted back into unconsciousness.

Sometime later that day, Father John regained consciousness. "Do you have my case?" he asked the nurse, getting the question out in a half cry since the pain had become almost unbearable.

"We do, Father." The nurse reached down under the bed and pulled out his case. She knew he wanted his prayer book and his rosary beads. "I believe you want these. I'll put your prayer book on the foot of your bed and wrap your rosary beads around your hand. It that what you want, Father?" She spoke gently and quietly. "We have a Sister of Mercy who will come tomorrow and pray with you. She works here as a nurse, but she is in the operating room today. She's here from Ireland."

Father John nodded his head in acknowledgment.

"I'll call Doctor Emmanuel and he will increase your morphine. Hopefully, you'll rest then."

Father John Coombs' condition worsened. Knowing he was on the verge of dying, his prayer was for God to take him quickly. When the agony subsided for a few moments he longed for life to continue. He thought about Sarah. Would she remember he loved her or would she only recall his rejection of her love? He had heard she'd married and he hoped she was happy.

He prayed to his mother and father, asking them to guide him and meet him when he joined them in paradise. France was the last place he wanted to die, alone and far away from home.

In his life, he had never fulfilled his desire to find complete unity with someone. Not even God had provided the bonding relationship he so craved.

The night passed and Father John Coombs lingered on.

Morning arrived and with it a nun dressed in the habit of a Sister of Mercy.

"Good morning, Sister. I guess you had a busy day in the OR yesterday?" The nurse was addressing Sister Mary Joan.

"Yes, but today is another day. Days like today I live for, Marlene." The nun hung her coat on a rack just inside the door. She reached for the clipboard which was usually handed to her as soon as she came into the room.

The nurse reached out to touch her arm. "Sister, we have a dying man, a priest, in fact. I don't think he'll be with us much longer. He is a chaplain with the Newfoundland Regiment. The poor men have been taking heavy causalities near Masnieres."

Sister Mary Joan's heart dropped when she walked over to the bed and saw Father John Coombs lying there. There was a chair beside his bed and she sat down in it. It was immediately apparent he had little time left.

His hands were on top of his blanket and wrapped around his left hand was a rosary. The rosary beads looked familiar. She peered closely and realized she was looking at handcrafted rosary beads. Beads made from whalebone. The rosary beads from Nowlan's Harbour. Her rosary beads. She felt faint.

If she hadn't been sitting down she would have fallen. She looked at the priest's face and knew she was looking at the face of her son. This was her child, the little boy she had held but once. Tears rolled down her cheeks.

She leaned forward and put her arms gently around him, all the while aching to hold him in her arms as tightly as she could. She pressed her face against his and softly kissed his cheek. Tears kept streaming down her face.

In one final, partially lucid moment, he opened his eyes and whispered, "I know you? Do you remember where I belong?"

"You belong to me, my loving son. You belong to me," she said through her tears.

Father John smiled and took his last breath. Sister Mary Joan, Johanna Hamilton, tenderly closed his eyes and kissed her son a final farewell.

The End

Non-Fictional Characters

Johanna Hamilton
Patrick Geehan
Jane Geehan
Garrett Sears
John Drake
John Fitzgerald
Catherine Fitzgerald
Patrick Fitzgerald
Catherine Hearn
John Hearn
Daniel Shugarue
Mrs. Shugarue
Thomas Morrissey
Father Michael Howley
Judge Byron Robinson
Mr. R. Raftus
Mr. Emerson
Inspector Foley
R.W. Lilly J.P.
Constable Fallon
Constable Hutcher
Constable Daley
F.T. B. Carter
Father Falconia
Archbishop Thomas Power

Fictional Characters

Father John Coombs
Sarah Keough
Sister Madonna
Catherine Drake
Mark Coombs
Theresa Coombs
Mrs. Donahue
Martha Hollett
Captain Foster
Mr. Apsey
Sister Edward

Although this story is historical fiction, the integrity of the true story of the murders of Jane Geehan and Garrett Sears is kept intact. Patrick Geehan was hung on July 1, 1872, in Newfoundland's first private execution and was buried in Her

Majesty's Penitentiary. Johanna Hamilton was sentenced to hang the same day. Her sentence was respited until November 20, 1872, because of her pregnancy. Her sentence was commuted to life imprisonment on October 21, 1872, when she was exonerated from being an accomplice in the murders. She was deported to Ireland on May 24, 1880. It is not known what happened to her child.

During my research, I discovered that the newspaper article, which was published by *The Evening Post* and is repeated in the prologue of this book, was bogus and was written for an Australian circulation in 1872. Johanna was not executed. Her death sentence was respited, as recommended by an empaneled jury, on the very same day she was sentenced to hang.

Footnotes

[i] *The Evening Post,*Volume VIII, Issue 119.21 June.1872.paperpast.nattlib.govt.nz

[ii] Murray, Myles. *The Geehan Murders of Harbour Grace, 1871.* Centre For Newfoundland Studies, Memorial University of Newfoundland, 1963

[iii] *The Morning Chronicle,* June 1, 1872

[iv] *The Morning Chronicle,* June, 1872

[v] *The Morning Chronicle,* June 1, 1872

[vi] *The Morning Chronicle,* June 1, 1872

[vii] *The Express.* St. John's, Newfoundland. June 3, 1872 paperpast.nattlib.govt.nz

[viii] *The Morning Chronicle,* June, 1872

[ix] *The Evening Post,* Volume VIII, Issue 119, 21 June 1872

[x] *The Newfoundlander,* July, 1872

[xi] *The Morning Chronicle,* June, 1872

[xii] *The Morning Chronicle,* June, 1872

[xiii] Mosdell, Harris, M. *Events in Newfoundland.* St. John's, Newfoundland, 1922

Bibliography

Butts Edward. *Ghost Stories of Newfoundland and Labrador.* Dundurn Group, Toronto, 2010

Mosdell, Harris, M. *Events in Newfoundland.* St. John's, Newfoundland, 1922

Murray, Myles. *The Geehan Murders of Harbour Grace, 1871.* Centre For Newfoundland Studies, Memorial University of Newfoundland, 1963

Barbara A. Crosbie, *"Michael Francis Howley,"* in The Dictionary of Canadian Biography. Volume X1V University of Toronto /University of Laval, 2003

The Express. St. John's, Newfoundland. June 3, 1872

The Express. St. John's, Newfoundland. July 6, 1872

The Express. St. John's, Newfoundland. June 8, 1872

The Evening Post, Volume VIII, Issue 119, 21 June 1872

The Evening Telegram, St. John's, Newfoundland, July 29, 1899

The Morning Chronicle, June 24, 1872

The Morning Chronicle, May 21, 1872

The Morning Chronicle, June 30, 1872

The Morning Chronicle, July 8, 1872

The Newfoundlander, July 1, 1872

Office of the Colonial Secretary fonds. Execution of Patrick Geehan, GN 2.34 1872. Provincial Archives Division. The Rooms

THE FULL CONFESSION OF PATRICK GEEHAN AS TAKEN FROM THE MORNING CHRONICLE JULY 8, 1872

I, Patrick Geehan, hereby solemnly declare that there never was any plot or conspiracy between me and Johanna Hamilton to get rid of either Mrs. Geehan or Garrett Sears. I never, up to the time of Garrett Sears' death, said one word to her on such a subject, nor did any conversation ever take place between us to that effect. I therefore freely submit my written confession as given at the knee of Father Michael Howley to my Savior the Lord God Almighty.

My wife had a cross and peevish temper. Every year up to the last four I used to have a quarrel with her. For the last four years I let her have her own way. When she'd begin to scold I'd go away. I used to be afraid I would do something that I would be sorry for.

Herself and Sears could not agree at all. They'd always be fighting. He was as savage as a beast in his manner. Still, if I turned him away I'd have to turn her away too. I hove his bed and box out twice and she brought it back in spite of me.

It ran in my mind to put him out of the way in Labrador where no one would know anything about it, and still I couldn't find it in my heart to do so. When I came home last fall I never saw them so united. They'd be always talking together, same as a young married couple. I thought in my mind that there was something that was not right betwixt 'em. I was afraid of them. (He stated one incident about Sears and Jane that was not unfounded, but I dare not publish!) This was in my mind ever since. I could not trust her. When I saw them so great together, I bethought her actions before, and I said I was not safe.

On the morning of November 20th, 1871, I was putting out

nets on the fence and I had a barrow of twine. I called out to one of them, either Johanna or Mrs. Geehan, to come and lift up the barrow. She found a bottle under the twine with a noggin or so of rum in it. I put that there myself for she was always jawing me about it. I used to take a little drop about my work. She didn't like me to have it unbeknownst to her. She took it up and went into the house with her hands abroad. "I'll make a holy show of you," says she.

I followed her in and took the bottle from her. I put my hands on her shoulders and gave her a couple of shakes. I did not strangle or choke her. I sot her on the chair and left her there. I did not put my fingers on her throat. My hands or fingers may have gone near her throat but not at all so much as to strangle her.

Johanna Hamilton was out about somewhere during this time. After I was out in the porch and came back in, I bethought myself that she looked queer. I thought the color of death was in her. I didn't think she was dead when I left her, for what I did could not kill her.

When I came back she was on the floor, stretched out and there was a little bit of skin off her forehead. She must have tumbled off the chair head foremost and knocked her head against the table. I took her up, rubbed her and shook her. I saw that she was dead and left her there. Johanna came in then and saw her; she clapped her hands and began to roar and bawl around the kitchen.

I sat down and began to console with myself for about an hour. I shut the door where she was. I said to myself if I didn't put Garrett out of the way now he would certainly do it to me. I couldn't tell if Johanna heard me say this aloud or not; but it occurred in my mind. I told her to tell me when she would be calling him in to dinner. That's all I told her; and I had not the gun in my hand at that time. 'Twas about an hour after the death of Mrs. Geehan. I can't recollect whether she let me know afterwards or whether I saw her going to call him. At all events, I took the gun. 'Twas at the westward end of the house. I put it there about a half hour before he was killed.

I was at two minds whether I should do it or not. I done it and it was in spite of me that I done it. When I was doing it I was sorry for doing it. And I still couldn't help it. As soon as the shot was fired, he bawled and called me by name. He then wheeled and fell face under, and with the fall stunned himself. I thought he was dead. I made sure the shot went into him. If I thought he was dead, I wouldn't meddle with him, but I thought he wasn't dead. I had to put him out of his pain. I gave him one blow with the pole of the hatchet and that's all. I wasn't in a passion. I didn't want to mangle or cut him up. I only wanted to put him out of punishment.

When I went out in the night to bury him, I saw the pigs and what they were doing. I laid down the light and grabbed the pitchfork and made a clout at the pigs. The man was covered with straw. The clout forced its way down through the straw and stuck either in the man or the beam. I fear it was the man.

Johanna came out. She was so frightened. I forced her to come. She was like a little fool. She was so frightened. She didn't know what she was doing. I buried this man in the clay for a few days, until I'd get the woman buried. I had to arrange for the prayers of the Church and the rites of the Church offered up for her soul. I was going to see John Fitzgerald and make the whole case known to him. I was going to get him to bring the Crowners and give myself up. I never dreamed about hanging.

Jane had no friends. I knew that she'd want none of them around her. I clear Johanna Hamilton's totally out of the whole of it. She had nothing to do whatsoever in it. The four witnesses that swore against her were false. She did not hand me the pitchfork as I stated in the prison. "Twas in derision I stated that; spite to her because she said I killed the man. What I said about her wasn't true.

This is my free and voluntary statement and contains the truth.

(Signed) Patrick Geehan
Michael F. Howley
Jonathan Martin

JOHANNA HAMILTON'S STATEMENT AS TAKEN FROM THE MORNING CHRONICLE JULY 8, 1872

Penitentiary
St. John's, Newfoundland
June 30th, 1872

Patrick Geehan used to say often that he wasn't leading a peaceful life on account of his wife. She was bad-tempered. He used to say this in the presence of others. He never said this to me alone, but before the neighbours. He said he was afeared he'd do something he'd be sorry for that – that there would be neither luck nor grace in the house with her. He often said that it was hell on earth.

She and her brother used to curse frightful. She used to be giving bad wishes. This was going on as long as I was with them. She used to be jawing with Sears too. I never saw Geehan raise a hand to Sears. He used to say: "God Almighty grant him patience." I saw Sears a couple of times rise his hand to strike Geehan. They had no quarrel to my knowledge on the 20th of November, the day of the death of Garrett Sears. I said both in the court house in Harbour Grace and here in the Penitentiary that Garrett and the skipper had a squabble that day. That was not true: but there was a squabble between him and his wife about the liquor she got under the net in the cellar house. I told that lie because I thought it wouldn't be as hard on him.

I never was in a court house before. I'm sorry I didn't tell the whole truth then as I am telling it now. I wanted to make the best of it for him. 'Twas around eleven or twelve o'clock when she found the bottle of rum. I was down by the back door in the yard. She ran into the house bawling and clapping her hands, and he ran after her. I stayed out in the yard. I was cleaving stumps to put under the pot to boil water to go washing. I came into the back house, not into the kitchen. I hove the stumps into the back house. I did not go in because I heard them jawing inside.

They were in the kitchen. I saw them - the door was open. I thought it was no more than usual. I often saw them quarrelling, and went between them once about a year ago when he gave her a slap. I got the most of the slap myself. I did not go between them this time because I did not think they were going to do harm to one another.

I went away towards the upper house in the garden for about half an hour – it may be more or may be less. I came down then. He was stood on the floor in the kitchen. I went in without saying anything and hung on the potatoes for dinner. The first thing I would do in the morning when I'd get up, before I eat my breakfast, was to wash the potatoes and put them in the corner by the fire. I did that morning and most always had water on them. The water was on them that day and they were ready to put on the fire.

I then sot down on the bench. I looked at him - he was in the middle of the floor. The room door was shut. He asked me was his face scrawled much. I looked at him and seen it scrawled and a little blood coming out of it - not much I told him. He told me that it was his wife who scrawled him. After that he says, "Her ways and her manners are after putting an end to her now." I think them are the words he said. I thought he was after killing her.

He told me to go to my work and not to mind anything. "Well," says I, "I'll go call some of the women." And he would not let me. I went to prepare dinner-meat, pork and cabbage for their dinners. He went to wax for cobbing and when 'twas made he brought it out to the back house. 'Twas near two o'clock when the potatoes were boiled and the meat warmed, he was out sowing straw. I was laying the table for dinner and going about the house and clearing up a couple of basins and doing other things. I strained the milk and put it to set. I put three plates on the table, one for skipper, one for Garrett and one for myself. This took up time till near two o'clock. I was just after straining the potatoes in the back house when he came in and asked if I had dinner almost ready. I told him I had. This was before I laid the table. I was just going to lay it. He told me not to pretend anything before Garrett. I was crying. He told me to tell him when I go to call Garrett. He said nothing more than that.

I did not know what he wanted him for. I thought he may want him about the straw or something he had to tell him. I had no thought that he was going to kill him. It never ran in my mind. He had nothing at all in his hand. The gun used to be on the rack in the kitchen. I can't say if it was there then. I didn't see him take it out of it. I didn't hear him take it down. He could take it down with his hand without a chair. I had my back turned. I was laping the table. 'Twas beside the fire. I did not see him going out. I never thought about the gun.

When I laid the table I called Garrett to his dinner. I came back into the house and shut the door. I heard the shot outside. I had the dinner on the table for the three of us. When I heard the shot I didn't mind but I heard Garrett bawling out "Oh, my God. Pad! Pad!" 'Twas just near the back door. I got great fright. I went to the back door and seen the man stretched. I seen Geehan walking away towards the stable. I reared and bawled. I ran back into the house and ran up and down. I did not go into the yard. I didn't hand him anything to kill him. He was killed dead when I went out. He did not speak or make any noise after I went out - and did not move. There was no pitchfork there. I never saw the pitchforks nor the gaffs. The gaffs were up in the upper house all together. They were never took out of it for years, as long as I was there, till they were taken to the Court. They were covered with rust.

I did not see him striking Sears at all. He was walking away when I came out. He had nothing in his hand. I did not help put the body in the stable. I did not eat any dinner that day. We did not go to bed till after two o'clock. 'Twas handy to two when he went out to the stable. I was lonesome to go out handy to the dead man. He forced me to go out. He said there was no fear. He said – Did I want to leave him (Sears) there all day; he said I should go. I said I can't go look at him. He said I must. He was sorry to have to do it himself, let alone me-so I went out.

There was boughs over Sears. You could only see some parts of his trousers. He went in first. I went in after. "I believe," says I, "the pigs are at him." "I believe they are, sure enough," says he. I seen one of the pigs rooting at his head. The pig had his nose through the boughs, and it was tearing and eating at his ear. I saw myself where the ear was licked clean off him. I looked sideways, but saw plain. It looked smooth and white. I seen the pig chewing – 'twas his right ear. The man's head was to the eastward. He was lying on his back and the car was to the Northward. I did not look anymore, but Geehan said they had his hand eaten.

He took up a pitchfork and made a prod at the pig. I did not see whether he prodded the pig or the man with the fork. There were three pigs rooting at the man. Geehan was mad when he saw the pigs. He put him on the handbarrow then. I don't remember whether I helped put him on the barrow or not. But I carried him with Geehan out of the stable. I went first. Garrett's feet were towards me. I was going of a shiver with dread all the time. He told me to go where he had the clay dug. We let him down on the ground and put him in the pit on his back. I did not see his hand; 'twas too dark.

I stood there for a while. He hove a little clay on him. I did not go near the pit after. I fought hard for my character from him. I said over and over again I'd leave the house. He used to tell me there'd be no fear of me. He used to say if I'd leave I'd be sorry for it. I was afraid to stay and afraid to go, and still I made up my mind to go. I told my brother-in-law, John Drake, I'd leave on Monday. He told me the Sunday after she was buried to leave, for "I expect Geehan will be taken," says he, for there was mistrust at that time. I said I would leave on Monday, and I intended to do so. That Monday, early enough, I was taken at about nine o'clock in the morning."

Johanna Hamilton
Michael F. Howley, R.C. Clergyman, Witness
William P. B. Doutney, R.C. Clergyman, Witness

I would like to thank DRC Publishing for their confidence and guidance during the writing of this book and my previous published works. I would also like to thank the following readers for their honest and supportive response:

Betty Simmons
Maureen Callahan
Thelma Manning
Shirley Collins
John Martin
James Callahan
The Salt Water Writers' Circle

Courthouse where Patrick and Johanna were charged - 1800

Spaniard's Bay Road

Chimney like the one in Geehan's home

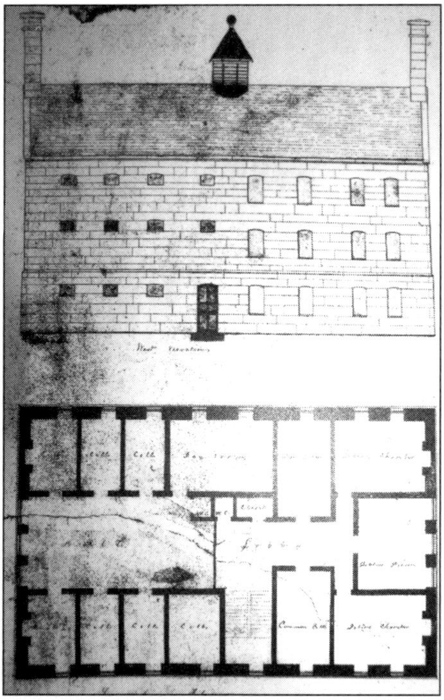

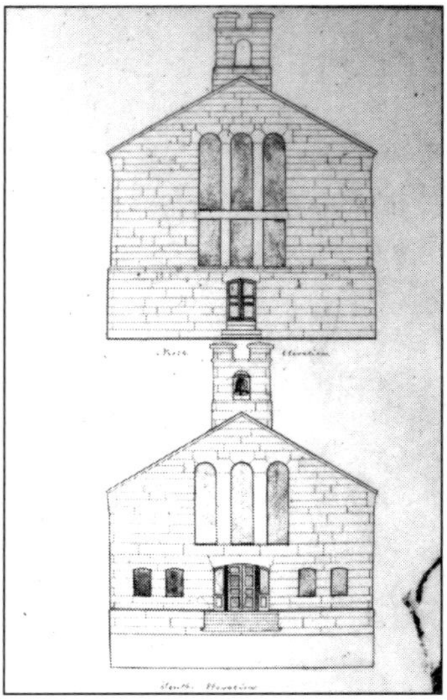

Original drawings and
floorplan of Her Majesty's
Penitentiary, 1859,
St. John's, NL

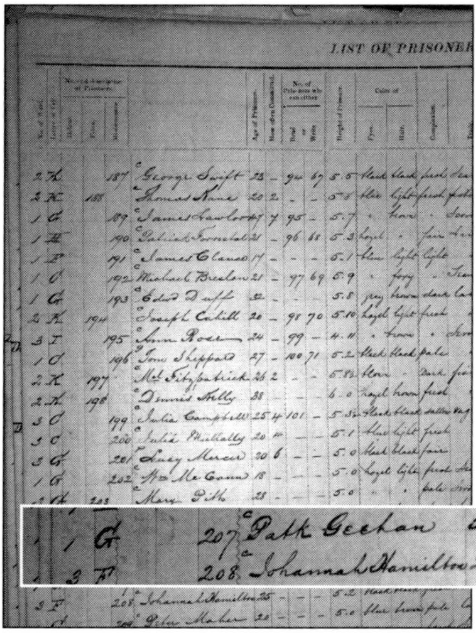

Prisoner's list from HMP, on
the day of Geehan and
Hamilton's incarceration

William Munn

J.R.McCowan, Superintendent who released Johanna Hamilton, 1880

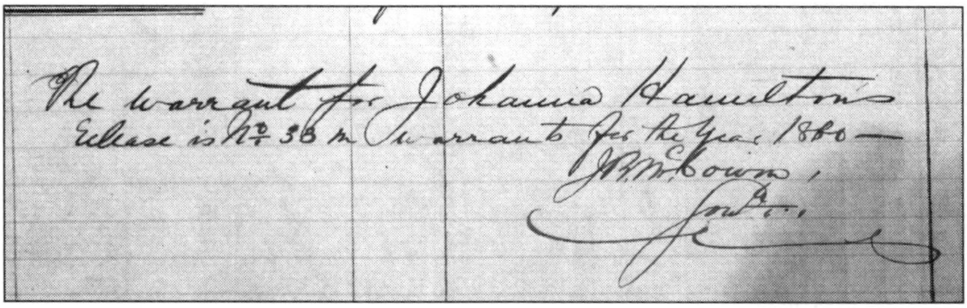

The warrant for Johanna Hamilton's
Release is No. 38 in Warrants for the Year 1880 —
J.R.McCowan,
Supt.,

Release warrant for Johanna signed by McCowan

About the Author

Patrick Collins is a retired educator who taught in various communities throughout Newfoundland and Labrador. He finished his teaching career in education as a Curriculum Program Specialist, working in School Districts on the Avalon Peninsula. Patrick also worked as Sales and Marketing representative with Lifetouch Canada until June of 2011. Recently, Pat has been working as an instructor for the Canadian Training Institute, Bay Roberts, NL.

This is Patrick's fifth book. Other works include a biography called *Dr. Charles Cron. A Doctor for All Time: A Man Who Cured Our Hearts; The Harbour Grace Affray; The Spirit of the S.S. Kyle; and Murder at Mosquito Cove, Harbour Grace: The Murder of Elfreda Pike, 1870*

Born and raised in Riverhead, Harbour Grace, he continues to enjoy teaching, researching and writing.

He may be reached at his email address: pjcollins@eastlink.ca